DISTRUZIONE DELLA ROCCIA

Also by Frank A. Ruffolo

Gabriel's Chalice

Tres Archangelis

Trihedral of Chaos

Jack Stenhouse Mysteries

Stuck in Traffick

Blue Falcon

10048

Xanthe Terra

DISTRUZIONE DELLA ROCCIA

A NOVEL

FRANK A. RUFFOLO

This is a work of fiction. Names, characters, and incidents are either products of the author's imagination or are used fictitiously. Certain events, locales, and business establishments are mentioned, but the characters and situations are imaginary.

DISTRUZIONE DELLA ROCCIA, a novel by Frank A. Ruffolo

www.frankaruffolo.com

Printed in the United States of America

First Edition, June 2021

ISBN: 978-0-9836803-9-0 (printed version only)

DISTRUZIONE DELLA ROCCIA

CHAPTER ONE

"Hey, Chic, what the hell is this?" asks George "Geo" Jackson, pointing to a wall carving along a street in the ancient city of Pompeii.

Steve bursts out laughing at what his friend is pointing at. "Oh, come on, Geo," he snickers. "That may be small by your standards, but it's *exactly* what you think it is…a penis etched in stone!"

"I can see that, asshole. But what the hell is it doing here?"

"Some think they used signs like that to point the way to the brothels. Others think the population here had a fondness for erotic art. In any case, that one is pointing to the entrance to the red-light district. Just wait till you see the mosaics in that section of the ruins!"

On this beautiful autumn day, three friends, Steve "Chic" Ciccone, Frank "Angie" Angelo, and George "Geo" Jackson, are exploring the famous ruins of Pompeii. As they walk through the city, they're amazed by the beautiful mosaics and frescoes that still grace homes and temples, like the House of the Faun, and the Temple of Apollo. They're also fascinated by the Roman cobblestone streets still rutted with the tracks of carts and chariots that were the mainstays of everyday life.

The day is warm, and it seems like these "three musketeers," as coworkers dubbed them long ago, have the famous place to themselves. Most of the usual hordes of tourists have thinned out from the busy summer months, and the fall travelers haven't arrived yet. Without the crowds, the men can see everything without having to jostle others for a good look.

Friends Frank and George are visiting Italy for the first time since Steve and Diane moved to Ravello, so Steve is happy to show them around today. However, the primary reason he arranged this excursion is because he wants to spend time alone with his buds. He misses the familiar closeness the three of them have developed over the years.

The men become hungry as the morning wears on, so it doesn't take long for Frank and George to start pestering Steve about eating some "real" Italian food.

"You promised to take us to Naples, remember?" whines George.

"Yeah, I'm dying for a slice of pizza napolitana," adds Frank. "If that don't say Italy, I don't know what does!"

"All right, let's go," says Steve. "We've seen most of Pompeii anyway."

On the way to Naples, the buddies reminisce about old times, joking back and forth with ease, recalling each other's foibles and quirks.

During a lull in their conversation, Frank pipes up with an announcement. "Hey, guys, I have some news!"

"What, is your hair growing back?" jokes Steve.

"Funny, man. No, I finally sold my saloon in Florida. And guess what? I'm seriously thinking about retiring to Italy, like you and Diane!"

"Hey, man, that's great!" congratulates George, slapping Frank on the back. "How the heck did you keep that a secret?"

Steve's reaction is more moderate. "Are you sure?" he asks. "You were hesitating last time we talked. You said you didn't know if you could live so far from home."

"I know, but that was before taking this trip. Now that I've seen this beautiful country and sampled its delicious food, I don't think there's anywhere else I'd rather spend my golden years!"

"You mean your graying years, right?" laughs George.

Steve looks at Frank in his rearview mirror. "If you're really serious, Ang, you can stay at my place while you look for a house. That way, you can take your time searching for your dream home. I can also recommend the real estate agency I used to purchase my villa. They did an excellent job for us."

"Hey, thanks, buddy!" replies Frank. "I think a small place with a view of the bay will do just fine!"

Steve Ciccone and Frank Angelo were buddies long before they met George. They've known each other for years, ever since they served together in the Vietnam War.

The intense fighting and highly charged issues surrounding that conflict forged many deep friendships, including Steve's and Frank's. Shared experiences made them inseparable, and their bonds remained strong, even after their discharges. Though they stayed connected over the years, they didn't see each other often, until they found themselves on the same SWAT team at the New York City Police Department.

The war buddies met the third member of their trio on the job. George Jackson, a bomb squad officer, came into frequent contact with the SWAT officers on shared calls, and they all developed a close friendship during and after work hours.

After a time, the three became thick as thieves, spending time at each other's homes and listening to each other's problems. Years later, they followed each other to Florida, hoping for relaxing moments in the sun after their stressful careers in

New York.

When they all moved to the Sunshine State, Steve was married with two young sons. Not long after they got there, his wife died in a horrific car accident. He became a widower, and his friends were there for him through it all. They've stuck together through thick and thin, and each of them would do anything for the others.

After the crash that claimed his wife, Steve received a sizeable settlement, which improved his finances dramatically. The sudden infusion of capital was a significant help in raising his sons, however, it did nothing to assuage Steve's grief.

The widowed father became increasingly lonely as his sons grew and formed their own families. Though he dated, he never found anyone he wanted to grow old with. He had even resigned himself to never marrying again when a fortuitous encounter changed his entire outlook.

One day, he stopped to help a stranger, and stumbled upon renowned actress Diane Summers. Surprisingly, the two clicked instantly, and married soon afterwards. Neither saw any need to wait; both knew they had found something special.

Soon after their wedding, Steve retired from the FSA, an agency created by the president to deploy the military within the borders of the United States. He bought a villa in Italy, where the Ciccones now live fulltime.

Though the couple moved far from family and friends, they frequently invite Steve's sons and Diane's family to Italy, and when they return home for important family events, they make time to visit close friends.

George Jackson has also been married at one time or another, but his love life hasn't been as happy as Steve's. Married and divorced three times, George considers himself fortunate that he never had any children. That doesn't mean he doesn't like kids. To him, Steve's sons have always been the family he never had.

George dates, but after his last marriage ended, he vowed never to marry again. Financially, he can't afford to risk another failure. The sum of his three alimony payments is so large that he's had to work at least two jobs for a good part of his adult life.

George's principal occupation is stressful; he runs the Fort Lauderdale office of the FSA, the Federal Security Agency Steve started. Though that job keeps him pretty busy, he still makes time to work at buddy Frank Angelo's old west-style saloon — his finances demand it. Holding two jobs is tiring and George doesn't see a light at the end of the tunnel. With his high financial obligations, he frequently grouses that he'll never be able to retire.

The third member of the trio is a lifelong bachelor. Frank Angelo has no children and no living relatives, so Steve and George "adopted" him as family. The three friends are often together anyway, so it just seems natural.

When Frank's not hanging out with the guys, he's at his bar, Duke's Saloon, named after John Wayne, his favorite actor. The saloon provides Frank with sufficient income and keeps him busy, while also giving him a sense of purpose. It also allows him to meet new people, something that he insists keeps him "young."

CHAPTER TWO

When the guys enter Naples, the overpowering stench of rotting garbage assaults their senses.

"Ugh! There's crap piled ten feet high all over the place!" complains Frank. "I thought this city was supposed to be beautiful!"

"Thank God we're not here in the heat of summer!" grumbles George, holding his nose against the horrible odor. "What's going on, Chic?"

"The Mafia controls the garbage companies and the unions, and they've been on strike for months."

George looks surprised. "I thought the Mafia was only in Sicily."

"There are many different criminal groups in Italy, and they're all known by different names. The Sicilian Mafia is based in Sicily. Around here, the major one is called the Camorra."

"And I'll bet the police don't do anything about it," shrugs Frank.

"Well, the Carabinieri, the country's military police, have pushed it back somewhat, but there's way too much corruption," responds Steve, driving slowly along a side street. "You know, money talks."

Looking around, Steve says, "I'll park along the bay. We can walk from there. The restaurant I want to take you to is just a few blocks away. The pizza there is the best."

The restaurant Steve chose for today's meal is crowded, as are all the others at mid-afternoon. Most Italians eat their main meal at this time of day.

The men have decided to order wine and linger over their food for a while, then do some sightseeing in the touristy parts of Naples. Since George is scheduled to leave for home in the morning, this will be the last time he can take in the sights. But Frank's going to stay a little longer.

After a short sightseeing tour of Naples, the friends return to Steve's villa. "Make yourselves comfortable," Steve says, tuning the TV to an overseas news channel.

"You don't watch Italian news?" asks Frank.

"I do, but I also like to keep up with the American perspective on world news. Let's see what's going on today."

As the men settle down to listen, Diane sets out glasses of Campari mixed with soda, the classic Italian *aperitivo,* or before dinner drink.

"This is John Thomas with Fox News in Rome," says a correspondent. *"A stunning announcement was made by the Holy See this morning. A statement issued on behalf of Pope Urban IV announces that the pontiff has taken the extraordinary step of excommunicating all Catholic members of the Mafia — La Cosa Nostra. This development, along with recent declarations from the Vatican condemning ongoing criminal activities in Sicily, Naples, and the rest of Italy, has unsurprisingly drawn the ire of the ruling capos and nervousness among Italian law enforcement. Many Italians can remember that when an earlier pope criticized the Mafia, the criminal organization detonated car bombs around Rome in a chilling display of arrogance. Italians throughout the country hope*

that today's announcement won't trigger another aggressive re-sponse. This is John Thomas reporting for Fox News."

That same evening, a group of people watching a re-broadcast of this report turns away from the TV when the station switches to other news.

"*Il Papa* has overstepped his bounds," says one of the capos at this secret meeting in a small room at the rear of a neighborhood restaurant in Cefalù, Sicily. "He has been too critical lately. We must send a message like we did before. But this time, it should be impressive enough to circle the globe."

"What can we do, Don Vito?" asks another Mafia boss. "We were angry when John Paul II criticized us, so we blew up some cars. He received our message, and nothing more was said or done."

"Yes, but this pope is different. I suspect that he will not be as easily intimidated. Our power is formidable, and what-ever action we take will make a powerful statement."

An elderly capo with an enormous potbelly and a reced-ing hairline agrees. "We control all the ports, all the unions, all the drugs, and all the human trafficking operations in and out of Italy. I am sure we can find some way to get his attention."

Don Vito looks around the table at his fellow crime lords. "You know that group in the Middle East that wants to con-front the Vatican?" Several heads nod in response. "They have said many times that they want to kill the pope and blow up the basilica. Perhaps this is the right time to do something with that information."

"What do you have in mind, Vito?" asks another king-pin.

Don Vito tents his fingers under his chin and squints his eyes in thought. Staring hard at the faces before him, he says, "I will call my man in Tripoli. We will give the Caliphate the keys

13

to do exactly what they have been threatening to do."

Sergio Fittipaldi, an Italian citizen working in Libya, scrambles to answer his private cell phone. "*Pronto*," he says, a little out of breath after running to where he left the phone in a small office at Libya's Port of Tripoli. "*Sì*, sì. I will call Amil and tell him to come to my office. No? Then I will go in person — no phone contact. Sì, I understand. Very well, we will speak again tomorrow morning. *Ciao*."

According to seaport officials, Sergio is a dock consultant from the *Confederazione Generale Italiana del Lavoro*, or CGIL — the Italian dockworkers union. But that isn't the only job that occupies Signore Fittipaldi's time.

A certain capo back home pays Sergio well to do occasional things for him that Sergio has learned not to question. The capo has made it clear that he will not hesitate to retaliate if the dock consultant doesn't do as he asks. In return, the mob boss takes good care of Sergio's family. Over the years, Sergio has learned to jump when the man calls.

With his phone lodged safely in his pocket, Sergio heads onto the dock. "Let us go," he says to an armed guard lounging against a wall, smoking a cigarette. "I need to go to a café on Swalim Road."

Sergio doesn't go anywhere without an armed escort. He has been in Libya long enough to know that foreigners are open targets for kidnappers and muggers, so out of necessity, he pays this man to keep him safe.

That same evening, George savors the scent of a nearby

lemon grove from Steve's Italian veranda as the friends chat. "Damn," he says unhappily. "I'm going to hate going back to the States! You got it made here, bro: no hassles, no bullshit, a beautiful view, and a gorgeous wife to boot."

Glancing at Frank, he asks, "And you're going to join him here, too, Ang? Both of you are abandoning me to face the chaos back home alone?"

Steve drapes a comforting arm around his old bud. "Geo, we're just a phone call away. And you're welcome to come here anytime."

Frank walks over to the wall overlooking the blue waters of the Gulf of Salerno. "A toast to the sun!" he says, raising his glass high. As the men watch, the golden orb sinks slowly into the horizon, sending rays of orange and yellow onto the sea.

"Geo," says Frank after the sun sets, "I'd like to make a toast to our friendship. I haven't mentioned this yet, but the place I buy will have room for you, too. You'll be able to come and live the good life with us whenever you can."

The friends raise their glasses again, this time, to the promise of good times to come.

Behind them, Diane opens the French doors and pushes a serving cart onto the balcony. "Ready to eat?" she asks.

The cart is laden with plates of food — a large bowl of pasta and sepia immersed in Diane's best tomato sauce, a side dish of broccoli rabe mixed with local sausage spiced with flakes of the area's best hot pepper, a basket of fresh bread, and an assortment of cheese and fruit.

"Steve, get a bottle of that good Lambrusco," instructs Diane. "Let's enjoy this evening without any talk of chaos or missed opportunities. Look around, there's no chaos here!"

Diane portions the meal out to her guests, then sits down to enjoy the men's company in the delightfully cool breeze blowing off the now-dark bay.

Steve smiles at his wife in the dimming light. Though Diane Ciccone is no longer a spring chicken, she's as beautiful as she ever was when she was on the silver screen.

Farther south, an evening meal is just ending on the coast of Africa.

Sergio Fittipaldi finishes the customary cup of green tea and stares into the eyes of the short, dark-skinned Syrian sitting across from him. "Time for business, Amil. I am sure you know that I did not come here only for a good meal. Don Vito needs to speak to you. I will return here at eight in the morning so he can tell you what he wants."

"Eh? Why you tell me here? Why you not call?" asks Amil Bacdadi.

"Too many ears listen to phone calls. This is important. Be ready tomorrow at eight. Thank you for dinner. I must leave now. *Ma'a salama.* Ciao."

"*Ila-liqaa.*"

CHAPTER THREE

At six the next morning, Steve and Frank drop George off at Naples Capodichino International Airport. It's chilly from the night before, so as they say their goodbyes in the departure lane, a warm mist forms around their words.

Frank is looking forward to moving to Italy and finding a home there. He's heard so many stories about the country from his father that he already feels comfortable. And because his father was born in Cefalù, he wants to apply for dual citizenship. He didn't know that he could do that until Steve said he was looking into it because his father was born in Naples.

An hour outside of Naples, SS145 becomes Corso Italia, the main thoroughfare in the heart of downtown Sorrento, a well-known town on Italy's southwest coast. As promised, Steve is taking George to his real estate agency.

"Wow, these streets are narrow," Frank comments when they arrive in Sorrento. "It's no wonder the cars are so small in Italy."

"Yeah, there's no way a full-size American car will fit in some places," responds Steve, turning sharply to avoid a woman on a scooter. "But I miss my Corvette. I'm thinking of having it shipped over."

"Wow, that'll really piss Mike off, won't it? I thought he

was driving it now," says Frank, referring to Steve's oldest son.

"Yeah, I'm sure he'll be disappointed. But it's still my car!" replies Steve.

Near the Hotel Villa Maria, Steve spots a place to park just past a Hertz Rent a Car store on Via Rivolo S. Antonio. "We'll walk from here," he says. We're not far from Sorrento's main piazza."

Hoofing it, the duo walks past a small-town square, and the imposing Cathedral of Saints Philip and James. Across from the cathedral, they spot one of many *gelaterias* in the area, so they stop in for a light breakfast of pastry and cappuccino, the intensely flavored Italian coffee known the world over.

That morning, Italian dock consultant Sergio Fittipaldi and Caliphate associate Amil Bacdadi have been staring at plaster walls and cheap furniture at the Tripoli dockyard since 7:00. The unlikely accomplices have been waiting for a phone call in a small room with two burly men in expensive suits.

When the promised call from Cefalù finally connects, Sergio answers, *"Pronto. Sì, è qui,"* and places the call on speaker.

"Amil," says Don Vito through the phone's microphone, "I have a great interest in speaking with you today. It is well known that you and your comrades desire to give a special message to Pope Urban, a message that will shake the world to its core. I am pleased to tell you today that I am the man who will help you deliver that message."

Amil listens but is uncertain that he understands correctly. The words he has just heard are almost unbelievable. If they're true, it would be an answer to many prayers. He looks questioningly at Sergio, who reassures him with a nod and a smile.

"Give Sergio a list of the people you want to send on your mission," Vito orders. "We will need information about them before my associates can prepare documents for entering Italy. We will also get everything you require to get your point across. Do you understand what I am saying, Amil?"

"Yes, I understand," answers Amil, almost giddy with excitement. "I am certain that my superiors will be happy to hear this news."

"I do not doubt it," says Don Vito. "I will take that to mean that we have an agreement. We will begin the process when Sergio receives those names and the list of what you need. It should not take long to get everything ready."

The call ends, and Amil stares wide-eyed at Sergio.

"Perhaps you are still unsure," says the mob negotiator. "But make no mistake. My associates are eager to help you achieve the outcome you have longed for. The sooner you get me the information we need, the sooner we can set your plans into motion. There is a saying, Amil: The enemy of my enemy is my friend. We know what your great desire is, and I assure you that our desire is the same."

Sergio rises from his seat and becomes serious. Leaning close to Amil, he jabs an index finger into the man's chest. "Make it clear to your superiors," he stresses, "that this is a business contract between our two organizations, nothing more. Do not void this agreement. Our offer will come only once. *Capisce?*"

"Yes, but what will happen if—"

Amil's question hangs in the air unanswered, as the two burly men grab him by the arms and march him out of the office.

Sergio waits until the men leave, then he turns to face a grimy, second-story window. Smiling with satisfaction, he stares out over Tripoli, knowing that the message he just delivered is sure to earn him a reward from his capo.

CHAPTER FOUR

Frank sets his coffee cup down, then sits back to watch the tourists promenade down the street outside the gelateria.

"Angie, let's go down to the seaside," says Steve. "We still have an hour or so before the real estate office opens. I know you want to see homes in Positano, but the costs there are astronomical. Let's see if they have any homes here first."

"I wish I had a hefty sum of money like you did when you bought your villa," says Frank wistfully. "I know what I want, but I'm not sure I'll be able to pull it off."

"Don't worry," Steve replies. "Diane and I can help you out. We're happy to do it for you. Just find something you like."

Outside the gelateria, the men stroll past shops lining the road with apartments above on their way down to the shore.

"Thanks," Frank says after a while of thinking. "I'm grateful for your offer, but I don't want a handout. If you'd consider a loan, we can work out a payment schedule, and I'll pay you back."

"Sure, if that's what you want," responds Steve. "Oh, let's turn here. Via Luigi de Maio changes names a couple of times, but this road will eventually take us to Via Marina Grande, and that will lead us down to the Gulf of Naples."

The route they're taking twists along cobblestone streets with crumbling terra cotta and stucco walls that look as if they're aching to expose signs of past civilizations.

"Just imagine the history here!" exclaims Frank, looking at the old stones.

"Yeah, it's mind-boggling just thinking about it."

Suddenly, Steve stops and looks down at the sidewalk. "Oh, wow!" he exclaims, pointing to crushed berries beneath their feet. Looking up, he spies a low branch full of ripe white fruit and picks a handful. "Taste this!" he says, holding one out to Frank.

"What is it?" asks Frank warily.

"Mulberry! They're delicious! My grandmother had a huge tree in her yard."

"Isn't that what silkworms eat?"

"Yeah," responds Steve, stuffing another handful of berries into his mouth. "But they only eat the leaves. Try one! They're really good!"

Frank takes a small bite, then opens his eyes wide. "This is delicious!" he says, gobbling down the rest of the fruit. "Why haven't I heard of this before?"

"Mulberry trees aren't popular in the U.S., but they're pretty common around here. There used to be a huge silk trade in Italy, but it died out years ago."

The pair grabs more of the sweet berries, then continues walking. On the road down to the marina, they pass small shrines to the Virgin Mary decorated with plants and colorful flowers.

When they reach the beach, they stroll casually along the shoreline, inhaling the refreshing aromas of the sea, and occasionally stopping to watch fishermen with their colorful boats.

After more walking, Steve says, "Angie, there's a larger marina at the other end of town that's close to the town center.

It's where the cruise ships dock. Let's make our way back up to the city. The real estate agency should be open now."

"Okay, but I'd be happy to stay right here. It's so pretty and peaceful."

"I know what you mean, and there are many places like this. After we look at properties around here, we can drive to the Amalfi Coast. There are some other towns on the way to Amalfi that are less expensive than Positano."

"Chic, it feels like I *am* home, right here," says Frank, eyeing the fishing boats over Steve's shoulder. "I don't think I want to look anywhere else. From what I've seen, this town has the feel of a big city packed into a small seaside community. I'd be happy to die right here."

"Hey! Why are you talking about dying?" retorts Steve, narrowing his eyes at his best friend. "You're not old enough for that yet! You have too much life left to live. Come on, let's go house shopping!"

Back in the center of Sorrento, the men thread their way to the real estate office through crowds of tourists. "These visitors are the mainstay of this town," says Steve. "Every day, they fill the streets and shops to the brim."

"That's what makes this town exciting," replies Frank. "There's always someone new to meet, and you know how much I love meeting new people!"

While Steve and Frank explore Sorrento, a joint meeting of two sub-agencies of the Republic Information Security System, the Italian equivalent of the FBI and CIA, is being held across the river from Rome's Castel Sant'Angelo. Representatives from AISE, Agenzia Informazioni e Sicurezza Esterna (External Intelligence and Security Agency), and AISI, Agenzia

Informazioni e Sicurezza Interna (Internal Information and Security Agency), are in attendance at this impromptu gathering.

"As you know, Pope Urban has excommunicated all Catholic members of Cosa Nostra," says Agent Vincenzo Bennini of AISI, "and the ruling capos are not happy. The last time the Vatican confronted the mob, car bombs and terror attacks occurred across Rome. The Mafia is bolder now, so we fear their retaliation will be worse this time. The American NSA and CIA assisted us in monitoring cell phone chatter in Libya and Sicily, and what they heard suggests that a level of cooperation has developed between the mob and the Syrian Caliphate. Agent Caputi will tell you more. Sal, please continue."

Salvatore Caputi, a twenty-year veteran of law enforcement, began his career at the Carabinieri. However, he's been with AISI for the past ten years. Now in his late forties, the six-foot-two agent has begun to turn grey, but still cuts an imposing figure.

"Thank you, Vincenzo," says Caputi. "Ladies and gentlemen, multiple informants inside Cosa Nostra have reported that Don Vito Scarapelli has placed a mob hit on Pope Urban. They say he has contacted the Caliphate through the mob's criminal operations at the Port of Tripoli. We do not have details of this threat to Pope Urban or the Vatican State at this time, however, we are monitoring the situation."

The real estate office of Immobiliare Gennaro is on Corso Italia, not far from where Steve parked his car. This agency is the one that helped Steve buy his villa, so he's confident they can also help Frank.

While the men wait for an agent to put together a list of

properties, Steve's cell phone rings, so he walks outside to get better reception.

"Good morning, love," he says to his wife, Diane. "We're waiting for a list of homes for Frank to look at. What's up?"

"You received a call from a Mr. Bennini. He said he's from AISI, and he left his number. What's AISI?"

Steve knows what the acronym means, but he's not ready to tell Diane — not until he finds out what the man wants.

"It sounds like a government agency," Steve replies. "Did he say what the call was about?"

"No, he just asked that you call as soon as possible. This doesn't have anything to do with your old job, does it? Remember, you're retired from all that hoopla."

"Yes, and happily so," contends Steve. "I'll give that guy a call when I get home. Hey, they have nice lemons here in Sorrento. I'll bring some back with me. Love ya."

Steve sighs as he ends the call. He knows that Diane will Google AISI to find out what it is, and he's not happy that the agency is trying to reach him.

Steve re-enters the office. "That was Diane checking in," he tells Frank. "Are we all set to go house hunting?"

The real estate agent is a young woman in her late twenties who doesn't look like a typical Italian. Rather than being on the short side with dark hair and dark eyes, this five-foot-nine woman has blue eyes and blonde hair.

Real estate agent Stefania Rossi holds a folder under one arm while addressing Frank. "I have three properties you can see today. Two are here in Sorrento; another is a few kilometers south of the city. The third is on a hilltop farther inland, but it has the good views you are looking for. That one is not as expensive as the ones on the Sorrentine coast. It needs some upgrades and is quite a good deal."

Stefania says to Steve, "I have explained to Mr. Angelo that prices are a premium along the coast."

Steve nods. "That's what I said before, Ang. All the properties along the Amalfi Coast are prime real estate. The farther you get from the water, the less expensive they are, just like anywhere else. However, in this area, all the homes are pricey to begin with."

Frank shrugs. "I hear ya. But ya can't take it with ya, right? I'm lucky that when I sold the bar, I was able to work the deal so Geo could manage it for the new owner; providing he's not busy with his FSA terror thing."

"What's gonna happen when he's not available for the bar?" asks Steve.

"He's gonna hire an assistant. I worked out a good deal for both of us. I got myself an ample nest egg, and a guarantee of ongoing employment for Geo. The egg may not be from an ostrich, but it's still from a decent-sized chicken."

"It better be from an effin' large chicken to buy something around here!" chuckles Steve. "But remember, I got ya," he adds, as the men follow Stefania to her Fiat 500 parked outside the store.

Amil Bacdadi is now in a small compound in the middle of the Libyan Desert, sipping tea with Muhammad Salim Muhammad and other Caliphate officers before their meeting begins. For a suitable amount of time, the men exchange pleasantries and chat about inconsequential matters. Then, they get down to business.

"Let us now talk about why we are here," says Amil, putting down his cup. "As my contact reminded me, the enemy of our enemy is our friend. The Italian Mafia controls all the ports in Southern Italy, therefore, they can ensure our safe passage to Rome by way of Sicily. While we all agree that their offer is tempting, I must advise you that they already believe we have accepted their terms. These men are serious. We cannot tempt fate with them. If we go ahead with this, our people will be in their element once they get to Italy. At that point, the operation will be out of our control."

"There is much to consider," says Muhammad, rising from his seat on a soft cushion. "I must think about this."

As the Caliphate chieftain considers what Amil said, he paces back and forth in a small room covered with brightly covered fabrics, while his thawb shifts softly with every step. Respectfully, the others remain at their places until their leader is ready to speak again.

Muhammad is in no hurry; he takes his time with his thoughts. He knows his decision will have major consequences, so it is essential that it is the right one.

After a long while, the chieftain stops and faces the men. "Taqiyya permits us to deceive and lie for our cause," he says thoughtfully. "Therefore, we will tolerate these infidels for as long as they are useful to us. Amil, you may contact the Italians. Tell them we are ready. I will choose three of my best men to accompany you back to Tripoli. Give them the information they ask for. That is all. Allahu Akbar."

CHAPTER FIVE

The Governorate Palace of Vatican City State, a majestic building within the stone walls of Vatican City, is where AISI officer Salvatore Caputi is waiting for Colonel Theodore Accola. Colonel Accola is Commander of the Pontifical Swiss Guard, the military unit in charge of protecting the pope, and Salvatore has scheduled an impromptu meeting with him, so he is being patient.

When Colonel Accola appears, he moves briskly behind his desk. "What is going on?" he asks crisply. "Why did you tell my secretary that this meeting is urgent?"

"Theodore, we are tracking a threat against Pope Urban. Cosa Nostra did not accept the excommunication of their Catholic members very well. We have reason to believe that the criminal organization has been in contact with representatives of the Middle Eastern Caliphate. We believe they are planning to work together to assassinate the pope."

The news stuns Colonel Accola but he tries to hide his shock behind a mask of doubt. "Are you serious?" he frowns at the man in front of him. "They will not threaten Pope Urban, Salvatore. That is unheard of."

"I assure you that they are discussing it as we speak," Caputi replies. "Our contacts inside the mob's organization have told us that they have put a contract out on the pope. As we know, Muhammad Salim Muhammad, the head of the Caliphate, has stated many times that they want to attack the Vatican."

"Yes, but where is your proof of this outlandish assertion?" asks Accola.

"Colonel, this is not a training exercise," Caputi declares bluntly. "Representatives of the mob have talked with the Caliphate, and I have come to warn you of the situation. You need to put your men on full alert. Be advised that we must manage this quietly; no statements can be made to the public."

Salvatore places an official folder on the colonel's desk. "God willing, we will stop this," he says as he goes through the door.

Colonel Accola reads the folder's name, DISTRUZIONE DELLA ROCCIA (Destruction of the Rock), and picks up his phone. "Come to my office," he orders.

Alone with his thoughts, Accola places the handset back into the cradle and stares with growing uneasiness at a photo of Pope Urban IV on the wall in front of him.

In a few minutes, a tall man in a black suit stands in front of his desk. "Sit, please," the colonel states grimly. "We have a problem."

As soon as Salvatore left the colonel's office, he began to formulate a list of tasks in his mind. Running through past procedures, he knows there are a number of things he'll need to do in the next few days to get things started.

Still thinking, Salvatore stops at the top of the steps just outside of the building's doors. At the bottom, a beautifully manicured lawn and garden flows into the vast expanse between this building and the rear of Saint Peter's Basilica.

Salvatore shakes his head at the job before him and walks down the steps to street level, then turns back to stare at the opulent, palace-like structure housing the Vatican City State's governing body.

"Accola better get moving quickly," he mumbles, walking through the garden to his car in a tiny lot at the rear of the Sistine Chapel.

Later, Salvatore steers the car through streets swamped with tourists and Italian citizens. As he goes, he wonders what they would say if they knew about the events he just set into motion.

Stefania Rossi stops her car at the first property on her list, a villa along the Via Bernardino Rota, a road overlooking the Gulf of Naples.

Steve and Frank follow Stefania through a cobblestone entryway that leads up to a wrought-iron gate. Through the gate, the group sees a stone and brick building with a majestic, hand-carved double wooden door adorned with cherubs and clouds.

Frank admires the details, but suspects the home is out of his league. "How much is this place?" he asks.

"It went on the market for about one million euros, but —"

"Wait," Frank interrupts. "I can't afford that. Let's not go inside. I'll only be disappointed to see what I can't have."

"Mr. Angelo," Stefania replies, "I understand your concern. This is what you would call a fix-her-up. It is quite affordable because it needs loving care. I would like you to see it because you should know what to expect at the lower end of housing costs in this area."

"Oh. So how much is it now?"

"The owners are asking five hundred and fifty thousand euros. It has been on the market for three years, and they just reduced the price again. They are anxious to sell, so I believe we can offer an even lower price. But you would need to do some work. Come," she says, unlocking the door. "Let us take a look."

When Colonel Accola and the man in the black suit finish discussing the information presented by Salvatore Caputi at the Governorate Palace, the man stands and reaches out his hand to the commander of the Swiss Guard. In doing so, the cuff of his stiff white shirt pulls back just enough to reveal a dark image tattooed on the inside of his wrist: a black raven perched on a cross.

Colonel Accola looks at the familiar shape on the man's wrist, then up into the man's eyes, hoping to see some semblance of humanity there. But there is nothing — no emotion, no reaction, no conscience. With a shudder, he shakes the man's hand and thanks him for coming.

When the door closes, Accola crosses himself and mouths a quick prayer.

In Sorrento, Stefania pushes on the villa's oversized wooden door, causing its rusty hinges to creak and moan from lengthy periods of disuse.

Inside, Frank is pleased to see that they've stepped into a decent-sized great room with a white but grimy marble floor. His initial delight turns into disappointment, however, when he looks more closely and sees that many of the floor tiles are missing, and even more are broken or cracked.

Dismayed, he trails Stefania into a small, unfurnished area at the rear of the house.

"I assume that was the living area," Frank says.

"Yes, that is correct," Stefania responds.

"So what is this room?" he asks.

With an expansive sweep of her arm, Stefania proudly explains, "This is the kitchen."

"Huh? How can this be the kitchen?" asks Frank, looking dubiously around the empty space. "Where are the appliances, the cabinets?" he asks with mounting incredulity. "What about the sink? There's nothing here except a bunch of pipes poking out of the walls. And it's so tiny! How can anyone prepare a meal in here? There's not even a window! This is crazy!"

"I understand that you are confused," says Stefania, trying to calm the American. "But this is common in Italy. The kitchen areas in our country are not large, and many sellers take their appliances and cabinets with them when they move. But that is good, you see. The buyer can then purchase what they like and set up the room however they want. You understand?"

"Well, I guess so, but it's so smal..." Frank starts to complain again, until Steve pokes him.

Aware that Steve is warning him to shut up, he asks instead, "Um, okay. Can we see the bedrooms?"

"Sì. Follow me."

Frank hesitates, so Steve prods him to move forward on the cracked tile floor. "Let's see the rest," he whispers to his friend.

Frank is not impressed. Down a short hallway, Stefania points out two bedrooms and two bathrooms. The floors in the first two rooms definitely need to be replaced, and the walls look like they need major repairs. They're cracked and peeling, and in some areas, foundational brickwork is playing peek-a-boo with the plaster. The rooms are small, and there are no closets inside either one.

"Where do we put our clothes?" gasps Frank, looking aghast at the real estate agent.

"You would need to buy wardrobes. Ah, you say, closets," replies Stefania. "You can place them there, along the far wall."

Frank pokes his head into one of the bathrooms, not expecting much after seeing the other parts of the house. With dismay, he notes that it's like the kitchen. Although it does have a toilet, the appliance is cracked, and the room is otherwise empty, with capped pipes coming out of the walls.

Frank frowns at Stefania.

"Yes, it *is* dated," the woman agrees with a broad smile, "but the tile is intact and in good condition. You can also fix the bathrooms the way you like."

"More work," sighs Frank. "But I guess it could be done."

Stefania nods and leads them back into the living area.

Frank makes a beeline for some windows at the other end, hoping for a pleasant view through the broken panes. This time, he's not disappointed. Just outside the windows is an overgrown garden area with an intact wall overlooking the sparkling blue sea.

Frank inhales deeply. "That's a pretty view. But this place needs *a lot* of work," he says, taking stock of the entire house.

"Yes, Mr. Angelo," Stefania responds matter-of-factly. "Minor work will have to be done. But this is easy and simple. I have many connections who can help in this regard. Do not worry, we will offer a low price. The owners need to sell; I am sure they will accept your offer."

Frank is uncertain, so he looks to his best friend for guidance.

"Ang," says Steve, "this is a million-dollar house that's priced to sell. It's perfect for you and Geo; you'd have your own rooms and bathrooms. Geo said he'd help with the down payment, and so will I. And you can stay with me and Diane while it's being fixed up."

"Yeah, but…"

"Look, the view alone could make it well worth the hassle," goads Steve with a smile. "You should definitely see more properties, but just about everything will need some work done. You think you can suck it up, buttercup?"

"Hmm. I'll think about it."

Salvatore Caputi and Interpol officer Henri Franchi are apprehensive about talking to U.S. Ambassador John Connelly. The man is a twenty-something official, new to his position, with no prior international experience. He also has no knowledge of the Italian language and is unfamiliar with Italian law and customs. However, he is the son of a wealthy contributor to the U.S. president's successful reelection campaign. Ergo, his coveted appointment.

"Come right in, gentlemen. Sorry for the delay," says the well-groomed bureaucrat. "Julie, please bring us some caffè," he instructs his secretary before closing the door.

Unsurprisingly, the interior of Ambassador Connelly's office is elegant. Fitted out with a well-designed marble floor, attractive walnut paneling, and tasteful Italian furnishings, the ample space exudes power and prestige. The ambassador's opulent desk, placed strategically in front of a large photograph of the current U. S. president surrounded by the Stars and Stripes and the Italian flag, completes the look.

"Thank you for seeing us today," remarks Salvatore in heavily accented English. "I am afraid we do not have good news."

"Oh? I'm listening," replies Connelly. "But before we begin, please tell me something about yourselves. My secretary supplied me with basic information, but I'm new here and I haven't met everyone in your government yet."

"Yes, of course. My name is Salvatore Caputi, and I work for AISI, our Internal Information and Security Agency. It is comparable to your CIA. My companion—"

"Pleased to meet you, Ambassador," interjects Henri. "I am Henri Franchi, with Interpol. I assume you have heard of us?"

"Yes," smiles Connelly.

Salvatore resumes, "Mr. Ambassador, we have disturbing information to share with you, and we are here to request help from the United States government to deal with it."

At that moment, Connelly's secretary walks in with coffee and biscotti, which she serves to each of them.

When the secretary leaves, Connelly states, "You have piqued my interest, signore. Please go on."

Caputi glances sideways at Franchi, who nods imperceptibly. He places his cup on a small table and says, "Ambassador, we have intercepted communications between the Scarapelli crime family in Sicily and the Caliphate in Libya. As you have most likely learned by now, Pope Urban recently excommunicated all Catholic members of Cosa Nostra. The Italian crime families are not pleased, and Don Vito Scarapelli has taken it upon himself to seek revenge on behalf of the other families. He is working with the Caliphate to help them carry out their well-known desire to attack Saint Peter's Basilica and assassinate the pope."

"But they can't do that, right?" asks the ambassador. "Don't you have procedures in place to uncover criminal activity, especially when it involves the pope?"

"Yes, we do, sir. But it will be easy for Don Vito to bring a suicide squad into our country undetected by law enforcement. The Mafia controls all the seaports in Italy. They smuggle many things into our country, including people. We are here to ask the United States to help our security forces block this assassination attempt."

Connelly stares at the men over his coffee. "How do you know about this?" he asks uncertainly.

Franchi says, "AISI and Interpol have informants in the Mafia, as well as agents in Tripoli. And we have received information from your intelligence agencies. We know that talks between the Mafia and the Caliphate have already occurred, and we expect members of ISIS to enter Sicily within days, if they are not already here. We would like assistance from your FBI. Your advanced technology will be of immense help to us, and we know that you have had many successes in stopping terror attacks in your country. Your FSA has proven to be quite effective."

"I agree," responds Connelly, "but it is an ongoing battle. FSA is always on the alert. Of course, I will have to contact our State Department, but I'm sure they'll support you in every way. However," he adds cautiously, "there may be a way for us to go ahead without official government confirmation. A former director of our FSA is now living in Ravello. I can arrange a meeting for you so we can get our partnership started."

Salvatore says, "We know about Mr. Ciccone, Ambassador. We have already contacted him, but he has not responded. We welcome your involvement."

CHAPTER SIX

Frank looked at several other houses, then offered five hundred euros for the "fixer-upper," and the sellers accepted it. Though he got the house at a great price, he was still unsure about laying out so much money. So when the euro took an unexpected tumble before he signed the final papers, he was happy that his actual cost became a more acceptable number.

"You know," says Frank to Steve after signing the last of the purchase papers, "I appreciate that you and Stefania will be overseeing the repairs while I'm back home."

"Happy to do it, bro," responds Steve. "Besides, it'll give me something to do. I can't stare at the water *all* day long!"

"Yeah, must be hard," laughs Frank. "Can't wait till I'm as bored as you!"

When the day comes for Frank to leave Italy, Steve drives him to the airport, then returns home to find Diane waiting for him with a kiss and a cappuccino.

"It's going to be great having your friends here full-time," says Diane. "But until they move here permanently, let's enjoy our quiet times together. Take your coffee out to the balcony. I bought sfogliatelle while you were out."

The couple relaxes in comfortable outdoor chairs, sipping coffee in silence. Neither of them is aware of the black

Mercedes cruising slowly up their *viale d'accesso*, the short access road to their home lined with cypress trees and white and purple bougainvillea bushes.

On the balcony, the couple stares peacefully at the blue Gulf of Salerno far below, until the soft tinkling of their doorbell cuts the mood.

"I'll get it," says Diane, rising from her chair. "Wonder who that could be."

Steve cranes his head to look past Diane when she opens the door, and he doesn't like what he sees: three strangers standing on his doorstep in dark business suits. He can't hear their conversation, but he frowns when each of them hands Diane a business card.

"Who are those assholes?" Steve asks when Diane goes back outside. "What do they want?"

"They want to talk to you," says Diane, showing him the cards. Knowing her husband well, she implores, "Please don't do anything that will get you into trouble."

Steve's frown deepens as he reads each card. "Fuck," he sighs. "I guess you should show them in."

While Diane returns to the door, Steve finishes his coffee, then walks over to the garden wall. Looking out across the water, he stares with unseeing eyes toward the ever-present sailboats caressing the gulf.

Diane knows that her husband will require privacy to deal with whatever the men want. So after she brings them onto the balcony, she retreats into the house.

But Steve makes the men wait.

With his back to them, he continues staring at nothing, letting several minutes pass in silence. Then he sighs and turns toward his visitors.

"Look," Steve says grimly, "I was trying to decide whether to let you speak or kick you the hell out of my house. Lucky for you, I decided to hear your story. But only because one of you is a member of my State Department. So okay, talk."

Giuseppe Seminara, shortest of the three and assistant to Ambassador Connelly, says, "Mr. Ciccone, these gentlemen have asked the United States government to help them with a delicate situation here in Italy, and the State Department has agreed to assist with whatever they need."

"Oh yeah? How does that involve me?" asks Steve.

"What they need, sir, is you."

"Ha," Steve snorts, unimpressed by the man's compliment. "Is that why Bennini called? Never mind, you don't need to answer that. Now, what's this 'delicate situation' you're talking about? That's political speak for shit hitting the fan. Just tell me what the hell is going on, and what the hell you want from me. You know I'm retired, so this better be *very* important."

Steve leans against the balcony wall with his arms crossed over his chest, waiting for one of his visitors to explain why they have come to his home.

"May we sit, Signore Ciccone?" asks Salvatore.

"Sure. Just make this quick."

"Very well. I will get to the point. We have credible data that proves that the Caliphate in Libya is actively working to kill the pope. We have received word through our undercover people in Sicily that the Scarapelli crime family—"

"You mean the Mafia," clarifies Steve frostily.

"Yes, the Mafia," concedes Salvatore. "The Pope excommunicated them from the Church, and they want to make a statement to protest his decision. But they do not want to do it entirely on their own. They are plotting their retaliation with the Caliphate, telling them that they will assist with their frequently-expressed desire to assassinate the pope."

"LOOK!" erupts Steve. "Stop with all the political double-speak! 'Make a statement,' my ass! The Mafia put a hit out on the pope, and they're getting the Caliphate to do their dirty work! Am I right? That way, the Arabs will get the blame, and the Mafia will walk away unscathed! What the hell do you need *me* for? Get your Carabinieri to go after them!"

"Signore Ciccone, it is not that simple," replies Salvatore. "The Mafia has tight control of all Italian ports. Hundreds of ships come into those ports every day, and with the crime lords' influence over the local police — and Carabinieri — we cannot be assured of their cooperation. Your State Department has agreed to help us by sending agents from the FBI, and Interpol will send officers from their headquarters in France. What we need from you is your expertise. We want you to oversee a group that we will form to stop the attack. Your reputation with the FSA has followed you here, signore. We need a man with no political connections to manage this international team — a man who is known to get the job done."

On the pretense of being helpful, Diane brings out coffee and pastries. But what she's really doing is making sure to catch Steve's eye to gauge the gist of the conversation. When she does, she knows immediately that he's going back to work, and is deeply concerned.

Steve knows that his wife is upset, so he turns his back on the men to stare out at the sea again.

After a while, he sits down and pours himself a cup of coffee. "I'll do this, only because it involves the pope. And there will be one condition. We do things my way, or I'm out. I must be the only one in charge, and I don't want any political bullshit. If you agree, grab a pastry. If not, I'll escort you to the door."

As three hands reach for a dessert, Steve smirks and looks pointedly at the Italians. "So the French will be in Sicily again?" he says, referring to French Interpol officers working with the group. "I hope those guys will keep their nuts this time," he sneers, assuming that the Italians know that the Mafia castrated Sicily's 13th century French occupiers and sent their testicles to Paris. "I hope you won't have to protect them again!"

CHAPTER SEVEN

The room Amil Bacdadi is working in at one of Tripoli's piers is hot and stuffy. But that's not why he's sweating. The day he's been dreaming of has arrived, and everything he's doing is on the line. He's anxious and edgy, and his emotions are strained to the max.

Bacdadi wipes his moist hands on his shirt before handing out the three sets of fraudulent IDs, work permits, and visas he paid dearly for. His organization's volunteers will need those items to conduct their mission, so he's careful not to soil them. Watching him, the three men are also sweating and tense.

"Study your information well," orders Amil. "You may have to answer questions and your answers cannot be unclear or hesitant."

Amil settles in a chair while the men, Bashir Sarcoom, a munitions expert from Pakistan, and two soldiers from the Syrian Caliphate — Abdul Al-Hakim and Harun Al Rachid — attempt to commit the unfamiliar facts to memory.

After a time, Bacdadi tells the men that they will board the cargo ship *Dammam Jeddah* after the meeting is over. "You will pose as crewmembers, but you will not be on board for the entire voyage. You will disembark at Trapani, a small city in western Sicily, the ship's first port of call. In Trapani, you will be met by soldiers of the Scarapelli crime family. They will bring you to Cefalù, another city in Sicily."

Amil watches the men closely. "The captain is the only

one who knows you are not crewmen. Keep low profiles. Stay in your bunks as much as possible, and do not interact with any of the others aboard the ship. When you arrive in Trapani, go directly to the Hotel Moderno. Here is the address. We booked one room for all of you under Bashir's name. Wait in that room. Do not leave it, except for food. Send one person out each day to get enough for the group; you will not be there long. Wait in that room for someone from the crime family to contact you." Amil wipes sweat off his forehead and gestures toward the dock. "Now, follow me. I will take you to the ship."

"Allahu Akbar!" shout the men.

The three novices are excited but nervous as Amil threads his way through the dock's bustling activities. When they see the *Dammam Jaddah*, Amil explains with disgust that they're loading textiles and spices for infidels in Italy. "But we need the money," he says.

At the approach to the gangway leading up to the cargo vessel, a potbellied older man moves to block their way. Motioning for them to stop, he asks, "Who sends you?" Amil replies, "I am looking for the office."

When the captain hears the code phrase, he grunts in approval. "Speak," he says.

"These are your new 'crewmen,'" says Amil, and goes on to explain the reason for the men being on the ship.

When he's done, the captain waves at the first mate, standing at the top of the gangway. "New men!" he shouts, motioning the impostors aboard with a flick of his wrist.

As the volunteers ascend the gangway, Amil mouths a silent prayer for their mission's success. Then, he turns around to begin the short walk back to the hot and stuffy room.

On the way, Amil concentrates on the critical task set before him, wondering not for the first time whether the three he chose were the best he could find.

With his mind occupied with a thousand such worries, Amil neglects to pay his usual careful attention to his surroundings. He gives only a cursory glance to an unmarked van when it's directly upon him. And when it passes, he returns to his musings.

Amil's lack of caution will soon prove to be a grave mistake.

A few blocks past the Mafia collaborator, the vehicle makes a sharp U-turn and speeds back in the opposite direction. When it comes alongside Amil, it slows down long enough for the side door to slide open, and a strong arm to reach out and grab the unsuspecting person around the neck.

Prey secured, the arm jerks back, and the door closes.

The last thing Amil saw was a tattoo of a black raven perched on a cross.

CHAPTER EIGHT

By the time the clock strikes midnight, the distinctive stars of Orion the Hunter are clearly visible over the Amalfi Coast. The sky is moonless, and if Diane and Steve were on their balcony, they could stare down at the calm black sea and see stars twinkling "hello" in reflections on the water.

But Steve and Diane are not on their balcony. They're snuggling up against each other in their bedroom, trying to reach the familiar state of mindlessness that keeps eluding them.

Knowing that Diane is just as awake as he is, Steve sighs and turns toward his wife. "You know I can't say no," he murmurs, referring to the meeting on the balcony earlier that day. "I thought I was done. But this is something I have to do."

"I know," Diane replies quietly, "but I'm worried. I want you to be careful. You're not as young as you think you are."

"Huh!" snorts Steve, throwing the covers aside and rolling onto his wife. "I'm young enough when it counts!"

When morning comes, Steve and Diane don light jackets so they can sip their cappuccinos comfortably on the balcony, their favorite place in their new home. The sun hasn't risen yet, so it's still a little chilly, but they love this time of day. It's quiet, and the sea is usually calm.

When the sun begins to rise, it throws sparkling rays onto the water, which delights them every time they see it. They often tell each other how they have to pinch themselves to believe they're really living in such a beautiful place.

Although neither slept much the night before, their time together was invigorating, to say the least. Thinking back on it, Diane tilts her head and smiles at her husband, getting Steve's attention. Smiling back, Steve gives her a peck on the cheek, just as his phone rings inside the house.

"Don't go anywhere," he winks.

Steve answers the call, then rejoins Diane with his cell phone in hand. Placing it on the tiled table, he looks at his wife sheepishly. "They work fast," he says. "They're sending a car to pick me up. It'll be here in an hour."

"Not today!" replies Diane petulantly. "We're supposed to go into town today to shop for new cushions!"

"Guess you'll have to do that on your own. I have a meeting in Naples; looks like I'm going to meet my crew today." Steve pushes his chair away from the table and says playfully, "I gotta go do my three S's before the car arrives."

"I'll wait out here!" Diane calls after Steve. "Just make sure you use air freshener!"

Diane swallows the last bit of coffee as Steve chuckles inside the villa.

It's been twenty-four hours since Amil's captors led him into a building and strapped him to a wooden chair, and he hasn't left that chair once, not even to relieve himself. Having no choice, he's pissed and shit himself several times since then, so the space he's in is now filled with an extremely foul odor.

Amil doesn't know it, but he's in a fifteen-thousand-square-foot building with cement floors and walls, and nothing else. He can't see his surroundings because of a burlap bag tied securely around his head. But Amil wouldn't be able to see anything even without the bag. The windows in the old warehouse are so dirty that they may as well be tinted.

The frightened man is fairly sure he's alone. The entire time he's been in the chair, he hasn't heard any sounds except his own breathing. He's called out several times, but all he heard back were echoes.

Amil had been in the chair so long, that he had begun to think that whoever captured him intended to leave him there to die. So when a weak light suddenly filters around the corners of the burlap sack, he grasps at the possibility that he could get out of his dire situation.

"Is someone there?" he asks hopefully.

No one answers, but what he does hear is the sound of shoes slapping toward him, and something dragging along the floor.

Suddenly, a strong stream of cold water hits Amil square in the chest, sending him and the chair backward. With no way of protecting himself, his head hits the concrete, and he's knocked unconscious.

The hooded men who brought in the hose are counting on the water to flush away the fetid smells.

"What else could we do?" they snicker as the dirty water circles a drain in the floor near the unconscious man. "That bastard desperately needed a shower! He was stinking the place up to high heaven!"

The men pass the hose over Amil a few times, then one of them sets him and the chair upright. Another man pulls the burlap sack from Amil's head, while a third waves a small vial under Amil's nose, causing him to open his eyes with a start.

Wincing from the pain in his head, Amil blinks rapidly at two men in dark masks and black clothing standing over him. "Who the hell are you?" he asks, noticing bird tattoos on the insides of their wrists. "What do you want?"

The taller of the men slaps Amil across the mouth. "*We* are the ones asking the questions here, so listen closely to the first two: Those men you put on the ship... Where are they going, and who are they going to meet?"

Amil knows his position is desperate, but he is loyal to his cause. "They are crewmen, and they will go where the ship goes," he responds coolly. "You want more information? Ask them."

"Oh, we will definitely ask them," replies the hooded man, his arms folded tightly across his chest. "But not now. Now, it is *your* turn to talk."

"We know they are not crewmen," growls the second man. "They are Caliphate, like you, and you are all working with Vito Scarapelli. So, we ask again: Where are they going, and who will they meet?"

Amil purses his lips. "I am a dead man, whether I answer you or not. So, *adhhab 'iilava aljahim*. Go to hell."

With a sigh, the taller man reaches into a bag on the floor and lifts out a bolt cutter. At the same time, the other man grabs Amil's left hand and holds it securely to the arm of the chair.

Amil is horrified. He knows what is coming, so he struggles and shouts. "You are animals! Fuck you!"

Swiftly, the taller man wraps the bolt cutter's jaws around Amil's pinky finger, and squeezes. With a bone-shattering snap, the finger falls to the concrete floor, accompanied by Amil's screams and blood squirting in all directions.

The taller one picks the finger up from the floor and throws it into Amil's lap. "We can do this all day. You have nine more fingers and ten toes. After that, we move to your dick.

That is, if you are still conscious at that point. So, let us try this again. Where are they going, and who will they meet?"

This time, Amil responds, but his words are interspersed with curses and moans of excruciating pain. "*Akh!* You son of a whore! Oww, eat shit, you son of a bitch! They will be contacted when the ship docks!"

"Where is it going?"

"To Sicily, you filthy dog! That is all I will say! Oww, umm..."

"Who will contact them?"

"I will say no more! My children are not safe!"

The man snaps off another finger, and Amil passes out. To wake him, they turn the hose on again.

As more blood drains from Amil's body, he grows weaker and weaker. "I cannot," he says softly, staring at his mangled hand and the blood flowing onto the floor. "I have made a vow. I will be shaheed."

Angrily, the interrogator grabs Amil's hair and jerks his head upward. "We will kill your wife and daughters if you do not talk! Is that worth becoming a martyr?"

But Amil says nothing. As the masked men continue to try to get him to divulge the Caliphate's plans, more bones snap, and Amil screams and screams.

Frank called George a few days after he returned to the U.S. from Italy and asked to meet for breakfast at their favorite diner. He chose a time an hour earlier than usual, because even though he was uncomfortable with Italy's chilly weather, the heat in Florida can sometimes be unbearable. And true to form, at only eight a.m. on the appointed day, the temperature is already close to eighty degrees.

Frank requests a booth toward the back of the restaurant, and George concurs; his choice would have been the same. The friends' days at the police force trained them to be wary of eavesdroppers and to always keep their eyes on the door.

Frank is dying to tell George his big news, but he waits until they place their regular orders: short stacks with a side of grits. As soon as the waitress leaves, Frank blurts out, "I did it, Geo! You're looking at the proud owner of a villa in Sorrento!"

"No way!" splutters George, nearly choking on his coffee.

"Yup! Now you can give your two weeks' notice and start learning Italian!"

"How did you find one so quickly? You didn't even ask for my share of the down payment!"

"Shit, I know you're good for it," Frank smiles. "Besides, Chic has deep pockets. Hell, he offered to help me out with a loan for the whole thing, and I might take him up on it. But I got a great deal on the place. It's been on the market for a while and needs some work, so the sellers came down on the price."

"Where is it?"

"Not too far from Chic and Diane; about an hour and a half away. I can't wait to move in! They say it shouldn't take long to get everything done to fix it up, barring problems with craftsmen and government regs."

"How you gonna manage repairing a house in Italy while you're here? You going back soon?"

"Nah. Steve's gonna oversee things, and the real estate agent is gonna help, too."

"Sounds like you have everything under control," comments George. "I'm impressed." Then, George leans toward

Frank and lowers his voice to a whisper. "Got some info. There's a bunch of shit going on in Italy."

"Oh? What's happening?"

"It's big," whispers George. "The Caliphate wants to kill the pope. Word's out that the Mafia's involved, too. The FBI sent a crew to help the Italian authorities."

When their pancakes arrive, they stop their conversation and busy themselves with their meals.

Between bites, Frank declares, "Dollars to donuts, Steve gets involved."

George nods. "*Scommetto che anche il nostro amico ci coinvolge.* That means, I bet he gets us involved in that crap, too. See? I've been practicing!"

Frank laughs. "*Sono d'accordo. Saremo nella merda profonda!* I agree, buddy. We're gonna be in deep shit!"

"I'll probably be back late," Steve tells Diane when a Mercedes arrives to drive him to the meeting. "When I get home, let's go into Ravello for dinner."

Steve settles into the back of the car for the hour-long ride to Naples. He's unsure about what he'll be doing, so his mind goes to past missions.

Steve trusts the AISI driver, so he looks absentmindedly out of the window, until the car turns toward Ravello's town center instead of Naples. "Hey, what's going on?" Steve asks, suddenly suspicious. "Naples is the other way."

"Sì," responds the driver, looking at Steve in the rearview mirror. "But the helicopter is not."

Steve is confused. *Should I be worried?* he wonders. Ravello is a small, compact town on a mountaintop, so he can't imagine where a helicopter would find a place to put down. The road they're on — Via della Marra — will eventually lead them to the Duomo di Ravello at the town's main piazza. However, Steve is supposed to be going to Naples to set up an anti-terrorist group. He knows Salvatore sent the driver, so he decides to keep his mouth shut and his eyes open.

Things get clearer when the car approaches Piazza Centrale in front of the Duomo. Surprisingly, the entire area is cordoned off, and an AgustaWestland AW139 helicopter is sitting in the center with its long rotor blades turning lazily.

Looking into the rearview mirror, the driver says, "Signore, we will bring you back here when your meeting is over. We will notify your wife to pick you up here."

The chopper is waiting for its solo passenger like a dragonfly sitting on a lily pad — to the intense dismay of the surrounding shopkeepers and restaurant owners.

Crouching down, Steve sprints toward the helicopter's open door and buckles himself in. When the pilot gives a thumbs-up, he lifts the black bird skyward.

Below them, the air wash blows over the same tables and chairs the annoyed shop owners had already righted once that day. Upset for the second time, they curse and shake their fists skyward.

Spotting a set of headphones, Steve puts them on so he can talk to the pilot. "You made some people pretty angry down there," he says. "And they're not going to like me very much, either. But I'm going to have to face them. I live here."

The pilot laughs and banks the chopper southward, giving Steve a view of the land below.

"Hey, that's my house, and that's my wife!" Steve shouts, surprised to see Diane looking up at the loud machine flying overhead. Chuckling, he tells the pilot, "Wait till I tell her that it was *me* she flashed the bird at this morning!"

CHAPTER NINE

At the American Embassy in Naples, introductions are made in a small conference room among the members of the team Steve was asked to lead. Present are Vincenzo Bennini and Salvatore Caputi from AISI, Colonel Theodore Accola from the Vatican Swiss Guard, Kathryn Samuels and John DeMaria from the Washington D.C. office of the FBI, and Henri Franchi from Interpol.

The group is now sitting at a round table, reading from folders placed in front of each of them.

"You know," confides FBI Special Agent John DeMaria, speaking to the person next to him, "I always wanted to visit Naples; my grandfather was born here. I never thought I'd be working when I got here, though. But I'll take it!"

Steve checks his watch, then rises to start the meeting.

"Let me say something first," whispers Vincenzo Bennini, grabbing Steve's arm.

"Okay," Steve replies, retaking his seat.

"*Saluti a tutti!*" begins Vincenzo loudly enough to get everyone's attention. "Let us welcome Signore Steven Ciccone from the United States FSA! We are honored to have him lead our group!"

"No need for formality," protests Ciccone. "I'm okay with just Steve."

"Very well," responds Vincenzo. "I am sure that most of

you have heard of Steve before today. His multiple successes at the FSA in stopping terrorist attacks are well-known through-out the world, so we are fortunate that he has agreed to help us. We will discuss the information in your folders in a minute. Before we begin, I need to update you with the latest informa-tion. We have just learned that several members of the Caliph-ate cell that is working with Cosa Nostra are already in Sicily. A photograph of the Mafia's Caliphate contact person is in your folder. His name is Amil Bacdadi."

While the team shuffles through the papers, Bennini explains. "Earlier today, Bacdadi was found by *la polizia* in an abandoned warehouse in Tripoli. He was alive when they found him, but he was tortured so severely that he died shortly after. He couldn't say much, but he did give the authorities a clue about who his killers are. He said he was tortured by masked men who had a tattoo — a black bird on a cross. They were—"

Across the table, Theodore Accola gasps so loudly that Vincenzo stops mid-sentence.

"What do you know about this, Colonel Accola?" asks Steve with eyes narrowed at the Swiss Guard official.

"Um, il Papa, he is a very powerful figure, and his life must be protected—"

"Yes, I'm sure everyone here agrees with that... That's why we're here," retorts Steve. "What I want from you is an ex-planation of your reaction to what Signore Bennini just said."

"Sì, if I may continue..."

Steve waves a hand to go on, so Colonel Accola says, "*Allora,* to ensure the pope's safety, the early Vatican Council created a, how you say? 'special organization' to see that he and the Church are saf—"

"I see," interrupts Steve. "So the Vatican has a hit squad

of 'ghost operators' at their service. And I bet they identify each other with that tattoo and work outside of all Italian laws and jurisdictions. Am I right?"

Steve sees a lot of blank faces staring back at him. "Well, well," he says. "It seems that I'm going to be leading a group of people charged with breaking up a partnership between the Mafia and radical Islamic fanatics, while also worrying about radical *Christian* fanatics. Chime in if anyone else here knows about that 'special organization'. Or if none of you wants to talk, should I just go home and leave you all with this stinking pile of *merda* to take care of on your own?"

No one else speaks, so Salvatore Caputi volunteers what little he knows. "Signore, the organization we are talking about is the Order of the Raven. It was established at the time of the Crusades to protect the Catholic Church, the pope, and the Holy See. It is a secret underground society, and no one knows much about it. However," he adds, looking pointedly at the colonel, "I believe Colonel Accola can tell you more."

The colonel doesn't respond, moving Steve to stand and stare daggers at the man. "Look," he states sternly, "tell us what you know, or I won't have anything to do with this group, and I'll direct our FBI to head home as well. Then you and the rest of your *Keystone Cops*-style system can take care of this yourselves. I won't work with anyone who keeps information from me."

Clearly uncomfortable, Accola looks down at his hands while slowly shaking his head side to side. After a moment of this, he sighs. "As head of the Swiss Guard, it is my responsibility to keep Pope Urban safe. Therefore, I am obliged to inform the Order of the Raven of any threats to His Holiness. But I use the word 'obliged' as an understatement. If that group ever thought I was part of this group and did not tell them... Well, one day, I would no longer be among the living. The Ravens are prepared to do whatever it takes to stop an attack on His Holiness, and it seems they already know something about it. If they think we are getting in their way, they will not hesitate to get rid of any of us as well. They consider everyone but themselves to be expendable."

"Fuck this!" shouts Steve as his blood pressure rises. "Then why don't you get the Ravens to take care of the Caliphate and the Mafia? That's what they do, isn't that what you're telling us? What the hell do you need us or the FBI for? Handle this yourselves! John, Kathryn, let's get the hell out of here. This is FUBAR! We're not going to get involved in this *merda*!"

Steve pushes his chair away from the table. "I'm going home. If that chopper isn't up on the roof waiting for me, send for it. And if it doesn't get here soon, I'll take one of your cars, and someone can pick it up at my villa."

Turning on his heel, Steve storms out of the meeting room with the two FBI agents right behind him.

Vincenzo Bennini frowns at Salvatore and the colonel, while Henri Franchi rolls his eyes.

"Go and stop Ciccone," Vincenzo instructs Salvatore. "He is upset; he does not understand how things are done here. Speak with him calmly; do what you can to fix this. And Colonel," he turns to Accola, "contact the Ravens to get them on board. This is not a request, Theodore. Do it. *Capisce*?"

Outside the conference room, Salvatore Caputi takes the stairs two at a time, reaching the rooftop helipad just as Steve boards the chopper. "Signore Ciccone!" he shouts over the engine noise.

Steve hears someone calling his name, so he twists around to see who it is. Spotting Salvatore waving his arms, he shrugs and takes his seat.

As the bird's rotor blades bob up and down in the breeze, Steve shouts out the open door, "Sorry, I'm out! Your group of

Keystone Cops will have to handle this without me. Good luck to you! You're going to need it!"

Salvatore is still panting from running up the stairs, but he shouts again, "Signore Ciccone! Steve! Please! We are going to try to get the Ravens on board! Can I call you? Can we regain your cooperation if they join us?"

"You can call!" responds Steve loudly. "But I don't know if I'll answer!" Steve engages his headset microphone and tells the pilot to take off.

When the craft's engines erupt in an increasing, mechanical whine, Salvatore backs away. He shields his eyes from the dust and debris kicked up by the prop wash, and watches with dismay as the chopper lifts off and heads south.

Frustrated that he couldn't change Steve's mind, Salvatore walks back into the building, Googling *Keystone Cops* as he descends the stairs.

Cosa Nostra capo Vito Scarapelli is not happy. He looks critically from one Mafia soldier to another, aware that they are uncomfortable in his presence. Normally, they would be eager to meet with the don to talk about their latest successes. But not today. The mood at the don's table is worrying.

Keeping his voice low, Vito probes for the reason why. "Tell me about our new Libyan 'refugees,'" he commands.

Now, the men are more upset than before. From past experience, they know that when Vito uses a soft tone, he means business, so someone must speak. But none of them do. The three officers only look at each other with increasing unease.

Across the table, Vito remains outwardly composed, but the soldiers can see that he is becoming impatient.

Drumming his fingers on the embroidered restaurant tablecloth, Vito stares at them, one at a time. "I see that you are troubled," he says. "My time means money. What do you need to tell me?"

The chieftain's first lieutenant, an experienced Mafia soldier built like a fire hydrant, bravely explains the problem. "My don, it is our contact in Libya. He was tortured and is now dead."

Vito narrows his eyes dangerously. "*Che cazzo?*" he bellows. "Who did this?" Vito is shocked that someone was able to breach his ranks.

The lieutenant swallows his nervousness and declares shakily, "It, it was the Order of the Raven."

Vito is furious. "The fucking Vatican sent their hit squad?" he screams. "And none of you could stop them? Did they get our Muslim guests, too, you morons?" Vito is now seriously upset, and the men know their futures are not guaranteed.

"No, Don Vito," replies the soldier, happy to impart some good news. "They are still at the Hotel Moderno in Trapani."

Vito angrily slams his fist on the table, causing the men to jump. "Ah, so you imbeciles can do *something* right!"

Turning away in disgust, the capo looks off into the distance. "We must not attract the Ravens again," he says decisively. "Kill our guests. We will start over with new ones."

CHAPTER TEN

Late in the afternoon, a BMW navigates the crowded streets of Trapani. The populace is just returning from their midday meals, so when the driver sees an empty spot in front of the Hotel Moderno, he considers himself lucky.

Before the car stops, two dark, olive-skinned men jump out from the back. Single-minded in their purpose, they walk straight into the hotel and look for the elevator. Finding it, they cross the lobby and stand in front of its doors, watching with impatience as the numbers slowly count down.

While they wait, a young couple joins them, whispering and giggling to each other in a private lovers' conversation.

When the elevator car arrives, the couple steps forward to enter it. But one of the stocky, well-dressed men holds out a meaty hand to block them.

The young man is annoyed by the slight. He puffs out his chest, and in loud and rapid German, appears to insist that he and his companion should be allowed in with the others. He tries to push past the burly man, but the doors close in his face with a mechanical whoosh.

In the privacy of the elevator, the two men get down to business. In practiced silence, they un-holster their semi-automatic Berettas and screw on black suppressors.

When the bell announces their floor, they march down the carpeted hallway to Room 403. Knocking sharply, they expect to barge in as soon as the door is cracked open. But no one answers. They try again, and still no response. The larger of the two kicks the door in, and they step into the room cautiously.

"What the fuck?" they whisper when they see their targets bound and gagged on the floor. All three Caliphate soldiers are dead, shot in the backs of their heads.

The two Mafiosos look around briefly but find nothing of importance. So they shut the door as best they can and leave.

Back in the lobby, they find an entirely different scene there than when they first entered the hotel. It seems that while they were upstairs, word spread about the earlier events on the fourth floor, and now the staff and guests are milling about, discussing what they heard.

The men thread their way through the crowd, eager to leave the premises. When they're safely outside, they sprint toward the BMW, jump inside, and exhale in relief when it pulls away without incident.

Vito Scarapelli frowns when he sees his first lieutenant walking toward the rear of the small restaurant in Cefalù. The man catches Vito's eye and nods toward the back room, indicating something urgent. Vito is dining with his wife tonight and isn't happy that something is apparently amiss.

The mob boss takes one last forkful of his pasta puttanesca. "I'll be right back, *cara*," he says to his wife, giving her a peck on the cheek. "There may be more labor problems in Trapani. Order dessert."

Vito walks quickly to the private room, knowing that something isn't right. Inside, he makes sure the door is closed, then turns to his confidant. "What is it?" he asks coolly. "You look green."

Giuseppe Sarducci, Don Vito's first lieutenant and long-time friend and brother-in-law, hesitates to answer, a sure sign of trouble that is not lost on Vito.

"Out with it!" Vito demands. "I am having dinner with Giulia tonight!"

"*Sì, mio capo*," complies the lieutenant. "We went to the room where the men from the Caliphate were staying, but they were already dead. Shot in the head."

Vito throws his hands in the air. "*Figlio di puttana!*" he spits on the floor angrily.

"It was the Ravens," adds Giuseppe.

"Those *bastardi* got to them before we did? The shadow militia from the Vatican? They are relentless; they will not give up! Even with all the power and influence we have in this country; we have never been able to find out where or when that group will strike next! Those Vatican bandits have been around for hundreds of years, and still, no one knows much about them! Beppo, are you sure it was them?"

"Sì, I am sure. Our men report that they saw foreigners in Tripoli with tattoos of a raven and a cross."

"Ah, the tattoos. Tell everyone to beware of strangers. They should trust no one they do not know."

"Sì, *immediatamente.*"

Giuseppe watches as Vito paces the room, a worrying sign of decisive action to come.

"So now, we have no choice," Vito growls, his voice rising in anger. "We will have to go to war with those sons of bitches! *Ai dei materassi!* Set up a meeting for tomorrow, there is much to discuss. And tell Sergio Fittipaldi to come to Cefalù now, no delays. Tell him to get on the very next flight!"

Vito narrows his eyes and searches his lieutenant's face.

"Is there anything else?" he asks, dropping his voice in controlled rage.

"No, mio capo."

"Then I will go back to my dinner now."

When the AISI helicopter drops Steve off in Ravello, the central square's business owners swarm out of their shops to raise their fists at him again. But Steve merely smiles and waves back. With his cell phone to his ear, he's waiting for Diane to answer his call.

"Hey, babe," he chirps when she picks up. "Got done earlier than I thought. Put on something cute and meet me at the Hotel Rufolo."

Steve sits alone at the crowded bar reviewing the day's events, unaware of the scowls and whispers of the people around him. Nursing a Bourbon neat, he wonders what will happen to the task force now that he's no longer involved.

Half an hour later, a tall blonde in a slinky black cocktail dress sidles up to him, grabbing the attention of male and female bar patrons alike.

"I see you're alone," the beauty purrs into Steve's ear. "Need some company?"

Pleased by the striking woman's attention, Steve replies, "Well... I *was* waiting for my wife, but I guess that's changed now." Sliding off his stool, Steve offers it to the woman. "Please take my seat," he gestures gallantly.

Signaling to the bartender, Steve orders two glasses of prosecco. "What's a nice girl like you doing in a place like this?" he asks, running his eyes from the woman's slingback heels up to her attractive face, lingering at all the good places.

The lady in black looks into Steve's eyes, drapes her arm around his neck, and draws him close. "Come on, babe," she whispers, "couldn't you think of a better line than that?"

"Hey," Steve laughs, "it's the best I got right now. I'm out of practice, you know. And anyway, when you dress like that, my mind freezes."

Diane gives her husband a playful slap on the shoulder.

"Ow!" Steve responds with a mock frown. "You know, every time we're together, people wonder why you're with me. It's a damn shame you're no longer making movies. Everyone loves you."

"Stop putting yourself down!" retorts Diane. "You know I love you more than the screen, you jerk."

While the bartender sets down their drinks, Diane asks, "How did the meeting go? I guess not too well since you're home early."

Steve sighs deeply. "Just a total screw up, Dee. Come on; let's get dinner. I'll fill in the blanks while we eat."

Swiss Guard Commander Colonel Theodore Accola is startled by a knock at his door. He's in his Naples hotel room, getting ready to go out for a late dinner. Accola isn't expecting anyone, so he grabs his firearm before approaching the door. "Who is it?" he asks cautiously. When the reply is, "A very good friend of the family," he sighs and opens the door.

Pushing into the room, a tall man with gold-rimmed sunglasses perches on a corner of the hotel bed.

Accola sighs again and closes the door. "So, you killed Bacdadi? Now what?" he asks.

"We also took care of the Caliphate targets."

Accola struggles to keep his emotions in check. "Your actions were well-intended," he declares, "but you cannot kill everyone. Some will always get through, and eventually, Cosa Nostra will succeed; terrorists will be smuggled in. Work with us. We need your cooperation. You can still operate behind the scenes, but I ask that you join our efforts. AISI has even brought in an American specialist."

In the tense silence that ensues, Colonel Accola has the distinct feeling that the man is boring holes into him from behind those dark sunglasses. Accola waits indulgently, knowing what the man is capable of.

A fair bit of time passes while the man remains silent. Then, he stands. "We usually work alone," he declares coolly. "No police, no Carabinieri, no Frenchmen from Interpol. And certainly no 'specialists' from the United States. But this time, we will help — from the shadows. Unless they get too close. You will give us the information you discover, and we will update you with what we find out."

The man walks back to the door and stops there with his hand on the doorknob. "We will talk again; I will let you know when and where. I want to meet Mr. Ciccone now. Make the arrangements."

Without another word, the man opens the door and leaves.

Accola waits about thirty minutes to make sure the dangerous man is gone. Then he picks up his phone and clicks on one of his contacts.

"Vincenzo, call Ciccone," he says to Vincenzo Bennini, the AISI agent. "The Ravens want to meet him. They have agreed to cooperate."

In Ravello, the Ciccones have moved from the bar to a corner table.

While Steve enjoys the house specialty — pasta and sepia in a light cream sauce — Diane picks at a salad garnished with fresh vegetables. Steve looks at Diane's plate and asks, "You sure you don't want something real to eat? I hear the food in Italy is pretty tasty."

Diane shakes her head sadly. "I barely fit into this dress today. So...no."

Steve wipes his mouth after swallowing the last bit of his pasta. "Okay, then. I guess it's time to tell you about the meeting. But I have to swear you to secrecy first."

"You bully!" teases Diane with a sly grin. "You know I'm good for it."

"I know, but this is mega-serious," Steve replies, not returning the smile.

"Oh? You sure you want to tell me, then?"

"Yeah, but like I said, you can't breathe a word of this to anyone."

"Lips are sealed, boss."

"Okay," says Steve solemnly. "The Italian government has a problem. They believe the Mafia wants to kill the pope, but they don't think the mob will be doing it themselves. They picked up some chatter that said they're going to use Islamists for their dirty work."

"Islamists?" questions Diane. "I never thought those groups would work together!"

"Neither did anyone else. Apparently, they think by

doing it this way, they won't take the blame when the pope dies."

"Wow. This *is* serious."

"Exactly. But the team the Italians put together to stop the attack is a total wreck, and a secret death squad already killed the hitmen."

"Wait, I'm confused," says Diane. "If the people who are supposed to kill the pope are dead, that's a good thing, right?"

"Normally, yeah," Steve replies. "But this plan was hatched by the mob, and they're banking on religious fanatics to carry it out — not a good scenario. In addition, swirling around this whole mess is a hush-hush organization that no one wants to talk about. Neither group will give up easily, and with the Italians keeping secrets, it'll be hard, if not impossible, to get anything done. So I told them to get their shit together. And then I stormed out of the meeting."

"I'm sure you said a little more than that, hon," Diane jokes lightly.

"You know me well, wife, and you're right. I wasn't very politically correct. But if they fix things soon, I may still help them. But first, I gotta be satisfied with what they did."

Diane tilts her head and flashes her best movie star pose. "Be careful, babe," she warns dramatically. "I've said it before, and I'll say it again. You're not as young as you think you are."

"And I'll reply as I always do — I'm still young enough to take care of a fox like you!"

At that moment, Steve's phone interrupts their private one-liners. "Fuck, it's Caputi," he declares glumly.

Clicking a button, Steve turns the phone off and drops it back into his pocket. "He can call again tomorrow if he's still interested in talking. Right now, my attention is all on you, babe."

The next morning, Steve's clothes are still on the floor, partially covering the little black dress where Diane dropped it the previous night.

Unusual for Steve, he wakes after nine and finds Diane's side of the bed empty. Hearing noises, he gets a wicked idea, and leaves the bedroom in only his birthday suit.

Expecting to see his wife puttering around in the kitchen, he stops short when Diane looks up from the breakfast bar and gasps, then bursts out laughing.

Sitting next to Diane is a shocked Salvatore Caputi.

"Damnit, Dee! You... Aw, crap! You should have warned me!" stammers Steve with his face flushing crimson. "Morning, Sal," he adds awkwardly.

"*Buongiorno, Stefano,*" laughs Salvatore, using the Italian version of Steve's given name. "I can tell that you are glad to see me."

Steve shakes his head peevishly and returns to the bedroom, returning only when he's properly dressed.

"Here ya go, stud," says Diane, suppressing a grin as she hands him a cappuccino. "I'll leave now so you two can be alone."

With a giggle, Diane opens the door to step onto the balcony, but she quickly retreats when the brisk fall air hits her. Turning around, she grabs a sweater from the sofa before stepping out again.

At the breakfast bar, Steve downs his coffee in one shot and slaps the cup on the table. "Why are you here, Sal?" he asks curtly.

"It's about the Ravens. Accola convinced the 'ghosts,' as you call them, to cooperate with us. One of their members wants to meet you."

"Why the hell should I meet him?" responds Steve sourly. "What's the catch? There's always a catch."

Caputi stares at the far wall. "The Ravens do not want Interpol involved, or any of our local or federal police. They agree to share their information with us, but they want to continue to work behind the scenes."

"Look, I told you—"

"If this isn't acceptable, you can negotiate with them yourself."

Steve leaves his seat and walks over to the French doors framing the Gulf of Salerno. He sees Diane outside and returns the kiss she sends him, then turns back to Caputi. "Okay, I'll talk to this guy. But I'm gonna tell him that I control the group, and I choose who's in it. Things are gonna be done my way, or I will happily leave it all up to you. Capeesh?"

Salvatore smiles at Steve's use of the colloquial Italian-American expression. "*Sì, io capisco, Stefano*. I will call the group together for another meeting in Napoli. Is ten o'clock tomorrow all right with you?"

"Yeah, that's good," responds Steve. "But I want you to send your chopper again. Not to the same place, though. The shopkeepers in Ravello weren't happy with me yesterday."

"*Va bene*. Where is a better location?"

"I saw an open field about eight hundred meters south of my house. Tell your guy to land there at 9:15. That's 9:15 a.m. sharp, Sal; I won't wait for it. If the bird's not there by 9:16, I'll gladly go home. Now, thanks for making my morning interesting. I'll see you to the door."

Outside the Ciccones' villa, Salvatore sighs with relief.

"*Grazie a Dio*," he murmurs as he climbs into his car. "I did not think I would be able to convince that stubborn American to return."

As Steve clears the cups from the breakfast bar, he hears his phone ringing from where he left it last night. Running into the bedroom, he moves clothes around to find it, then clicks on the call. "Angie?" he asks quizzically. "Man, it's early in the States! What's wrong?"

"Nothing, it's all good!" replies Frank excitedly. "Geo retired from the FSA! We're both so excited that we can't sleep. He's helping me pack my house up right now!"

"No shit! I never thought that snake would do it!"

"Ha! I'll be sure to tell him about your undying confidence in him!" Frank snickers. "Look, I put the house up for sale, so as soon as everything's done here, we'll be heading your way. Construction on my new place is scheduled to start in two weeks. I know you said you'd take care of it, but I want to be there."

Steve is beyond pleased. "You know I got plenty of room for both of you to stay here! I'll also get you a storage facility, so you can start sending stuff over."

"Thanks, but I won't need one. I'm selling all my furniture here; too expensive to ship. I'll shop for new stuff over there."

"Good idea."

"Hey, bud, gotta go now. Kiss Diane for me, okay? *Sayonara*, old pal!"

Steve snorts. "What's up with the Japanese? You're coming to Italy, dumbass!"

"Oh, yeah! I should have said, 'Ciao, *bello!*'" replies Frank, laughing happily.

Miles away, a disembodied voice on another phone says, "*As-salamu alaikum.*"

"*Wa alaikum as-salam.*"

"I have unwelcome news," says the voice. "Amil is dead, and so are your three men."

"What?" screeches the Caliphate leader. "Who did this? CIA?"

"I do not know. I will ask Scarapelli when I see him. One of his men told me to go to Sicily right away. Muhammad, we must move forward more carefully now. I will call you after my meeting."

Dockworker consultant Sergio Fittipaldi paid a premium for the next flight out. But his plane lands in Naples, not Sicily, and he's met at the airport by a member of AISI.

"We must hurry," says the government official. "Accola, Bennini, and Caputi are waiting for you at the office. We will have a quick meeting. Then you can go on to Cefalù."

As they exit the terminal, a watchful Carabiniere takes out his phone and punches in a familiar number.

CHAPTER ELEVEN

After a short flight from Naples, Sergio lands at Palermo International Airport in Sicily. With no luggage to wait for, he goes directly to the curb to find the car Don Vito sent for him.

Sergio sits alone in the back seat of the sleek Maserati, too nervous to enjoy the scenery along E90, a two-lane highway that skirts the northern Sicilian coast. Sergio anxiously wonders if he's been discreet enough to stay alive. He's afraid that his recent decision to cooperate with the Italian government against the Caliphate and the Mafia, may prove to be his undoing.

An hour after leaving the airport, the Mercedes slows down before turning into the entrance to Vito Scarapelli's estate overlooking the ocean.

The way to the house is secure. The car must first pass through a guardhouse in a ten-foot-high wall, then follow a long drive lined with scented plumeria trees that hide high-definition cameras. The cameras watch the car the entire way.

Sergio swallows hard when the drive ends at a large courtyard. Standing in the sun waiting for him, is mob boss Vito Scarapelli.

Sergio places his hand on the car door handle, breathes deeply, and puts a smile on his face. Steeling himself for whatever comes next, he exits the car and greets Vito with an enthusiastic kiss on each cheek. "I hope I haven't kept you waiting long," he says.

"Come inside," responds Vito, patting Sergio's back. "We have much to talk about. I heard you were in Naples."

Beside the don, Sergio's face grows pale.

Steve is in the open field, staring at his Bulova. It's 9:15, and there is no helicopter. Turning to Diane, he points insistently at his watch.

"I know," she says, rolling her eyes in exasperation. "But you told them you'd be here till 9:16 at the latest."

When popping sounds drift over the water, Steve looks at his watch again. "They just made it," he says grimly.

Diane stays a safe distance away while Steve runs to the bird's open door, bending low to keep from having his head chopped off.

The chopper brings Steve to the same building where the anti-terrorism group met before, and he arrives there before anyone else. With no one to talk to, he stares mindlessly at the Italian flag.

Just past ten, Salvatore, Vincenzo, and Colonel Accola enter the room, accompanied by an unfamiliar man dressed in a finely tailored suit. Steve can't see the man's face; his eyes are hidden behind fashionable, mirrored sunglasses.

"Buongiorno," greets Salvatore. "I hope you had a nice flight."

"I did," says Steve. "Keep the chopper warmed up in case I decide to leave early again." Nodding toward the stranger, Steve asks, "Who's the suit?"

Colonel Accola responds, stiffening against Steve's casual informality. "Our guest will represent the Order of the

Raven. While he is here, he wishes to be addressed as Marco."

"Hmm, keeping a low profile? All right," says Steve, holding his hand out to the new arrival.

When Marco extends his own hand, Steve pulls it closer to get a better look at the famous tattoo. "I like your ink," he says. "Take a seat."

When everyone is settled, Steve looks again at Marco. "I read a report about Amil and the dead Caliphate killers," he states dryly. "What the hell were you thinking? We must be careful! No more killing people until we can talk to them! The Mafia's probably going to recruit new—"

"We met with a Mafia contact named Sergio Fittipaldi," interrupts Vincenzo. He told us that Don Vito Scarapelli has called him in for a meeting, so we are bringing some of our people down from the North. We fear things are escalating, and we do not trust the local polizia and Carabinieri to do what needs to be done."

"That's all well and good," responds Steve. "But let's get something straight, right off the bat. If you want me to remain involved with this group, I must be the only one in charge. When I make a decision, it stands. I won't put up with anyone going behind my back to do whatever they like. I don't trust anyone, and that includes *your* group," he declares, eyeing Marco. "I don't want your guys killing off potential leads just to please your vicious natures. We need to get all the intel we can on this jihad. Nothing, and no one, is unusable!"

Steve waits a few minutes to see if there are any reactions to his stipulations from Marco or anyone else. When no one makes a sound, he says, "All right, it's settled, then. Vincenzo, the first thing I need you to do is to contact the CIA. We need eyes on the ground in Libya. But you know, if the Muslims were smart, they'd recruit new assassins from among their followers who are already in Italy. Damn, there are so many

Muslims in Italy now that it looks like the Moors are invading again! Marco, I want to put your group in charge of finding the new Muslim recruits. You work out of sight, and we need strong intel."

Marco nods and rises from his chair. "I will get started immediately," he tells Steve. "The Ravens will never deviate in our commitment to protect the pope and the Church. But I must caution you. Our group has agreed to do things your way this time. However, if we feel that your way will not succeed, we will proceed on our own."

Marco turns gruffly and heads for the door, offending Steve with his retreating back.

"Leaving so soon?" Steve asks sarcastically. "We were just getting to know each other."

Steve eyes the rest of the group. "I just told you all that I insist on overseeing this mission, and you agreed. So Marco, if the Ravens get in *my* way, I'll have no problem eliminating that interference."

Marco laughs at Steve's threat, then turns and walks out the door.

Steve grits his teeth. "I don't know which is worse, radical Islamists or radical Catholics. You agreed to put me in charge of eliminating one of them, but I can easily do away with both. So I'm in... For now. I'll only stay as long as things are done my way. If there's dissension in the ranks, or meddling by nosy politicians, I'm out."

Colonel Accola speaks up to calm the situation. "I have activated the Swiss Guards' highest security level and alerted the ranks to the threat against the pope. I have also contacted the Swiss Embassy, and they will send more men that we will consider for training."

"Very good," responds Steve. "And the Ravens?"

"I will keep in close contact with them."

Bennini pipes up, "I will dispatch more AISI operatives from northern Italy and contact your CIA. I will also ask your FBI to send us more agents. We will contribute whatever you need, Mr. Ciccone."

"Steve. Just call me Steve."

"So, it is now Wednesday," remarks Salvatore. "Let us meet again next week, unless there is something new."

"That'll work," agrees Steve. "All of you have my email address, so I want daily updates. We can meet here once a week, and I'll come by helicopter; it's quicker than driving from Ravello. When things begin to hit the fan, I'll stay here in Naples."

Steve pauses for a moment, tapping his fingers on the table. "I think that's it for now; I have nothing else."

Steve dismisses the group, then walks over to Salvatore. "How about lunch?" he asks. "Your treat."

Sergio drapes one arm over the back of a long leather sofa, hoping to appear casual. He's trying hard not to let Vito know that he is nervous.

"So, tell me," says the mobster, eying the dockworker consultant intently. "How was your trip to Naples?"

Sergio lies, "It was distressing; my mother is not feeling well. I have not seen her for a while, so I made a short trip to visit her before coming here."

Vito nods thoughtfully. "I am sorry to hear that," he says somberly. "I hope she will feel better soon. Now let me tell you what we are going to do. We need to bring in new people. But this time, they will not be from Libya."

Sergio lets a faint sigh of relief escape from partially closed lips. He believes the mob boss accepted the story about his mother, since he's already onto another topic.

"There are too many ragheads in Sicily," complains Vito. *"Fanculo!* This country is overrun with them! I tell you, after we take care of the pope, we are going to have to clean up Italy. Now, I want you to get more men to replace the ones killed by the accursed Ravens. But choose them from people who are already here. I assume you have contacts?"

"Sì, Don Vito."

"They should know who can do the job. The Vatican's hit squad expects to disrupt our plans, but my men are now prepared for further interruptions."

"I understand. I will do as you ask."

"Va bene. That is all for now. I will pray a rosary for your mother's health."

Vito embraces Sergio warmly, then leads him back to the Maserati. He watches the car leave his property, then goes back into the house.

On the way in, he gives orders to his first lieutenant. "Keep an eye on him," he tells Sarducci. "I want a report on everything he does and everyone he speaks to."

CHAPTER TWELVE

After the AISI helicopter drops Steve off in the open field near his house, he waves to the pilot and starts walking home.

On the way to his villa, he passes large drifts of wild lavender on the hillside near his favorite place to think. Needing some quiet time, he steps through the flowers to find the large rock he likes to sit on.

In the peace and quiet of the secluded spot, he stares unblinking at a lone sailboat skimming the sparkling water far below. *I don't know how we're gonna get anything done if they're gonna keep secrets,* he muses dismally. *They're fucking all over the place. How the hell are we gonna keep the pope safe?*

Suddenly, out of the blue, an idea pops into Steve's head that has nothing to do with assassins and potential trouble, but everything to do with shutting out the noise. His mood brightens at the thought, and he resumes his walk home.

At the foot of his driveway, he's surprised to see Diane coming toward him. "I wanted to give this to you inside, but this is as good a time as any," he says, whipping his hand out from behind his back. With a slight bow, he gallantly presents his wife with a bouquet of lavender stalks from the hillside.

"How pretty!" exclaims Diane, giving Steve a peck on the cheek.

At that moment, a neighbor drives past on her way into town. Seeing the couple kissing, she waves and gives two beeps of her horn.

"What are you doing home so early?" asks Diane, waving back at the neighbor. "I thought you'd be gone all day. Is there trouble with the group again? I was just going out for a walk."

"No, it didn't take long to whip them into shape," quips Steve. "I was thinking—"

"Uh, oh. That could mean something good or something awful. Should I be worried?"

"It's good," smiles Steve. "I thought this would be a great time to go to the lake area in the northern part of Italy. You know, before the shit hits the fan down here and the snow hits the ground up there."

"Mr. Ciccone, funnyman extraordinaire. Did I ever tell you that you have an interesting way with words?"

"Yeah, I think you mentioned it once or twice. So, whaddya say? You wanna take a quick trip up to Lake Como?"

"That sounds wonderful!"

"Great! Let's go today."

Sergio Fittipaldi's calls to Libya don't usually take this long to connect. Impatient to get this over with, he drums his fingers on a table; the sharp, staccato rhythm magnifying his already tense frame of mind.

When the Caliphate leader finally answers, Sergio avoids the customary niceties. "We need to meet," he states curtly, "but not in Libya. The men sent from the Vatican are close."

"Greetings to you, Sergio," responds Muhammad stiffly. He's annoyed by his Mafia contact's blunt tone. "What is the rush? Do you not say how are you anymore?"

"There is no time for pleasantries," retorts Sergio. "I am

going to Cairo tonight, so I will meet you there tomorrow."

"Tomorrow? This is unusual, my friend," responds Muhammad. "I am not in Libya now. It will take me a while to get there."

"I see," states Sergio irritably. "Then I will give you time to travel. We can meet in two days."

"You will give me two days? I am grateful for your understanding," replies Muhammad, deliberately sarcastic with the infidel.

"Yes, well, things are getting serious now. Do not travel with your usual entourage; come with only one or two people. We cannot attract undue attention. We must take more than the usual precautions. Call me when you arrive so I can let you know where we will meet. That is all for now. Ciao, Muhammad."

"Allahu Akbar, Sergio."

The conversation leaves Muhammad in a pensive mood. Sergio's call intruded on a meeting Muhammad is holding in the war-torn Syrian city of Aleppo, once a vibrant and active urban center, but now a crumbling expanse resembling Hiroshima after the bomb.

"I must go to Cairo alone," he announces to his followers. "And I must leave right away. Tell everyone to be extra careful of people they do not know," he warns. "The Vatican has unleashed their hidden protectors."

After Sergio speaks to Muhammad, he goes online to search for flights to Cairo. He checks several popular sites, but none show any planes going directly to the Egyptian capital. Frustrated that there are no nonstop routes, he resigns himself to having a seven-hour travel day with a connecting flight in Rome.

Muhammad Salim Muhammad's trip will take about the

same amount of time, but it will be more involved than Sergio's. The Caliphate leader knows there are no flights at all from Syria to Egypt, so he asks the Syrians for travel advice.

"What is the best way to get to Cairo from Aleppo? I need to get there quickly, and I do not care about the cost."

Eager to keep their Caliph safe, the Syrians begin to debate the pros and cons of alternate methods of travel.

At first, the Caliph listens to his followers' discussion with interest, but their endless squabbling soon bore him. Hoping they will agree on something soon, he picks at a plate of dates and wonders why Sergio wants to meet right away.

"My caliph," says one of the men, drawing Muhammad's attention away from his full belly. "I believe a most suitable way for you to reach Egypt is to drive to Amman, then fly to Cairo from there."

"Hmm. Do the others agree with you?"

The men looking on nod their approval, however, the caliph has a question. "Would it not be better to drive the entire way?"

"You can certainly do that, but it would take at least eighteen hours, and you would have to pass through several checkpoints."

"Hmm…," Muhammad repeats, stroking his long beard. "Then how long will your route take?"

"The drive to Amman is seven hours, and the flight to Cairo is another one and a half hours."

"I see. Your way is better."

The drive to Jordan has been dull and uneventful so far.

The scene out of Muhammad's window has been nothing but sand for miles.

Things change fast, however, when the BMW joins a lengthy line of vehicles backed up behind a desert checkpoint at the Jordanian border.

Blocked by the other cars, the caliph's driver has no choice but to come to a complete stop. With the car at a standstill, swirling dust devils kicked up by the hot, dry wind quickly surround it, leaving a fine dust behind on every surface.

While groups of people in front of the car step out of their vehicles to stretch their legs, Muhammad and his driver remain seated. The other drivers leave their motors running, because it's too hot to allow the air conditioners to turn off in the searing heat.

When the line moves, Muhammad catches glimpses of the checkpoint guards up ahead, all of whom appear irritated as they go about their duties. It seems that they're deliberately taking their time with their inspections.

While the caliph's car inches along, Muhammad's driver begins to fidget behind the wheel. Muhammad tells him, "I know you are uncomfortable, Jamil. We will stop for something to eat as soon as we can."

Jamil eyes his passenger in the rearview mirror. "It is not hunger that concerns me, Caliph. The Jordanians know you, but they do not trust you. How are we going to get through—"

A blast of gunfire suddenly disrupts their conversation.

The men crane their necks toward the sounds, but neither is surprised to see Jordanian guards firing AK 47s at a small car. Every Arab knows that checkpoints can be dangerous places.

Looking away, Muhammad replies to Jamil as if nothing

has happened. "We pay well for smooth passage," he says. "We will be allowed to pass. Allah is with us."

Up ahead, a forklift comes out of nowhere. With business-like precision, it slides its forks under the bullet-riddled coffin and dumps it in the sand at the side of the road.

And the slow creep to the checkpoint resumes.

Another hour of boredom passes, then Muhammad and his driver reach the small command post.

As instructed, the driver puts the car in neutral, trying to appear calmer than he feels. While an armed guard scrutinizes their IDs and accompanying forms, he says nothing and keeps his eyes straight ahead.

The guard doesn't look happy about his job. He takes his time, glancing from the paperwork to the passengers, and back again.

Suddenly, he stiffens. Motioning to other soldiers leaning against a wall, he barks commands, and three more guards circle the white Camry with their rifles trained on the driver, the passenger, and the car's interior.

While the driver struggles to remain composed, Muhammad sits in the back, not overly concerned.

Alerted by the commotion, a more important-looking soldier approaches the Camry. The fancy insignia on his red beret distinguishes him as a high-ranking officer in Jordan's military police.

The military officer looks inside the car briefly. Then he straightens up fast and backs away. Turning to the armed guards, he yells something unintelligible at them, and they drop their rifles and stand at full attention.

With a mighty scowl, the officer grabs the ID and paperwork from the now-worried border guard. Poking his head into the driver's side window, he smiles broadly, hands the papers back to the driver, and waves the car on.

When the vehicle passes through the checkpoint, Muhammad says, "I told you. Money talks."

Later that day, Muhammad's Camry enters Amman's international airport. "Find a room nearby to wait for my return," he orders his driver. Then the Islamic leader walks into the terminal to check in for his flight to Cairo.

When Sergio arrives in the Egyptian city, he drives to a luxurious hotel overlooking the Nile River. After settling in, he sits in a comfortable chair near the window to compose a text. "I am at the Four Seasons Hotel," he dictates to Muhammad's voice mailbox. "Let me know when your plane lands. I will pick you up at the airport."

That afternoon, Diane and Steve enjoy a chilly sunset on the balcony of a vacation rental on Lake Como, a picturesque resort area at the foot of the Italian Alps.

Below them, the scenic lake is a beehive of activity. Though the Ciccones are accustomed to seeing boating traffic from their house, there are more upscale crafts in this resort area, and the couple is entranced.

But not even the most scenic views can overshadow hunger. "Come on," says Steve after a while. "Let's get some dinner. Later, we can take a walk along the lake."

"Sounds like a plan," replies Diane, shrugging into a warmer jacket. "You know, there are a lot of famous people around here. Maybe we'll recognize someone."

"You mean, like you?" winks Steve.

The following day, Diane is up early again. The rental villa came with light provisions, so while she waits for Steve to wake up, she makes cappuccino and sets a few pastries on a small breakfast bar.

Woken by the aroma of brewing coffee, Steve puts on his robe and pads out to the kitchen. "Morning, Mrs. Ciccone," he says, smacking Diane on the backside. "I know you made the coffee to get me up, so here I am."

Steve grabs a cup and looks back at Diane. "Are you expecting someone?" he asks, noting that there are too many cups on the table.

A knock at the door makes them turn toward the sound.

"Get that, would you?" requests Diane, feigning disinterest in the early morning intrusion.

Steve narrows his eyes suspiciously but pads toward the entrance, stopping to cinch his robe closed. When he's ready, he swings the door ajar, and opens his mouth in wide surprise.

Standing on the doorstep are buddies George and Frank.

Ignoring Steve's reaction, George pushes him aside and glides past him into the house. "Aren't you gonna let us in?" he teases.

Following George, Frank pats Steve's chest lightly. "What? No good morning kiss?" he jokes.

Both men greet Diane, then turn back to Steve, who is frowning at them from the doorway. "Don't just stand there, man," orders George. "Be a good boy and bring in our luggage."

Scowling, Steve flips George the bird, but drags in the bags sitting outside the door.

"What the hell are you two doing here?" he inquires rudely, looking from his friends to Diane. Settling on Diane, he asks, "Why didn't you tell me they were coming? I thought this was going to be a quiet weekend, just you and me."

"I know, but they wanted to surprise you," replies Diane with a raised brow.

George spies sfogliatelle on the counter and takes a bite. "So, are you surprised?" he asks Steve.

"You can say that," replies Steve crisply. He's not hiding the fact that he's a tad miffed at the change in his quiet weekend plans.

"Well, here's another surprise," says George, oblivious to Steve's frame of mind. "The guys at the FSA gave me a nice going-away party, and I quit the bar. So now, I have nothing to keep me in the States! I came to help Angie get his new place fixed up!"

"Okay, that's great. But that doesn't explain why you're at our rental house on Lake Como."

"Diane told us about your getaway, so we decided to join you for some sightseeing before we tackled the house. Instead of flying into Naples, we came here! Isn't that great?"

At long last, Frank picks up on Steve's mood. "Are you angry?" he asks.

"Well, I guess that's a good way of—"

"Look, Chic," Frank interrupts. "I want to thank you guys for offering to put us up during the construction on my place, but Geo and I talked it over. We decided that it would be better to stay at my house to monitor things more closely."

"Okay, if that's what you want—"

"Yeah, that's best," chimes in George. "Whatever stuff we didn't sell, we sent airfreight to Naples."

"Sounds g—" begins Steve, until Frank interrupts him again.

"Hey, this is gonna be a fun weekend! But I have to ask… What's this shit about the Mafia and the pope?"

When Sergio receives Muhammad's text that his plane has landed, he pockets his cell phone and grabs his keys.

Distracted by his upcoming task, he steps into the hotel hallway without thinking.

"Ooh, my sincere apologies, sir!" says a passing employee after plowing into him. "I did not expect you to come out of your room!"

"It is all right," replies Sergio kindly, brushing off the man's explanation. "I was not paying attention." Continuing on his way, the AISI official presses the button for the hotel parking garage.

Inside his rented Jetta, Sergio sets his phone's GPS for directions to the airport, then heads out to the street.

Immediately, a BMW driven by one of Vito's soldiers falls in line behind Sergio's car. But Sergio doesn't notice. He's paying too much attention to his phone's directions in this unfamiliar city to see what's going on behind him.

Strangely, the mob soldier driving the BMW is also unaware that he's being followed. A third car, a white Toyota van occupied by members of the Order of the Raven, has similarly joined the procession toward the main road.

Conflicting with their training, neither the Raven nor mobster drivers pick up on the fact that they're not the only ones interested in the rented Jetta. Both keep up with Sergio without seeing the other.

At the airport, the cars park within sight of the Jetta, and one person from each vehicle follows Sergio into the terminal.

At baggage claim, Sergio studies each passenger coming down the escalator from the arrival gates. But none of them look familiar.

"I am here," says a man, walking up to the mob informant.

"Ah! So you are," responds Sergio. "That is a good disguise; I did not recognize you." The Caliphate leader is now clean-shaven and wearing jeans and an NBA T-shirt, with a pair of fashionable Oakleys hiding his eyes. "How was your flight?"

"Uneventful. We will talk outside. Ah, there is my bag."

Sergio and Muhammad stroll freely through the crowded terminal, undetected by the armed Egyptian soldiers patrolling the building. However, on their way to the parking facility, a couple of men in dark suits take their photos and monitor their conversation.

Back at the hotel garage, the AISI official drives his rented Jetta up to the top floor, hoping that it will not be well occupied. "There are not many cars parked up here," he says. "We can have some privacy."

He chooses a spot far from the building entrance and turns off the engine. "Before we go inside, tell me whom I should talk to about the new hitmen," he says to Muhammad.

"You must contact Hussein Assan, the imam in Palermo. He knows what you need and is waiting for your call."

"Good," says Sergio. "Here is the key to your room. We will go to the room first, so you can drop off your bag. Then, we will eat dinner and talk more."

As they leave the car, two separate groups watch from the shadows.

"We have the name of the contact," says one of the watchers into his phone. "It is the imam in Palermo."

"Excellent," replies the voice on the other end. "Now, go take care of our problem."

As Steve listens to Diane laugh at Frank's and George's stories, he decides that he'd rather enjoy his weekend than continue to be upset. "It's a good thing I chose to rent the larger place this time," he says. "There are four bedrooms here, so find the two that are empty, and stow your luggage."

"Mind if I take a shower?" asks George. "We've been traveling all day, and I'm a little tired. A little hot water might perk me up."

"Sure, no problem," says Diane. "Towels and such are in the bathroom."

"Okay, see you in a bit."

When George is cleaned up, he sees Steve and Frank talking on the balcony, so he opens the door to join them. But when the chilly air hits him, he rushes back to his room to rummage through his suitcase for a jacket.

"It *is* a little chilly out here," agrees Frank when he sees George run back inside. "But I'm okay for now." Looking around, he asks, "Where's Diane? I haven't seen her in a while."

"She went shopping," says Steve. "We haven't had a chance to stock up for the weekend yet. Right now, all we have is coffee. But I'm glad she's out. It'll give me a chance to talk to you guys about our new gig."

"What's this 'our' shit?" asks George as he rejoins his friends. "I'm not gonna do anything crazy anymore." George pulls his jacket tighter around his neck. "But why the heck are we talking out here? I just came from Florida, and this is damn cold, even with my coat on!"

Rolling his eyes, Steve pushes his friends back into the villa. "You want some coffee, you wimp?" he asks George.

"Nah, I'm good now."

"Okay, then sit down and let me fill you both in with what I'm working on."

"Lay it on us," responds Frank.

"AISI, the Italian CIA, has a big problem, and they don't think they can manage it alone. They know about my work back home with the FSA, so they asked me for help. But I'm gonna need you guys with me."

"Oh, I don't know, Chic," whines Geo. "I just retired, for cryin' out loud! Can't I get even one month of nothing to do?"

"Yeah, I know, and I'm really sorry about the timing," replies Steve. "But I do need your help. I'm retired, too, and I thought all this crap was behind me. But you know, criminals never take a break, and we're the best, right?" he adds with a twinkle in his eye.

"Yeah, yeah, we're the best, blah, blah, blah," responds Frank with a wave of his hand. "Just get on with it. What's going wrong in the world now?"

"Have you heard that Pope Urban excommunicated all the Catholic members of the Mafia?"

"I heard something about that back home," says Frank, looking at George.

"Well, for some reason, they didn't like that," Steve declares wryly. "So, they issued a death threat on the pope. But," he continues, lifting his finger to emphasize his next point. "They're not gonna do it themselves. You know the saying, 'Keep your friends close and your enemies closer?' Well, the

Middle Eastern Caliphate has been saying for years they want to eliminate the pope, so the mob teamed up with them, and *they're* gonna do the deed. The Mafia's gonna help them get into the Vatican."

"Aren't we done with this crap now?" cries George. "It's serious, but can't the Vatican take care of it? Don't they have *ghosts* that can handle things like this?"

Frank shakes his head and stares out at the lake.

"I met one of their ghosts," says Steve. "The Mafia smuggled some of the Muslims' hitmen into Italy, but the ghosts — they call them the Order of the Raven — killed them all. So now, they'll probably recruit again, and I'm betting that this time, they'll take their new fall guys from the immigrants already in Italy."

"So?" says George.

"So I need you guys on board. You're the only ones I can rely on. I don't trust AISI, the Ravens, or even the Swiss Guard. Come on," he pleads, looking from one man to the other. "One last fling for the musketeers?"

Frank still isn't saying anything. He's staring out the French doors, not focused on anything in particular.

"One last job, guys?" implores Steve. "I'm getting tired of this shit, too. But the mob is teaming up with the Islamists, and that's too much to ignore."

Frank sighs deeply, then looks at Steve. "Fuck it all; I'm in," he says. "You need help. But for the record, we're all getting up in years, you know."

Steve turns expectantly to George, hoping that he can still get the crew together again. But George is sitting glumly on the sofa with his arms folded across his chest.

The third member of the trio remains silent for a long time. Then, he says, "Hmpf. I guess I gotta protect your asses like I always do, right? You and Angie are too reckless, *and* too old. So, I'm in as well."

"Too old, you say?" chuckles Steve. "Dammit, Geo, you're older than we are!"

Behind them, a voice calls out from the entryway. "I don't care who's older!" exclaims Diane. "Which one of you senior citizens is gonna help me with these groceries?"

CHAPTER THIRTEEN

Egyptian police are puzzled. An anonymous tip led them to the parking garage, where they found one man lying on the floor in a pool of blood, and another man standing nearby in a blood-splattered NBA jersey. Behind them both, blood and brain material is splattered on the wall like a macabre Jackson Pollock painting.

"Look what I found under his collar," says one of the responding officers, lifting the blood-soaked material of Sergio's shirt. "Someone heard what happened here."

Stepping over to see, a fellow officer whistles while he takes photos of the object: a small electronic device a quarter of an inch in diameter.

It seems that the hotel employee who bumped into Sergio earlier that day did his job well.

Nearby, another officer is looking through Muhammad's wallet and asking him questions. He believes the Islamic caliph to be Sol Conrad from Tel Aviv, the name he finds on Muhammad's ID card, credit card, and passport.

While the police focus on the crime scene, the BMW and white Toyota van use the distraction to leave the area.

At ground level, the BMW's occupants fall into tourist mode. None of the Mafia soldiers have been to Cairo before, so they pay more attention to the scenery than they should. Drawn by the sight of the famous Nile River, they chatter non-stop about ancient pharaohs on luxurious boats, and Cleopatra on gilded barges. Once again, they don't notice that they're being tailed — another major failure on their part.

Traffic along the Nile is thick, but after the two cars pass over Cairo University Bridge, it begins to thin. The Ravens in the Toyota have been waiting for a good place to make their move. When the cars are near Orman Botanical Garden, they act.

Weaving through the lighter traffic, the Raven driver pulls his vehicle alongside the BMW and keeps pace with it for half a block. Choosing his moment, the front seat passenger rolls down his window and raises his suppressed Glock 17. After two quick shots, the Mafia hitmen's BMW slams into the botanical garden wall.

With their mission completed, the van speeds off, and the backseat passenger clicks on a contact number.

Miles away, Colonel Accola's phone buzzes with an incoming call. He glances at the Caller ID and sighs. The number on the screen usually means trouble, so he steels himself before answering it.

But it's worse than he thought. While he listens, his eyes go wide and beads of sweat form on his face.

Shaken by what he heard, the Swiss Guard commander dials Vincenzo Bennini as soon as the caller signs off.

Diane and the "three musketeers" are in good spirits. They've been spending the afternoon on the balcony over Lake Como snacking on crusty bread, prosciutto, fruit, and creamy mozzarella, while trading endless stories about past adventures. As the men talk, they inevitably bring up each other's foibles, many of which they'd rather not remember. Every embarrassing story sends them into bouts of hysterical laughter that then need to be explained to Diane.

Diane enjoys listening to the men's stories. Their tight friendship is a joy to see, and their frequent anecdotes give her a glimpse into Steve's life before she met him.

Even though they're having fun, George continually finds himself distracted. Whenever the conversation lags, the endless parade of luxury yachts and boats on the lake catches his eye. At one point, he murmurs dreamily, "I could get used to living around here."

Steve hears George's comment. "That would be nice," he says. "But this area is really expensive. You'd have to be a millionaire to afford to live here."

"Well, that wouldn't be a problem for you, would it?" Frank cuts in, with a wink for Diane.

Diane smiles and cocks her head toward the house. "I hear a phone," she says. "It's probably yours, hon. I'll be right back."

A few minutes later, Diane returns with Steve's phone in her hand. "It's Salvatore Caputi," she declares somberly, handing the phone to Steve as he tries to grab the last piece of cheese.

With a roll of his eyes, Steve takes the phone and puts it up to his ear. "Sorry, guys, gotta take this," he declares, heading into the house.

Inside, Steve says irritably, "You took me away from a magnificent view of Lake Como, Sal."

"Sorry to interrupt," replies Salvatore, "but I have news, and it is not good. Our spy inside Cosa Nostra is dead. He was meeting with the Caliphate leader in Cairo to get us the name of his Sicilian contact. But he died before he could get it."

"Who was he?"

"He worked at the docks in Tripoli. His name was Sergio Fittipaldi."

"Do we know who killed him?"

"The Ravens say the mob did it. Their agents trailed Fittipaldi to Cairo and saw Mafiosi there as well."

"Shit. Now we're gonna have to figure this out on our own, without inside help. You say the Caliphate guy is in Sicily?"

"Yes, it seems so."

"Looks like we're gonna have to investigate every mosque on the island to find out who's collaborating with the mob. How many mosques are there in Sicily?"

"There are only a few. Most Muslims in our country do not meet in mosques. They gather in cultural centers — prayer rooms located in garages, basements, and warehouses.

"I assume you sent people down there?"

"We already have people there."

"Good. Tell them to sniff around; maybe we'll get lucky."

"It is already done."

"Okay. Now, listen. I was hoping to spend some quiet time with my wife, so please don't call again. I'll talk to you on Monday."

Steve ends the call and throws the phone onto the sofa. "Damnit! This isn't good!" When he rejoins the group, he opens a beer and downs it in one gulp.

"You don't look pleased," quips Diane, seeing an all-too familiar scowl on Steve's face.

"Right now, I could hurl that damn phone into the lake. But I don't want to think about problems anymore. We came up here to relax for a couple of days, right? There's supposed to be a hotel-casino around here somewhere. Let's go out and try our luck."

"But wasn't that a call about your case?" asks Frank.

"Yeah, but it can wait till Monday. Let's have some fun!"

Vito Scarapelli calls out to his youngest granddaughter, "Do not let him get away! Lorenzo, let her win sometimes! She is your sister!"

Chuckling softly, Vito watches his grandchildren chase each other through rows of olive trees from his terrace in Cefalù. Recalling his own carefree upbringing, he remembers how proud he was when his father said he was ready to take over the business. *I wonder, will one of this generation also remain here to work with the family, or will they think it beneath them?*

While Vito waits for Giuseppe Sarducci, a small power-boat patrolling slowly off the coast grabs his attention. Seeing it makes him feel safe; he knows that his men are out there guarding him and his family.

Footsteps behind the don announce his visitor.

"Don Vito," hails Giuseppe, bending to greet his boss with a kiss. "Our problem has been taken care of."

"Excellent, Beppo," replies Vito, using a pet name for his favored soldier. "Is everything back on track?"

"Yes, but we lost some men in the process. The Vatican killers got to them."

The don displays no emotion at the news of a few dead soldiers. "They will pay," he says, referring to the Ravens. "Make sure you take care of the men's families. Now sit with me. Who do we need to contact for new recruits?"

Giuseppe turns his head at the sound of laughter from the grove, then takes a seat next to his boss. "Hussein Assan leads a prayer center in Palermo. He will provide the men we need."

"It will not be long now," Vito declares smugly. "The pope will soon know who has control of this country."

Vito shifts his gaze to look at his grandchildren, who have stopped playing to inspect something on the ground. "Beppo, I do not want any more slipups," he states firmly. "You are one of the few people I can count on, so I want you to go to Palermo for me. Speak with this Imam personally. Take extra steps to cover your tracks."

"I will do as you say," replies Giuseppe, rising to reenter the house.

When Vito is alone, he picks up his phone. "Giuseppe is going to Palermo to talk to one of those Muslim leaders. *Sono tutti stronzi*," he says, spitting on the terrace floor in disgust. "Send some men to back him up. The Vatican bastardi will be watching."

CHAPTER FOURTEEN

Monday morning, Steve looks down from another black helicopter on his way to Naples. "Ah, there it is," he mutters, spotting Frank's villa. The home's bright blue roof and the multitude of construction vehicles around it are unmistakable, even from the sky.

Steve looks at the house until he can no longer see it. Then, he sits back and starts to review the latest intel about his mission. These frequent helicopter rides have become a perk that Steve has come to enjoy. The convenience of not having to negotiate Italian traffic whenever a meeting is called cannot be overstated, and Steve is grateful that it's available to him.

In Naples, Steve opens the door to an empty conference room. He's the first to arrive — again. "This is getting annoying," he mumbles. "Where the hell are the others?"

Too wound up to sit down, he walks to a window, but frowns at the mounds of uncollected garbage outside, spoiling in the sun.

The unpleasant sight is a powerful image of the Mafia-controlled sanitation workers' ongoing strike and a testament to how neither they nor the governing officials want to budge on the issue. Though he spies military soldiers working hard to clear the mess, their job seems insurmountable.

Steve turns to see U.S. FBI Special Agents Kathryn Samuels and John DeMaria flinging open the conference room door. "Morning!" they greet Steve cheerfully.

Steve is pleased that these American special agents are part of his team. He requested them personally from the United States because of rumors that the agents in Italy are a little too cozy with the ever-present Mafia.

"Welcome to another day at the office," Steve replies. "The Europeans haven't arrived yet, so help yourselves to fresh coffee."

While they're at the coffee station, the rest of the team trickles in.

After everyone has taken a seat, Vincenzo Bennini declares, "I have some unwelcome news. As you may know, our operative in the Middle East, Sergio Fittipaldi, was murdered in Cairo by a Cosa Nostra hitman. He traveled there to meet with Muhammad Salim Muhammad, the self-proclaimed Islamic Caliph. Theodore has more information."

Across the table, Swiss Guard Colonel Theodore Accola clears his throat. "The Ravens said they began to keep track of Sergio's whereabouts when he started to work with Don Vito Scarapelli, so they knew where he was. Fortunately, they planted a bug on Sergio before he was killed, so they were listening while he talked to Muhammad."

"What were they discussing?" Steve asks.

"Sergio was talking about getting new trainees."

"Oh, that's right. They'd need more because your guys killed the first ones," notes Steve with distaste.

"Signore, the Ravens are not 'my guys,' as you put it," replies Accola disdainfully. "They are not controlled by anyone."

"Okay, okay. What else?" retorts Steve, waving his hand.

"The Mafia is moving quickly. Our man inside Cosa Nostra says Don Vito has already sent a messenger to speak with the imam Muhammad recommended."

Steve groans loudly.

"The imam's name is Hussein Assan. He is the leader of an Islamic cultural center in Palermo."

"Why didn't we know the Ravens were watching this Sergio guy?" asks Steve irritably. "As far as I'm concerned, the Ravens aren't doing us any favors. Do you have plans to raid that Islamic center?"

"Not yet."

"What are you waiting for? You pulled me out of retirement to help you with this shit, not to make every damned micro decision! I still expect all of you to know what needs to be done! Why are you letting the Vatican hit squad continue to do their own thing? They don't give a damn about what we're trying to do! I'm going to have to consider the Ravens part of the problem. Theodore," he declares, staring hard at the colonel, "get that group under control. Make sure they work together with us, or nothing's going to get done! Remember why we're here! The pope is in grave danger!"

At the sound of a chair scraping along the floor, all eyes turn to Kathryn Samuels, who moves to stand beside Steve. Raising her voice, she declares forcefully, "I can't believe what I'm hearing! This group is losing control of the issue! None of you seem to want to work with each other! *Signori Caputi e Bennini*," she addresses the men from AISI, "you were the ones who requested urgent help from Mr. Ciccone and the FBI, so it is you who need to get this operation under better control! We are here to help, but we can't do anything without total cooperation! You must bring the Order of the Raven in, or they'll continue to go their own way. And we've already seen what happens when they have free reign." Kathryn fixes her gaze on the colonel. "Signore Accola, I agree with Steve. You're the one most closely affiliated with the Ravens, so you must convince them to work with us. If you can't or won't, we may as well disband this group. We cannot have one unit doing whatever they want!"

Colonel Accola shakes his head firmly. "I have already told you that I have no control over the Ravens. They report to three cardinals, and those cardinals only reveal what they feel is necessary. I am not even sure who those cardinals are. Only the pope knows."

"Well, isn't that special," retorts Steve with disgust. "Looks like I'm going to have to speak with the pope myself."

Colonel Accola begins to protest, but Steve says, "Set up a meeting for me with Pope Urban. I need to talk to the men the Ravens report to. From now on, we're going to have to monitor the Ravens' actions closely."

Colonel Accola shakes his head dismally.

"I have in mind two persons who would be able to work with the Ravens," continues Steve, "and I trust both of them completely. However, this will depend on whether I receive answers from the Vatican. If I don't, there's nothing more I can do, and all of you can go pound sand." Steve catches the eyes of Kathryn and John. "And I'm sure the FBI feels the same," he adds.

The special agents nod in agreement while Steve rises from his chair. "There's nothing more to do until I talk to the pope, so we may as well end this meeting now. I'm going up to the roof to catch my ride home."

Colonel Accola jumps out of his chair to intercept Steve. "Signore, please wait," he pleads quietly. "We need to talk... In private, *per favore*."

Accola leads Steve to an empty office down the hall. "I need to explain something to you," he states. "The Order of the Ravens does not officially exist, and it is impossible to get them to interact with us. They do not want anyone to know—"

"Don't give me that shit!" interrupts Steve as subtly as

a runaway freight train. "You're not telling me anything you haven't already said before! Look, I'm not going to have mysterious killers doing whatever the hell they want, whenever they damn well please! They already fucked up this mission once! Because of their recklessness, they've forced the mob to recruit from people already in Italy, so the new hitmen will be next to impossible to track! I want a meeting with the cardinals in charge of the Ravens, and I want a meeting with the Ravens as well. All of them need to cooperate with us!"

"Please, signore—"

Steve is surprised by the anguish in the colonel's eyes. "Okay," he sighs. "I'm willing to meet you halfway. I understand that the Ravens want to remain in the shadows. So how about this? Instead of meeting face-to-face, let their leader know that we can meet with him electronically, on one of those video chat services. He can even distort his voice and wear a disguise — a mask or a fucking paper bag. I don't give a shit. He can keep his identity hidden if he wants to. But I won't compromise on this: The rest of his operatives must be available to us, and he must assign one of them to our team. In return, one of our team members must accompany that Raven at all times. Period. If he doesn't like it, he can go fuck himself. And I still want a meeting with the cardinals."

Colonel Accola looks green.

Steve says, "If they won't cooperate and work together with us, someone higher up than me will pull the resources the USA sent. Get me those meetings. If they give me what I need, I'll continue on your team. Now, ciao. I'm going home."

As Steve climbs the stairs to the rooftop helipad, Salvatore tries to get his attention. "The rest of us agree with you!" he shouts up the stairs. "AISI will pressure Accola to arrange your meetings! Please do not leave yet! Will you join me for breakfast? I want to learn more about the people you want to work with the Ravens!"

"All right," says Steve, stopping his ascent. "But do you know of a place where I can get something American? I've had a monstrous craving for eggs, bacon, and grits lately."

"*Che diavolo è quello?*" asks Caputi with a puzzled look. "What the hell is grits?"

Steve chuckles. "My friend, grits are like polenta. Soft, runny, polenta."

The Muslim population of Palermo gathers to worship in an Islamic cultural center in an older part of the city. The neighborhood is rundown and not well cared for. Graffiti is everywhere, and rust-covered cars sit wherever they were left.

Typical of the area, the building housing the center is unremarkable. It's old and crumbling, covered by swirls of colorful street art and shredded political slogans that reveal nothing of its religious use. Equally commonplace is the center's entrance — merely a green, garage-type rolling door in an ugly concrete wall.

Despite this, certain parties have a keen interest in this building. From an abandoned apartment across the street, at least two men with cross and raven tattoos watch it 24/7. Through torn and soiled curtains, they note the comings and goings of all visitors. They log detailed notes of every one of them with great dedication, even recording videos and taking photos of surrounding activity, no matter how trivial.

Today, Giuseppe Sarducci is driving his Mercedes slowly down Via Cosmo Guastella, looking for a place to park as near as possible to the Islamic center. When he finds a spot, he parks his car and locks it, jiggling the handle to make sure it's secure.

At the green rolling door, he presses the button on an intercom to announce his presence. Seconds later, an electronic hum gives way to the rattle of moving metal.

As the door slides open, Giuseppe slips his right hand into his light blue suit jacket to feel for his Beretta — his constant companion, especially in unfamiliar circumstances. Assured of its presence, he tugs at his lapels and steps forward. As he does, the door slides closed behind him.

Giuseppe is mildly surprised to see that he has stepped into a spacious courtyard. Seeing no one there, he walks around and looks at everything, but the area is sparsely furnished.

The enclosure's main feature is a fountain of carved marble set into decorative floor tiles. Beyond that, two small pillars border a separate area nestled under a golden dome.

Giuseppe is relieved when he hears footsteps. Turning, he watches a short, bearded man dressed in an ankle-length thobe and white skull cap head in his direction.

The man's footsteps are loud on the tile floor. Thinking it odd, Giuseppe spots elegant leather dress shoes under the bearded man's long robe. *I always thought they wore slippers inside their religious buildings,* he ponders.

Imam Hussein Assan greets Giuseppe with a firm handshake. "Welcome," he says. "You are Giuseppe Sarducci, yes?"

"Sì, I am Sarducci. How do you know my name?"

"I have been in contact with your…capo? Vito Scarapelli. Please follow me."

Hussein leads Giuseppe to a place where worshippers' footwear is stored. "Place your shoes here, please. You may leave your socks on."

Ah, this is what they do," thinks Giuseppe.

The men put their shoes in individual compartments, then walk through an open prayer space to a side room.

"Please sit," motions the imam. Nearby, a woman in a black burka waits for instructions. "Please bring us some tea," he tells her.

When the woman leaves, the imam says, "Mr. Sarducci, I have been told that you need help solving a problem."

"Yes. I understand that you have four men willing to help my organization complete our mission. I have come to take them back with me to get things started. We are very interested..."

Giuseppe lets his voice trail off because the covered woman returns with the hot tea.

"We may speak in her presence," says Assan. "She does not understand Italian. However, I should warn you that we are always being watched here, which means that you are being watched as well."

"I understand," nods Giuseppe.

"Because of that, you will not take anyone with you today. The men I have chosen will connect with you in Cefalù."

The imam says something to the woman in a language Giuseppe doesn't understand, and she leaves the room, returning shortly with a plain manila folder. She hands the folder to the imam, then dips her head and retreats.

Assan slides the folder toward Sarducci. "These are the men who will help you. They will meet you at Palazzo del Marinaio. That is a restaurant owned by your don, is it not?"

"Yes, it is," replies Giuseppe, nearly choking on his drink. "I am surprised that you know of it."

Hussein stands, smoothing down his thobe. "We know more than you think," he smirks. "Take as long as you like to drink your tea and read the information. Leave the folder here when you are finished. A man will be waiting outside this room to lead you back to the street. Have a good day, Signore

Sarducci. May Allah be with you and our shared mission."

When the imam departs, Giuseppe flips through the files of the Caliphate's newest Mafia collaborators, trying to memorize as much as he can.

CHAPTER FIFTEEN

Swiss Guard Colonel Theodore Accola never wanted this meeting. He did everything he could to avoid it without absolutely refusing his colleagues' requests, but he knows he can no longer avoid them. So, while he waits for the three cardinals in charge of the Ravens, he cradles his drooping head in his hands.

At the sound of a sharp knock, he jerks his head up and jumps out of his chair, standing behind his desk in a stiff military pose.

With his hands clasped tightly behind his back, Colonel Accola readies himself to receive distinguished members of the Church. Instead, an unfamiliar person enters the room. Accola wonders nervously, *Did I schedule another meeting at this same time?*

Thankfully, the colonel's uncertainty fades to relief when three others sweep into the room, each one dressed in the distinctive black cassock, scarlet sash, and red zucchetto of the Catholic Church's leading bishops.

Cardinal Niccolo Amorello, the elder of the three and their self-appointed spokesperson, shoulders his way to the front with a warm smile for the commander in charge of the pope's protective guard.

"Colonel Accola, it has been a long time since we have talked," the cardinal says. "I would like to introduce my esteemed colleagues, Eminences Lafayette, and Ramon." Then he tilts his head toward the stranger. "The gentleman with us today will remain unnamed. He is simply here to observe."

Colonel Accola moves around his desk to kiss each cardinal's ring. "Please be seated, Your Eminences. I am sorry, but I have no chair for your guest."

"He will be fine," replies Cardinal Amorello.

"Very well." Colonel Accola is relieved that he has not offended the cardinals' guest. Something about him doesn't sit right. "Let us begin," he says. "You must have many important engagements today."

As the colonel moves to retake his seat, he sneaks a quick look at the unnamed man. At first glance, he thinks the man looks familiar, but he can't place him.

Seated at his desk again, Theodore glances at the man once more, this time more openly and with more than just a passing interest. The man looks back, calmly oozing a quiet but resolved purpose, mixed with a certain element of danger.

Unnerved, Colonel Accola breaks eye contact and moves to the task at hand. "Thank you for agreeing to meet with me today," he says to the cardinals. "I know all of you are well aware of the threat against our pontiff, and I am sure that you have heard about the group we put together to keep him safe. Unfortunately, we have experienced a problem with the pope's 'special guard.' They have placed themselves in the middle of the situation by acting without our group's knowledge."

"Are you speaking of the Order of the Ravens, Colonel?"

"Yes, Your Eminence. Our group welcomes their help, but AISI and the Americans insist that they cooperate with us."

"I see," comments Amorello suspiciously.

"Your Eminence, they want the Ravens to appoint a representative to join our team and attend our group's regular meetings in Naples. The American in charge, Steve Ciccone, would also like to meet with the three of you and Pope Urban."

Colonel Accola is not surprised to catch fleeting looks of disbelief mixed with distaste from each cardinal. "I know it is unusual, Eminences, but if you decide against talking with the American, he will no longer help us, and we will lose the services of the United States as well."

The cardinals seem unconcerned by the warning. However, they lean in close to confer with each other in Latin. To give them a bit of privacy, Colonel Accola rifles through a mound of paperwork on his desk.

When the cardinals turn back in their seats, they face the colonel with determined expressions.

Speaking for the others, Cardinal Amorello says, "May we remind you, Colonel, that the Order of the Raven has existed for over five hundred years, and they have never once needed outside help. We are confident that they will continue to do their jobs well."

Colonel Accola's heart sinks as he listens. *I tried to tell him they would never agree*, he reflects, recalling all the times he tried to convince Steve that the Ravens were untouchable. Then the cardinal speaks again.

"However, we understand that you may need the Ravens' expertise during the present 'situation,' as you call it. Therefore, we have decided that it would be in Pope Urban's best interest to combine our forces. To show our willingness to cooperate with the Americans and our country's intelligence and security agency, we will comply with your requests. However, if the Pope is ever in imminent danger, the Ravens will act quickly; they will not delay. There will be no meetings first."

"I am sure we can agree on that," replies Accola, clearly relieved by this unusual turn of events.

Cardinal Amorello continues, "In addition, we are aware of the complexity of coordinating the pope's defenses. Please inform Signore Ciccone that we will try to arrange a meeting with Pope Urban as soon as tomorrow." Glancing at the mysterious stranger in the room, he adds, "This agent will be our liaison with your team."

Colonel Accola is baffled. None of his prior requests have been granted this quickly, so he is fearful that the cardinals' goodwill may be short-lived. Hastening to add one last appeal, he says, "Mr. Ciccone has one more requirement. He has asked certain individuals known to him to join our team, and he wants one of them to travel with the Ravens to observe their actions at all times."

Accola knows that this demand is much rarer than the others. Therefore, he fully expects this wish to be firmly denied. However, Cardinal Amorello surprises him again.

"Theodore, the Ravens are deployed all over the world, so it will be impossible for the American to monitor everything they do. We will allow Mr. Ciccone's associate to interact with the organization, but with one man only, the man you see here today. There will be no more concessions. Do you understand?"

At Accola's nod, the cardinal rises. "Good. The pontiff's schedule is very tight, so we will have to leave now to arrange Signore Ciccone's meeting. *Buona giornata, Teodoro.*"

As the cardinals file out of the small office, Accola stands respectfully. Beside him, the silent observer remains behind.

When the Church officials are gone, the man says, "You may address me as Raphael. Send the details of your group's next meeting to Cardinal Amorello. I will attend that meeting to meet this Ciccone. Do not forget: The first time any Raven disapproves of what your team is doing, our organization will cut all ties with your group *immediatamente.* There will be no explanation or excuse for our decision."

"Steve... Angie and Geo are here," announces Diane, opening their balcony door a crack.

Steve is sitting outside, staring at the sparkling waters of the Gulf of Salerno from a comfy lounge chair. "Thanks, hon," he replies, his eyes still on the view. "Send them out with some beers."

Diane prepares some food while the three musketeers enjoy cold Peronis outside in the crisp fall air. Steve doesn't mind the weather, but Frank and George are cold. However, neither of them wants to complain again.

Steve watches with amusement as his friends position themselves to catch the sun's rays. There is something he needs to tell them, but he patiently waits until the sound of their chairs scraping on the tile floor stops. When the men are settled, he explains his reason for asking them to come over.

"Okay, guys, here's the skinny. The caliph is recruiting again after the first team he sent to work with the mob was killed. This time, instead of sending them here from the Middle East, he's taking them from among his followers already in Italy. So now, we have our work cut out for us."

"Gotcha," replies George. "Before, we could at least watch the ports and other entryways into the country. Now, if we don't know where the followers are coming from, there's no way we can figure out who they are."

"Right," agrees Steve. "So I requested a meeting with the pope and the cardinals in charge of the Order of the Raven. That's the Vatican hit squad no one's supposed to know about. The Ravens are supposed to have a good handle on what's going on in the country. That meeting's important, so I'd like both of you to attend."

"Okay, when is it?" asks Frank.

"AISI should be calling soon with details."

Steve says to George, "Geo, if the Ravens agree to work with us, I'd like you to link up with them. I'm gonna need someone to be my eyes and ears inside that group. We need to know what they're doing at all times, and I don't trust them to keep us informed. You okay with that?"

"You want me to be a Raven?" George asks, surprised that they would allow him to infiltrate their clandestine organization. "I'll do whatever you say, but are you sure they'll want me around? If they—"

When a sharp wind blows through the area, George's train of thought trails away. "Oh, shit," he complains. "I didn't want to say anything before, but now, it's getting to be too much. Tell me again why the hell we're out here and not inside."

Steve chuckles as George zips his jacket up as high as it'll go. "I don't know if they'll take you on," he replies, but if they don't cooperate with us, we won't work with them. I hope it doesn't come to that. They already screwed things up once, and we can't let that happen again. Oh, there's another thing. I should tell you both that there will be regular team meetings in Naples, so when the hoopla really gets going, we'll probably have to get temporary rooms there."

Frank walks to the concrete wall overlooking the sea. "You know, Chic, you never told us what we're supposed to do if we find the assassins who want to kill the pope."

When Diane pokes her head out of the door, the men stop talking. "Hey, you guys!" she calls out. "I prepared a little snack, but I'm not going out there in this weather. Come inside if you want to eat."

"Smart girl!" George responds, leaping out of his chair.

Close behind him, Frank wraps his arms around his chest as he hurries toward the promise of warmth.

Steve shakes his head at his friends, then follows them in after gathering up their empty beer bottles.

Frank and George are happy to be inside. They remove their outerwear, then chat happily as they partake of Diane's offerings. When Steve joins them, he grabs a plate and fills it with fruit, cookies, and a slice of cake.

Sitting across from Steve, Frank pops a piece of fruit into his mouth. "You know, from what you've said so far, I get the feeling that all the Italians want from us is to help them find the bad guys."

"Yeah, right," laughs George. "That's bullshit, and you know it. It won't be long before we're knee-deep in their shit." Turning to Steve, he asks, "What's the deal, boss?"

Steve can't answer because his cell phone rings at that moment.

"Yeah, okay, tomorrow morning," Steve says, looking at Frank and George. "You'll pick me up? Good. What? Already? Okay, look, two more will be joining me. Well, we'll make it happen. Right. Okay, ciao."

Steve disconnects the call and grabs more snacks.

"I guess the meeting's tomorrow," Frank surmises. "That was quick."

"Yeah. The meet and greet with the pope and the cardinals is in Rome at ten, and the chopper will be here at five. Can you guys be here before then? Oh, and the mob connected with an imam in Palermo. Looks like they're moving fast. They must have already chosen their new recruits."

When the rear door of the Palazzo del Marinaio restaurant opens, Giuseppe Sarducci approaches a large oak and marble desk and places several sheets of paper in front of his boss. "Here is what I remember about the new ragheads the Arabs are sending," he says. "That *pezzo di merda* made me memorize it all. He would not let me take any information out of the building."

Vito glances briefly at the papers. "Are they here with you now?"

"No, and that is another thing. He would not let them come back with me. He said they know where to find us and will contact us in a few days."

Vito sighs and turns his head sharply to relieve a sudden tension in his neck. "This better work. I will not tolerate any more fuckups. Now, tell me about these men."

CHAPTER SIXTEEN

When the AISI helicopter lands at Fiumicino Airport, the morning is cold, with a slight breeze. Steve, George, and Frank bundle up as they leave the chopper.

"Welcome to Rome," smiles Colonel Accola as he greets the group in front of a black Range Rover.

"Morning," says Steve. "These are the men Sal should have told you about: Frank Angelo and George Jackson."

"Yes, Salvatore gave me their names. Signore, I am sure you understand by now that the Ravens are hard to control."

Steve stares at the colonel with narrowed eyes. "Look," he declares. "We aren't here on a joy ride. The only reason I'm in Rome today is to meet with the pope about our wayward friends. However, it seems that you're saying his answer is a foregone conclusion. If that's the case, we'll just re-board that chopper and return home. The Italian government asked for my assistance, but I won't stay if they keep my hands tied behind my back."

"Come now," says the colonel, refusing to be swayed by Steve's swagger. "I am sure we can work together. Let us not leave His Holiness waiting."

After Giuseppe tells Don Vito about his talk with the Palermo Imam, he drives the don to Scarapelli Exports, where

Vito keeps a spartan, working office.

The office is a stark contrast to Vito's opulent home. There are no comforts here; it is strictly for business. The room is dark, and its only features are a metal desk and a few chairs. Nevertheless, the don likes it this way. He says there is less to mess up when things get nasty.

While Vito speaks on the phone to his shipping dock manager, Giuseppe sits nearby — business as usual for a typical workday. Giuseppe knows that his boss will probably have orders for him at some point, so he's content to wait.

When the call ends, Vito isn't in a good mood. "We're having problems with our oil shipments again," he growls. "The fucking dockworkers are back on strike."

"You want me to take care of it?" Giuseppe asks, ready to step in to do the boss's dirty work.

"No, not now."

"All right, boss. While you were on the phone, I received a message from the new recruits. They want to meet you at the restaurant before they start working."

"That is good," responds Vito. "Where will they stay while they train?"

"I will put them up in a safe house near Pompeii. We will teach them what to do and go over the assault plan at one of our empty buildings outside the city."

"How soon will they be ready?"

"If all goes well, I think they will be able to make the hit in about four weeks."

Vito is furious. "Four weeks? Fuck no!" he screams. "That is too long to wait, Beppo! This must be done quickly. The longer we delay, the more time we give those Vatican bastards to find us."

"But boss—"

"No! I will give you ten days, no more, no less. This is important. Get those ragheads ready! And take care of that cleric in Palermo. In fact, take care of that entire cultural meeting hall, or whatever they call it. I want no loose ends!" With a wave of his hand, Vito dismisses his lieutenant with an angry flourish.

Though Vito was upset about Giuseppe's estimate of when the attack could take place, he calms down when he thinks about all it will accomplish.

Confident that Giuseppe will do as he was told, he tents his fingers under his chin with a dreamy smile. He has no trouble imagining the glorious victory that he and all of Cosa Nostra will soon enjoy in their wicked vendetta against Pope Urban IV.

A black Range Rover drives under an archway near Saint Peter's Basilica, then parks in a small cobblestone lot. The four men that exit the vehicle enter a side door in an unremarkable building guarded by a tall Swiss Guardsman dressed in the order's traditional, striped uniform.

As the men walk along a richly decorated marble floor, their shoes click and clack until they enter a carpeted area. From there, a secretary ushers them into a conference room dominated by a large circular table with twenty leather chairs. Behind the table are two flags: Vatican City and Italy, the latter known to its citizens as *il Tricolore*.

"This is a seriously humongous table," whispers George, feeling intimidated by his surroundings.

"Yeah, but who are we waiting for, King Arthur?" asks Steve flippantly. "I feel like a fucking Knight of the Round

Table."

George winces at Steve's comment and hopes that Colonel Accola didn't hear it. But there's no time to find out, because Pope Urban enters at that moment, followed by three cardinals and a man dressed in a well-cut suit.

Taking turns, Steve, George, Frank, and Colonel Accola give the pontiff the traditional greeting, then everyone takes a place around the table — all except the man in the suit.

As Steve studies the man, he gets a decidedly aloof and unfriendly vibe from him. The unnamed person stands stiffly apart from the others with his hands clasped firmly at his waist. Steve can tell that he's tightly coiled, ready to spring into action at a moment's notice.

"Excuse me, Your Holiness," Steve says. "I need to express some concerns before we begin."

"Oh?" replies the pontiff. "I am interested in your comments. As I understand it, you are now in charge of the group that is trying to protect me from harm, yes? Please continue."

"Thank you, Your Holiness. It's an honor to be here. What I want to say is that the task force includes members of the Italian government, the United States FBI, my men here, and the Pontifical Swiss Guard."

"Yes, I have been informed."

"Well, I also want to say that your private hit squad agreed to join us, but their representative here today doesn't seem happy to be at our meeting." Steve turns to stare pointedly at the black-suited stranger. "I'm not sure they're actually willing to work with our team. Your Holiness, if we're going to protect you the best way possible, we need your assurance that we will have the complete support of *everyone* involved. There cannot be two groups operating independently of each other. Without the cooperation of your Ravens, I cannot guarantee that our FBI, or any other United States agency, will remain on our team for long."

Steve notes blank expressions around the table but continues with his appeal. "You may think I'm being dramatic and should not be taken seriously. But Your Holiness, if your Raven doesn't sit at this table with the rest of us today and show a clear desire to be involved with what we're doing, I don't see any point in continuing this meeting."

Pope Urban looks intently at Cardinal Amorello, then smiles at Steve. "Mr. Ciccone, I am not anxious to become a martyr. I personally guarantee that everyone at the Holy See will cooperate with you. Niccolo, please assure Mr. Ciccone of our support."

Cardinal Amorello flushes pink and nods at the suited stranger, which prompts the man to pull out a chair and sit down with the group. "The Order of the Raven is prepared to give you their full assistance," he states solemnly. "All of us are here today because we want the same thing: to stop any and all attacks on our Holy Father."

"That's good to hear," responds Steve.

Amorello gestures toward the Raven. "The man you see here today will be your new connection to the Order. He will be called Raphael, and he is at your command. I do not know how familiar you are with the Ravens, Signore, but that group is our version of your CIA. It is not as ruthless as—"

"Gentlemen," interrupts Pope Urban, "the silent soldiers of the Order of the Raven have been dedicated to the Catholic Church for hundreds of years. They originated with the valiant crusaders of the Knights Templar and have always held the interests of the Church close to their hearts. Now, I will leave you to your discussion. Cardinal Amorello, you have authority to speak for me. Later today, you will update me on what transpired in my absence. May God bless you all."

After the pope leaves, Colonel Accola says, "I recently received a disturbing report from Vincenzo Bennini at AISI. I believe Your Eminences know of him. The Mafia has met with an imam at a Muslim cultural center in Palermo, so we believe they already have the information they need on the second group of men they will supply for the assassination attempt."

"Our men have that mosque under surveillance," declares Raphael, "and we saw Giuseppe Sarducci entering it as well. For those who may not know, Sarducci is first lieutenant to Vito Scarapelli, the Cosa Nostra capo who ordered the hit. We followed Sarducci back to Cefalù, where he and Scarapelli entered an export house controlled by the crime syndicate."

"That's valuable information," replies Steve with a grateful nod to Raphael. He tells the Church's bishops, "I'd like to set up close collaboration with the Ravens so we can share information like this more easily. I want someone from our group to be out in the field with the Ravens, so I designated George Jackson to be my liaison with them, as your man Raphael is with us." Turning to George, Steve says, "Stick with Raphael as closely as possible."

The cardinals turn to each other, conferring in low whispers, while the others wonder what's going on.

"When can Mr. Jackson join the Ravens in Cefalù?" asks Cardinal Amorello.

"I can be ready as soon as you want," answers George. "But I hope there won't be a language problem; I don't speak Italian. Do the Ravens speak English?"

Raphael chuckles. "Most of us speak at least seven languages, Mr. Jackson. I personally speak eight."

CHAPTER SEVENTEEN

A few days later, Raphael arrives at dawn to pick George up from Frank's villa. The Raven asked him to be ready early so they could get to Naples International Airport before traffic builds for the day.

George is eager to get started. He knows he's the first outsider to work with the secretive organization, and he's excited.

At the same time, Giuseppe Sarducci speed-walks down Palermo's Via Cosmo Guastella flanked by two mob soldiers from Cefalù. The mobsters have just left the Islamic center run by Hussein Assan, and they're determined to leave the area quickly.

Inside the center, Imam Assan lies sprawled on the tile floor of the courtyard with a bullet hole through his head. Scattered around him, others are already dead or well on the way.

Down the street, Giuseppe quickly opens the car door and seats himself behind the wheel of the mob vehicle. After his companions duck inside, he removes a detonator from his pocket and presses its red button. Instantly, a deafening explosion erupts behind them, and the Islamic center goes up in flames.

At the force of the blast, windows shatter in adjoining buildings, and the Ravens in their rented room across the street jolt awake.

Inside the van, Giuseppe turns in his seat and shoots one of the soldiers with a suppressed Berretta. The other soldier slips the detonator into the dead man's pocket, then pushes him out of the van. When he closes the door, Giuseppe drives away.

Outside of Cefalù, a sixteen-foot speedboat skims across the Tyrrhenian Sea toward a secluded cove on the coast, where a one-hundred-fifty-foot yacht waits in the early morning light at a little-used dock.

Following a strict schedule, an oversized truck soon pulls up. As ordered, the driver positions the vehicle's bulk in front of the ship's boarding ramp.

With the ship shielded from prying eyes, four men file out of the truck. The first is Amid Tabul, a five-foot-two-inch man in his mid-twenties from Aleppo, Syria. Amid is un-usually small for this type of work. Normally, he would be taunted and ridiculed by the hotheads he hangs around with, but because he is muscular, and was trained in bomb-making in Iraq's Anbar Province, none of his associates mess with him.

The next to leave the truck is Josef Igmani from Tehran. Igmani is also a trained explosive expert, a specialist in IEDs, after several stints in Iraq, Syria, and Libya. At forty-five years old, he is the oldest of the four in this group, and the tallest. With fair skin, blue eyes, and a six-foot frame, Igmani appears more French than Iranian — one of the principal reasons he was chosen for this mission.

Moammar Sanjoni and Azim al-Hussan are the last to step out. They are young adults — each barely twenty years old. But both are expert snipers, trained by the Taliban in their native Pakistan. Each of them can pass for Sicilian. Their chis-eled faces, dark skin, and brown eyes belie their Middle Eastern backgrounds, a definite plus for blending into this Mediterranean country.

Each man came to Sicily several years ago as a refugee from his native land. They all learned enough Italian to get by and tried to find jobs, but none of them ever felt that they fit in. The only place these men felt comfortable was their neighborhood worship center. They spent so much time there, that Imam Assan noticed, and started talking to them every day about their religion. Eventually, the Imam instilled so much fervor in them that when he asked them to declare their faith with action, they readily agreed.

To boost their anonymity, all four of these Caliphate recruits are wearing typical western-style clothing: jeans, sneakers, and tee-shirts with the names of well-known sports teams and recording groups.

The men board the hidden ship silently, each of them knowing what awaits them at the end. Outside the yacht, a throaty growl announces the arrival of the speedboat. When it enters the cove, the pilot cuts the throttle and guides it alongside the ship, to a point where crewmembers can attach it to cranes and lift it into the ship's hull.

The yacht's destination is a private dock in Scilla, a seaside resort town in Calabria, on Italy's mainland. The four men will disembark there, then travel overland to Rome.

When their flight lands, George and Raphael deplane at Palermo's Falcone Borsellino Airport, then follow the signs to the luggage area. Raphael knows that some of his colleagues will be waiting for them there. Spying them in the crowd, he speeds up to talk to them privately.

"Mr. Jackson," says Raphael when George catches up to him, "you can call these men Antonio and Wilfred. They were monitoring the Islamic center in Palermo, but it has been destroyed."

"What the hell do you mean, it's been destroyed?" asks George.

"La Cosa Nostra blew up the imam and the mosque and everyone in it," clarifies Antonio.

"Ah, shit," sighs George. "Tell me you talked to the guy before the mob got there."

"No, we were not able to do that."

"So you don't have the names of the men he recruited?"

"No."

"How do you know it was the mob?"

"We have video of men leaving the building just before it blew up. We cannot identify them because their faces are covered, but they appear to be mob soldiers."

"What time did it happen?"

"It was early in the morning, before we woke up," says Wilfred.

"You were sleeping?" questions George. "How did you get the video?"

"We keep a camera running at all times. It is trained on the building from a window across the street."

"This isn't good," sighs George. "Those guys are managing to keep one step ahead of us at every turn. We're going to have to change that, and fast."

In Ravello, Steve and Diane are still in bed, but they're not sleeping, and they're no longer happy. One of their morning trysts was just interrupted by Steve's loudly ringing cell phone.

Cursing angrily, Steve swipes at the phone and answers the call without checking the number first.

"Look," he fumes, "this better be a fucking emergency or I'll hunt you down and make you pay!"

Instantly, Steve recognizes the voice, and begins a hasty apology. But George cuts him off.

The former FSA chief listens to the unwelcome news about the Palermo Imam, then hangs up and stares unseeing at the floor for a long time. When he finally lifts his eyes to his wife, he sighs heavily. "The time has come, Dee," he says. "The shit has just hit the fan, so I'll have to be in Naples for a while."

Steve's gloomy expression worries Diane. "What happened?" she asks, then changes her mind. "No, don't tell me. I'm going to get up and make breakfast." Without further comment, she rolls out of bed and wraps herself in a silky robe.

Steve sits back against the headboard, still unclothed from their attempted romp in the sack.

"Chopper will be here in two hours!" shouts Diane from the kitchen. "You gonna need Angie?"

"Yeah! I'll tell the pilot to stop for him in Sorrento!"

"We have a problem," says Colonel Accola when Vincenzo Bennini answers his call. "Cosa Nostra blew up the Palermo Islamic Center. The imam is dead. Mr. Jackson and Raphael are on their way to Cefalù, so I sent a helicopter to bring Steve and Mr. Angelo here. I will meet you in Naples. I am afraid things have become critical."

CHAPTER EIGHTEEN

The private yacht La Fiore Blu is now rocking gently in the waters of the Mediterranean, one hundred yards off the shore of Scilla. Her passengers are stepping into the craft's speedboat for the short trip to the mainland. "Keep out of sight," says the skipper.

The four men duck below the gunwale, but curiosity gets the better of them as they near the mainland. One by one, they sneak peeks over the side, to instant rebukes from the skipper.

Local police in Sorrento are having a tough time this morning. Their superiors alerted them to the arrival of a high-ranking official's helicopter, so they're scrambling to stop traffic and install blockades to keep people away. The only open space in the busy tourist town is Piazza Tasso, the city's popular gathering place, and as usual, it's crowded with visitors.

When the AISI helicopter lands, Steve sees Frank standing near the statue of Saint Antonino Abbate, the city's patron saint. He waves him over and watches his friend running in a crouch to avoid the dragonfly's deadly blades.

Frank straps himself in, then turns to Steve to complain — loudly — as the chopper arches into the air toward Naples. "Dammit, Chic!" he shouts, making himself heard over the engines. "I have to live in this town! They're not going to forget the *Americano* who closed their piazza and pissed them all off!"

Steve leans close to reply directly into Frank's ear. "Buongiorno to you, too! I already pissed people off with this thing in Ravello, so welcome to the club!"

Frank doesn't appreciate Steve's flippant retort, so he gives him the bird and mouths some choice words that Steve pretends not to understand.

As close friends do, Steve brushes off Frank's rebuke. Leaning close again, he asks, "How's the renovation going?"

"Going well!" Frank responds. "But after this grand exit, I'm sure they're gonna raise their prices! I just shut down their town, for cryin' out loud! Why the rush?"

"Tell you later! Too loud in here!" yells Steve. "Enjoy the view!"

Later that morning, a dark-colored Passat heads east along SS113/Via Roma in Cefalù, a narrow thoroughfare lined with apartments above small shops and eateries. Wrought-iron balconies overlooking the hustle and bustle hold clay pots filled with geraniums and other plants typical of the Italian countryside.

Raphael turns the car down Via de Pasquale, then makes a left at Via Maestro Pintorno and pulls into a parking lot along the beach.

Beneath circling and swooping seagulls, Raphael leads George to an apartment building across the street from Palazzo Del Marinaio, a restaurant owned by Vito Scarapelli. It's one of the businesses that Scarapelli uses often, so the Ravens keep it under constant surveillance.

Inside the apartment building, the pair walks up three

flights to Apartment 31A, where Raphael knocks five times in rapid succession, waits a minute, then knocks once more. When the code is recognized, the door swings open.

Raphael enters first and motions for George to wait while he speaks confidentially with two men standing near the windows.

George watches the exchange with narrowed eyes. *He's keeping me out of it again,* he thinks, annoyed by the rebuff. *There's a helluva lot of secrecy among these Ravens.*

During the conversation, Raphael looks back at George and seems to explain his presence to the two men, neither of whom appear to care very much for his being there. When the discussion is over, they turn around without acknowledging George's presence and enter a room off the living area, closing the door behind them.

"That went well," says George when Raphael joins him. "What's going on?"

"My men do not want you here, but they will not make trouble as long as you work only through me."

"I can live with that," George replies.

Raphael stares hard at his new shadow, not seeming to care if George agrees with him or not. "We have a problem," he says. "The new group of Islamic killers have already reached the mainland."

"That's just great," comments George dryly. "Can't anything go right?"

"We may have an edge," states Raphael. "Inside that room is the man who drove them to a ship early this morning. He is about to tell us the men's destination.

At that moment, the volume of a radio that was playing faintly inside the bedroom is turned up to its highest setting. However, this classic tactic doesn't work well. Through the din, George and Raphael can still plainly hear the pitiful sounds of a male's pleading cries.

For the first time since the Naples meetings began, Salvatore Caputi, Vincenzo Bennini, and Colonel Accola have arrived in the meeting room, ready to start. But neither Steve nor the other Americans are there yet.

To pass the time while they wait, the Italians drink Lavazza Oro espressos and chat about mundane topics. But Colonel Accola soon has his fill of chitchat. "They don't understand what we are doing," he mumbles, to nods of agreement from the others. "We need to inform them—"

"Yeah?" interrupts Steve, strolling casually into the room with Frank. "What the hell *are* we doing? I'm happy to see that you got here before me this time. I'd begun to wonder whether I'd have to start our meetings without you." Looking around, he notes scowls on the Italians' faces. "That was a joke, gentlemen. I hope your senses of humor haven't left you."

Samuel Caputi retorts, "I am afraid we are not in a joking mood."

"No, I guess not," replies Steve. "Okay, let's get started, then. Have a seat, Ang. Everyone, this is my friend, Frank Angelo. We call him Angie for short. He's going to be joining forces with us."

"Your other friend, George Jackson, is with the Ravens in Cefalù," says Samuel Caputi. "The new terrorists the Caliphate supplied to Cosa Nostra have already made it to the mainland. They came on a ship from Sicily, but we do not know where they landed. When the Islamic center in Palermo was destroyed, any records they may have had there are now gone, along with the Imam who made the deal."

"I may have some information about that," interrupts Colonel Accola. "The Ravens had the mosque under surveillance. They have photographs of four men leaving the building the day before the explosion. Their faces are not visible, but the same men were later photographed entering Palazzo del Marinaio restaurant in Cefalù. That's a place Vito uses for clandestine meetings." Accola flips open a file and displays the photos to the others.

Steve glances at the evidence, then turns to Bennini. "Why aren't the FBI agents at this meeting?"

Bennini shrugs. "They were called to Rome unexpectedly."

Steve rubs a rising tension from the back of his neck. "Send copies of those photos to them as soon as possible. And let's also send them to any other agencies that can help. We need to find those men quickly. If they're the assassins, they could disappear into the Italian countryside, and we'll lose them."

Steve crooks his fingers to motion Accola to pass him the photos, so the captain slides them across the table. He studies them more closely and inquires, "If these guys are no longer in Sicily, why are Geo and the Raven in Cefalù?"

"The Ravens are questioning the man who brought them to the ship," replies Colonel Accola.

While the loud music and screams continue, George paces the small flat near the sea.

Suddenly, the sounds stop. The two unnamed men exit the bedroom, then converse with Raphael.

George listens, but doesn't understand a word they're

saying. Raphael knows he only speaks English, so he thinks they're speaking French to exclude him intentionally, and his blood pressure soars.

After a minute, the Raven agents reenter the bedroom and close the door again.

"He brought them to Don Vito's yacht," says Raphael. "It was bound for Scilla."

"Where's Scilla?"

"On the mainland."

"What else did he say?"

"If he knew anything more than that, he can no longer tell us," sneers Raphael.

George is furious. He knows what Raphael isn't saying, but he opts to bite his tongue until the other Ravens aren't around.

"We need to go to Scilla," continues Raphael, "but I need to contact Accola first. Let us go back to the car. A helicopter is waiting for us, so we can talk on the way. Besides, this apartment needs to be cleaned."

George remains quiet on the way out of the apartment building, but as soon as they're back in the Passat, he explodes. "You dumb asses killed the only lead we had!" he shouts incredulously. "And now we're running blind again! Explain that shit to me, will you? Who allowed those assholes to murder the guy before we got everything we could out of him? Was that you?"

With unnatural control, Raphael doesn't react to George's fury. "I know your government uses enhanced interrogation techniques," he states calmly, reaching for his phone. "So I find your astonishment at our methods disturbing."

"Your methods? Yeah, we use waterboarding," declares

George. "But we don't use it to kill people! You guys did it again! You murdered someone we're trying to get information from, and that's insane! You guys are still fighting the Crusades, for cryin' out loud! What the hell are we gonna do now? For all we know, those Caliphate loyalists could be halfway to Rome by now! Make your fucking phone call, and let's get out of here!"

Colonel Accola neglected to silence his phone before the Naples anti-terrorist meeting began, so when it rings loudly, he leaves the table to answer it. The others know he's connected to the Ravens, so they suspend their conversation until he can rejoin them.

Accola moves some distance away, however, those watching know the call means bad news when his expression turns from curiosity to dismay.

"What's the skinny, Colonel?" shouts Steve. "Who screwed the pooch?"

Vincenzo Bennini rolls his eyes at Steve's offbeat phrase. He's been around Americans before, so he knows many of their colloquialisms. "You Americans have an interesting way of expressing yourselves," he says. "But not all of us understand." To the other Italians, he explains, "Steve believes there is a problem and wants to know what happened."

Colonel Accola returns to the table. "The four people in the photos are now on the mainland. A ship transported them to Scilla, a small fishing town across the strait of Messina. Raphael and George Jackson are on their way there now. That was all the information the Ravens were able to retrieve from the man they apprehended."

Though the colonel's comment was brief, Steve picked up on a hidden meaning. He's angry, and his face flushes beet red. In one abrupt movement, he pushes himself away from the table and stands with his fists clenched at his side. Dumbfounded, he points at Accola and yells at him accusingly, "The Ravens killed the guy? These are the dedicated and highly skilled people we have to deal with? What is *wrong* with them?" Using his foot, he pushes at his chair and retakes his seat. "Where else, besides Naples, does the Mafia have a presence on the mainland?"

"They are everywhere," answers Salvatore Caputi. "But Cosenza seems to be a favorite gathering place. They have a large compound east of the city."

Steve asks wearily, "Where's Cosenza?"

"It is about two hours from Scilla."

Steve raps his fingers on the table. "Get ahold of Raphael and Geo; tell them we're going to that compound. That's probably where the assassins are. Which airport is closest to Cosenza?"

"Um... I..." stammers Caputi, looking around the table for help.

"Lamezia Terme is the closest," offers Vincenzo Bennini. "I have family in the area."

"Okay," says Steve. "Angie, you're going to get on the next plane to Cosenza. Can you go with him, Sal?"

"Yes, but..."

"Good. Colonel, tell Raphael to meet Frank and Salvatore at the airport. Vincenzo, can you arrange their flight?"

"There are no direct flights to Cosenza from here," states Bennini. "The best way to get there is to drive."

"Seriously? No flights? That's not good! How long is the drive?"

"About three-and-a-half-hours."

Steve sighs loudly. "We can only hope those scumbags stay there awhile. But I bet they're already on their way to Rome. The mob probably won't waste any time now that their goons are so close."

"We should still check the stronghold."

"Yes, let's not let any stone go unturned. Sal, if your operatives in Cosenza spot the terrorists, tell them to trail them and take photos."

"Will you come to Cosenza as well?" asks Salvatore.

"No, I'm going to stay here. I want to bring the FBI up to speed when they get back. I assume you have an office in Cosenza?"

"AISI is in many cities."

"Right. By the way, you're gonna need hardware, Angie. Your personal firearm won't be enough for this job."

"We can get him what he needs," says Bennini. "You know," he adds thoughtfully, "if they are in Cosenza, they will most likely take the train to Rome. The trains don't have security checks."

"What? Aw, that's just great. I think I feel a headache coming on," sighs Steve. "Things aren't looking good, people. Between searching for killers to prevent the pope from getting hurt, we also have to watch the Ravens like hawks. No pun intended. They're exceptionally loose cannons."

CHAPTER NINETEEN

"How are you, hon? Miss you awful," says Steve, making effective use of rare downtime. After the meeting broke up, he remained behind at AISI to wait for FBI Agents Kathryn Samuels and John DeMaria.

"I'm fine," Diane replies. "But it's been too quiet around here since you left."

"I probably won't be back for a while," states Steve glumly. "But hey," he continues, his mood brightening with an interesting thought. "How about this? What if I send a car for you on Friday? We can have a nice weekend together in Naples. You up for a short trip?" Just then, John and Kathryn enter the room, so Steve cuts the conversation short. "Think about it," he says. "I'll call back later."

Steve pockets the phone and looks at the FBI agents. "Glad to see you guys. We have news: The shit has officially hit the fan."

"What happened?" John asks.

"Our terrorists are now on the mainland. Those pictures are for you," he says, nodding at the photos Colonel Accola displayed during the meeting. "We think they're the new recruits. I have a sneaking suspicion they went to a Mafia compound outside of Cosenza, so we sent a team there to raid the place. But my gut tells me that they're already on their way to Rome."

"Interpol has an informant inside the Cosenza Mafia," states John while he studies the photos. "He can let us know what's going on there."

When John passes the photos to Kathryn, Steve says, "Keep them. I'm depending on you guys to figure out who the hell they are. Let the mole know we're going to Cosenza in case there's trouble. I hope things don't go to shit."

Raphael is mostly silent on the long drive from Naples to Cosenza. That's not a surprise, but George is curious, so he tries to draw the Raven out.

Figuring that it's best to start with trivial questions, he asks where Raphael was born. But the Raven looks straight ahead without acknowledging that he heard George. George tries again. "Do you have any siblings?" Silence. "Are your parents still alive?" Nothing. So he tries a different tack: "When did you join the Ravens?"

That gets a reaction, but it's not what George hoped. Raphael looks so disturbed by the question that George is afraid he'll kick him out of the car. With a sigh, he turns his face to the window and watches the Italian countryside go by instead — a thoroughly enjoyable diversion on any count.

In Naples, Vincenzo Bennini gets in touch with AISI's Cosenza office. He informs the officer in charge about the raid and lets him know that several team members are on their way by car and that others will arrive by plane. He also tells him that the team will need to assemble somewhere private. "Is there anywhere at Lamezia Terme airport that is isolated from prying eyes?"

The AISI officer thinks for a moment. "There is a hangar that has not been used in a while. It should be quiet. There should not be anyone hanging around it."

Bennini sends the location of the hangar to Salvatore

and Raphael.

Relying on the car's GPS and a backup paper map, Raphael drives through Lamezia Terme airport and parks in front of the hangar. "It is best to wait in the car for Vincenzo's colleagues," he tells George. "If we walk around, we may attract unnecessary attention. This place is supposed to be abandoned."

Not long after they arrive, an SUV parks nearby, and someone steps out of the vehicle. Neither man knows who he is, so they finger their guns to keep them ready.

"*Sono la Benemerita!*" the man shouts, holding a badge out in front of him.

"What'd he say?" asks George.

"La Benemerita is a common name for the Carabinieri."

Raphael shouts to the new arrival, "Who are the others with you?"

"*Mostra le tue identificazioni,*" the man instructs the others piling out of the car.

When the carabiniere's companions flash their IDs, Raphael relaxes. He recognizes badges from AISI and Interpol, so he tells George they can get out of the car.

The carabiniere walks up to Raphael with an outstretched hand. "*È un piacere,*" he says charmingly. "I am happy to work with AISI again."

Raphael ignores the man's welcome. He asks stonily, "How close is the Cosa Nostra property?"

Disappointed, the officer drops his arm and turns to business. "It is not far. We can confirm that four men arrived there a couple of days ago, and there are no reports that they left."

The whine of an approaching plane forces the officer to

raise his voice to continue. "The Carabinieri are keeping eyes on them!"

As the noise increases, the men stop speaking to watch a small jet pull up to the hangar. When the door opens, Salvatore and Frank descend the steps.

Though the AISI team thought this hangar was out of use, an airport employee has been watching everything from behind a low wall. While the assembled team introduces themselves to each other, the eavesdropper relays what he sees into his cell phone like a raging Italian river.

As the talk continues, Frank pulls George aside. "Geo," he says quietly, "Steve wants us to keep an eye on the fucking Raven, as if we aren't gonna have enough to do with the mob and their fucking associates. He don't trust that sumbitch."

"Yeah, I know. How the hell did we let Chic pull us into one of his schemes again, Ang? Now, we're probably gonna get into a firefight in Italy, of all places. We're supposed to be relaxing at your villa, dammit! Remind me to smack Chic in the head when I see him!"

"You and me both!" retorts Frank.

Frank's expression turns grim when he sees the rest of the group starting to board their vehicle. "Let's roll," he says solemnly. "It's about to get real."

George responds, "Never thought I'd hear that again. I thought I put all this shit behind me when I left the States. But bad guys don't stay down for long. So…here we are again."

While Raphael drives behind the police SUV, George takes another stab at talking to him. "Those guys don't know you're a Raven, do they?" he asks.

"No, they do not," replies Raphael icily. "And the both of you better keep it that way."

"We're good," replies Frank from the back seat.

The cars drive for about an hour on E45, then both exit onto SP234. A short time later, they turn onto Contrada Malivicina, a narrow country road in a small village in Cosenza Province.

Raphael has no trouble keeping up with the SUV on this road. It winds around low hills dotted with farmland and vineyards, so the SUV slows down to negotiate the turns.

On a slight rise, a goatherder with a double-barreled shotgun slung casually over his shoulder watches intently as they drive by. This area is ordinarily quiet and peaceful, so the mechanized intruders aren't unnoticed. The goatherder waits until the cars disappear into a stand of trees bordering the road, then he turns on his phone and places a warning call.

Minutes later, the cars travel over an even narrower dirt road leading through an orchard of blood orange trees, known locally as *arance sanguigne*. There, they pull off the road and park under the dense tree cover.

"The mob's house is through those trees," says Salvatore as he disperses Beretta ARX100 semi-automatic rifles and flack vests from the trunk of the police vehicle. "We will proceed through the orchard on foot," he instructs. "The compound with armed guards is about three hundred meters out. We should be able to surprise them."

The group dodges orange trees on their way to the walled Mafia fortress, with George and Frank bringing up the rear.

"I got a bad feeling," whispers Frank. "There has to be some way for those goons to watch over their surroundings, but I don't see any cameras or guards. Whiskey Tango Foxtrot?"

"What about that goatherder?" asks George. "I don't care what Caputi says. Those fuckers know we're comin'. Just keep low and slow. Chic's gonna need more than one smack for this job."

Slowly and steadily, the men creep toward a tall stone wall poking through the brush. As they go, the superstitious Italians can't help but think that the ghosts of fallen Mafia hit-men are watching their approach.

Still believing they haven't been seen, the group gets within fifty yards of the stronghold before all hell breaks loose. Without warning, automatic weapons fire fills the air, and bullets whiz by the men's heads like angry bees, forcing them all to find cover.

As they come under attack, George and Frank instinctively go into SWAT mode. With practiced calm, they choose targets carefully and drop them one by one. The firefight continues for an undetermined length of time.

When both camps run out of ammo, there is a deadly quiet in the orange grove. Caputi takes a moment to survey his men.

"*Grazie a Dio,*" he murmurs, thankful to find that only two are injured, neither with life-threatening wounds.

Hearing a rustling on his left, Salvatore turns to see Raphael sprinting toward an arched opening in the stone wall. "*Che cazzo?*" he shouts, astounded at the Raven's recklessness. "That guy is crazy, but maybe he sees something! *Segui quel coglione!*"

As ordered, the Italians dart after Raphael.

"What did he say?" George asks Frank.

"It must mean, 'Let's roll!'"

Soon, the raid team finds themselves in a courtyard dotted with bodies lying near the wall, but there's no time to check on them. Engines are starting and tires are screeching, so all of them dash toward the front of the building, where three vans are leaving the compound in a hurry. Raphael gets several shots off, but none hit their targets, and the vehicles disappear into a line of cypress trees.

Cursing their bad luck, the men retrace their steps back to the courtyard to begin sorting through the bodies they passed earlier. "Here is one of ours! Someone gave him a 'Columbian necktie!'" shouts an Italian officer when he sees the Interpol agent who accompanied them in the SUV.

Salvatore kneels at the agent's side to search for identification. "One of those Mafia fuckers must have been alive," he says ruefully. "We should have checked them when we passed through." With a sigh, he pockets the Interpol officer's badge, then says a quick prayer.

Standing nearby, Frank clicks on a contact number. "We missed them, Chic," he says sheepishly.

"Fuck it all!" responds Steve, loud enough to be heard clearly by anyone standing near Frank.

CHAPTER TWENTY

While extra AISI and Carabinieri officers swarm the courtyard and surrounding orchard like ants searching for food, EMTs from the nearby town tend to Salvatore Caputi's injured men.

Inside the house, Frank, George, Raphael, and Salvatore look for anything that will give them useful information. Not knowing who or what they may encounter, they keep their rifles ready. But the large villa seems deserted. So far, they've searched eight bedrooms and a large media room, and they're not done yet.

After they pass through the living area, Frank opens a door onto a dark staircase in a small alcove. "Let's take this one, George. You guys go ahead."

While the pair descends a flight of well-worn steps, Frank voices a question he's been wondering about. "You know, there are a lot of orange trees outside this house, so they must get a good harvest. Could this be where they keep the equipment for processing them? They have to do something with them, right?"

The question goes unanswered, as they've come upon a locked wooden door at the bottom of the steps.

"Let's try to get it open," says George.

Bracing themselves against the steps, the two men put their shoulders to the door and heave, but it doesn't budge.

"Shine your light on it," says Frank. "It's too dark to see

what's here."

George reaches into a pocket and shines a small tactical flashlight on the lock.

"It doesn't look very sturdy," comments Frank, inspecting the setup closely. "I wonder why it didn't open."

"Hey, one side is just nailed on," George declares. "I have an idea." Reaching into another pocket, he takes out a knife and pries the lock off. "Eureka!"

Throwing the contraption aside, the duo swings the door open into utter blackness.

"There may be a switch somewhere," George mutters, feeling along the wall. "Ah, here it is."

When a bank of LED lights turns on, the room becomes brighter than daylight.

"What the hell?" Frank and George exclaim.

"It's a weapons depot!" cries Frank. "There must be enough firepower down here for an army!"

The men are stunned by the enormity of the room's contents. "I'll take this side and you take that," says George. The men separate to examine rows of orderly shelving to see exactly what's there.

"These guys are methodical!" Frank calls over to George. "They labeled every shelf! I'm gonna start taking photos."

"Do you believe this?" asks George from a couple of rows over. "There are boxes and boxes of automatic weapons, sniper rifles, and ammunition of every caliber! There are even containers of plastic explosives and detonators!"

Frank takes more photos, then hits "send" to let Steve know what they found. But all he gets is a spinning circle. "Damn. Let's go back upstairs," he says. "There's no service down here."

Suddenly, both of them freeze in place.

"Shh," whispers George, unslinging his rifle and pointing it at the door.

A moment later, Salvatore and Raphael enter the room, looking just as shocked as they did.

"Fuckin' shit!" exclaims George, lowering his weapon. "You almost got shot!"

"What the hell is this place?" asks Salvatore.

"They have fuckin' military weapons!" George replies, sweeping a hand toward the rows of shelving.

"Barrett .50 cal. sniper rifles, if you can believe that!" adds Frank.

Salvatore looks around in awe. "How much do you think is here?" he asks.

"We don't know, but all the shelves are labeled and stocked. There are a couple of empty boxes, though."

"What is missing?"

"We figure there were at least three ARX100s and one 82A1. We haven't checked, but I bet your ass some explosives are missing as well. I wouldn't be surprised if they're on their way to Rome…"

Frank's last sentence trails away as Raphael and Salvatore turn on their heels and storm out of the room.

"What the…?" calls Frank as he and George scramble to catch up, bounding up the stairs two by two.

Ahead of them, Raphael, a man of few words, exclaims fervently, *"Adesso dobbiamo andare in Vaticano!"*

Ordinarily, neither American would have understood what the Italian said, but this time, they did.

"Crap!" they shout in unison. "We're going to the

Vatican!"

When the scavenging ants in the courtyard make their way down to the weapons storeroom, they load the booty into their vehicles. Leaving them to it, Caputi, George, and Frank climb into Raphael's car for the drive back to the airport.

On the way, Frank calls Steve. "We got a fucking problem, Chic," he declares glumly. "We believe our targets are armed with ARX100s and at least one 82A1. They may also have plastic explosives with blasting caps."

"Holy crap!" proclaims Steve. "Explosives, too? That's a nice addition to their candy bags!"

"We're heading back now and should be in Naples in three hours. I'm sending you photos of the stash."

When Steve's phone pings, the photos appear one by one. As he views them, scenarios of what could happen pass through his mind.

"Vincent, we were too late," he informs Vincenzo Bennini at AISI's Rome headquarters. "The assassins are probably on their way to Rome right now. Take a look at the photos I forwarded to you from the Mafia compound. We need to get everyone up to AISI headquarters."

Steve ends the call without waiting for a response, then clicks on his contact photo of Diane. "Pack some bags, Dee," he says instead of his usual greeting. "I'm going to be in Rome for a couple of weeks, so you may as well come, too. I'll send someone to pick you up in the morning."

"Really? Anything you say, Your Highness," Diane replies in her typically sassy manner. "Now, would that be by land or air? And do you require anything else, Your Majesty?"

Steve can't say much; he's laughing too hard. "Ha, ha," he snorts. "You're a real trip, Mrs. Ciccone. I really needed that laugh right now!"

Raphael drives Salvatore, Frank, and George to AISI headquarters in Naples just after midnight. They write up some reports, then plan to meet again at the airport later that day.

With another trip in a couple of hours, Salvatore brings Raphael to his apartment to freshen up, while Steve takes a taxi to his hotel room to rest. Unwisely, George convinces Frank to walk to their hotel.

At two in the morning, George and Frank stroll down Corso Meridionale, a few blocks from Stazione di Napoli Centrali, the city's central train station.

At this hour, the only Neapolitans on the street with them are ladies of the evening and thugs. The two *amici* successfully avoid the former, but they run into the latter when they're close to their hotel.

In front of a darkened building, two young punks with more attitude than brains suddenly step out in front of the Americans. "Oh, no," says Frank tiredly. "What do you want?" He's in no mood for a confrontation; all he wants is a nice clean bed.

"*Ciao, vecchio,*" says one of the youths. "You *americano, sì*? I think you give us money now. *Capisci?*" he says in broken English.

The youths start tossing sharp knives from one hand to the other in a classic show of bravado intended to intimidate the older men. George and Frank watch the show, but only for a moment.

Chuckling loudly, George suddenly reaches out and punches one of the youths in the throat. When that one gasps for air and drops to the sidewalk, Frank grabs the knife hand of the other punk and bends it backward, forcing him to the pavement as well. As the would-be thief moans in pain, Frank relieves him of his knife and stomps his foot into his crotch.

"Hey, Geo!" Frank calls out. "Look at the souvenir I got from our trip to Naples! It's an Italian-made switchblade!"

Sniggering at the young men's plight, Frank pockets his memento and straightens his shirt collar. Then the friends resume their slow stroll to the hotel. At the end of the block, they pass hookers who offer each of them a high five.

Across from the hotel, George spies an open café. "How about a quick drink before we nod off?" he asks.

"Aw, come on, Geo," responds Frank. "I would if I were thirty years younger, but we have to be ready for another trip in a couple of hours. We're not gonna get much sleep."

"You're right," sighs George. "My brain needs to get in step with my body. Man, you got any aspirin in your room? I think I twisted my shoulder punching that jerk. The look on that asshole's face when his partner hit the deck was priceless!"

"Yeah! And what about the other jerk's face when I stomped his balls?"

Alone in her quiet house, Diane stares absently at the rippling waters of the Mediterranean while she drinks her first caffè latte of the morning. The beauty of the view outside her windows never fails to captivate her, and it always brings up pleasant memories. Today, her mind wanders to her last Oscar acceptance speech, and the first time she met Steve.

Choosing to reflect on Steve, she remembers the sweltering heat and how uncomfortable she was that day. She was in Florida, in a disabled limo at the side of a busy expressway. Still grateful that Steve showed up instead of the tow truck, she lingers on that pleasant memory — until her cell phone breaks the spell.

"Pronto," she answers.

As if her thoughts conjured him up, the voice of the man she'd been thinking about says, "Morning, Dee. Miss me?"

Diane smiles at her husband's voice. "More than you know, you sweet man," she replies. "I was just thinking about you."

Steve puffs out his chest with pride. He knows he's fortunate to have found such a wonderful soulmate in his second wife. "That's why I love you," he says appreciatively. "Now get ready, milady. Your ride should be in the clearing at any moment."

"What? I thought..." Diane stops speaking when the noise of blades slapping the air in the distance captures her attention. "Oh, I think I hear it now! See you soon, babe!"

Still sleepy from their early morning arrival in Naples, the three musketeers are quiet while they wait for their ride to Rome. Yawning frequently, they make sure to stand a safe distance from the large, circled H on the AISI building's roof.

Suddenly, George remembers something he forgot to do last night. Reaching forward, he smacks Steve hard in the back of the head.

"Ow!" shouts Steve, rubbing the spot where George hit him. "But I should have expected that, I guess. Feel better now?"

Frank cracks up, recalling what George said before the attack on the mob compound. "We both feel much better!" he smiles, giving George a high five.

Steve rubs his head while he focuses on a growing spec in the sky.

When the helicopter arrives, it circles the AISI building like a dog searching for a place to rest. Looking down at the roof, Diane waves at the three men while the chopper lands.

While the men strap themselves in, Steve leans over to kiss his wife. "We're going straight to Rome!" he shouts, straining to be heard. "You've been warning me about all the shopping you want to do, so now you'll have plenty of time to do it!"

Diane leans close to speak into Steve's ear. "You gonna update me about the mission? I was worried! What have you guys really been doing? Spill it, hon!"

"Everything's fine!" Steve responds, waving his hand dismissively. "I'll fill you in when we land!"

Frowning at how Steve made light of her concern, Diane reaches up and hits him in the back of the head. "You better!" she declares with firm, wifely authority.

Amused by the marital tiff, Frank and George high five each other again, while Steve winces at another sore spot.

CHAPTER TWENTY-ONE

The streets near Saint Peter's Basilica are crowded with tourists from around the world. Some are shopping in nearby stores, while others are on their way to Saint Peter's Square for Pope Urban's weekly address, typically held every Wednesday when he's in town.

North of the world-famous landmark, a two-bedroom apartment overlooks Piazza del Risorgimento, a popular city square near Via del Mascherino. Initially, the square was just another unimpressive stop for the city's public buses. However, after restaurants and hotels came to the area, along with food trucks and souvenir vendors, the city's residents started flocking to it.

Inside the apartment, Josef Igmani and Amid Tabul work side-by-side, quietly assembling a suicide vest and an IED at their dining room table. They are busy filling the weapons with bags of nails and plastic explosives they took from the villa near Cosenza. On another table, Azim al-Hussan has disassembled the Barrett 82A1 and is now cleaning and oiling his baby.

Seated on the living room sofa, Moammar Sanjoni watches the bombmakers closely. There is a lot of tension in the room, and he is nervous. "Hey," he says, "this apartment is not a good place to become martyrs. Be careful about what you are doing, brothers."

Josef smiles at Sanjoni's weak attempt to lighten the mood. "No, this is not a good place," he says. "But next week, when the enemy Urban has his audience, we will delight in killing him and his adoring infidels at their shrine to Satan."

"That is true, but that is for next week. Now, it is almost time for prayers, so finish what you are doing and get ready."

A few blocks south of the assassins, Pope Urban's specially built car has begun to circle through the crowd in Saint Peter's Square. While the pontiff greets the people and blesses them, the men in the small apartment change into different clothes before conducting their ritual purifications.

Diane and the three musketeers go online while they're in the chopper to Rome. They need to find a hotel close to Saint Peter's and AISI.

"Hey, here's one," says Frank, spotting a hotel within an acceptable distance. "It looks nice."

"Where is it," asks Steve.

"Not far from Saint Peter's, but we'll need a car to get to AISI. Their office is about six kilometers from the hotel. That's too far to walk, but by car, it'll only take fifteen minutes."

"Sounds good," says Steve. "Book three rooms."

When the group arrives in Rome, they check into Le Méridien Visconti, a modern hotel off the west bank of the Tiber River. After settling in, they spend the rest of the morning sightseeing.

At nearby Castel Sant'Angelo, they pay a small entrance fee, then receive informational brochures that explain the structure's history.

"Hey," says George. "It says here that this building had many uses over the years. It was built in 135 A.D. as a mausoleum for Emperor Hadrian and his family. But it was converted into a military fortress a few centuries after that. Then, in the fourteenth century, the popes started to use it as a castle. At one point, it was even a prison!"

"Hmm," muses Frank, searching through his copy of the brochure. "If this was a mausoleum for an emperor and a fort for Rome, why is it called the Castle of the Holy Angel? Oh, I see," he says, reading further. "Pope Gregory I led a procession through Rome in 590 to beg God to save the city from a plague, and when he came to the castle, he saw the Archangel Michael on top of the building. The angel was sheathing his sword, and the plague ended after that!"

"Wow, that's what's so interesting about Rome," marvels Diane. "There are so many legends connected with the city, not to mention actual history, that we could spend months here and never be bored!"

After the group tours the Castel, they return to their hotel around one o'clock, the time of day when many Italians stop what they're doing to take their midday meal.

"Are you guys hungry?" asks Diane. "Let's ask at the front desk for a nearby restaurant."

Instead of directing his guests elsewhere, the clerk recommends the hotel's newly redesigned rooftop dining area, which pleases the Americans. All of them are hungry and thirsty after their morning of sightseeing, and they don't want to travel too far to eat.

Happy that the hotel can accommodate them, they take the elevator up to a modern, open-air terrace, where groups of tourists are already eating. As they pass the diners, they overhear them chatting away in multiple languages.

The only seating available to them is a pair of sofas surrounding a small cocktail table.

"This'll work, right?" asks Diane.

The others agree and sit down, taking turns to look at the menu.

While Diane waits for her turn, she tries to get Steve's attention. She still wants to know what the guys have been up to, but Steve hasn't said anything to her yet.

Sitting beside Diane, Steve nods toward the tourists. "I always find it amazing to hear so many different languages spoken here. In the States, the only foreign language we can be sure to hear is Spanish. We don't have very much variety."

"I know what you mean," remarks George, picking up on Steve's comment. "When I hear someone speaking another language, I'm curious about what they're saying."

Diane doesn't want to interrupt the conversation, but she's anxious to talk to Steve. She fidgets and squirms next to him, hoping he'll notice her erratic movements. But he's oblivious.

Steve holds onto his train of thought. "So now that you live here full-time, you gonna learn some Italian?" he asks George.

"I'm gonna have to, right? I know many people speak English here, but not everyone does, and I don't want to stick out like an American idiot for the rest of my life."

Diane still wants Steve's attention, so she clears her throat loudly. But Steve continues talking to George. "There are classes you can take," he says. "You should look into them."

"Thanks, I will." George asks Frank, "You want to join me, Angie?"

"Absolutely!" Frank responds, while Diane sighs loudly. "I know very little Italian, even though my grandparents were born here. They wanted to assimilate into America as fully as they could, which was great. But they frowned on any of the family who would only speak Italian. I wish they had taught us."

When the waiter stops by for their orders, they request drinks and plates of food. Then they continue to chat amiably about unimportant matters, while none of them notice that Diane is getting more and more impatient. Diane wants to know what's been going on with Steve, but it seems that he's forgotten his promise to explain it to her.

While the men toss back Peronis, Diane sips a cold Pellegrino with lemon and decides that she's had enough.

"Steve!" she declares, commanding her husband's attention with a stern, spousal look. "It's time. I'm not going to wait any longer."

"Wha...? What do you mean?" Steve asks, confused by the sudden change in Diane's demeanor.

"What the hell's been going on with you boys these past few days?" Diane asks, crossing her arms over her chest. "Things are getting tense, and I'm getting nervous."

George and Frank have known Diane long enough to know that she's pissed. Glancing between her and Steve, they hope they won't have to witness marital fireworks this afternoon.

Fortunately, the waiter appears with their food at that moment. While he accepts more drink orders, Steve uses the time to organize his thoughts.

When the coast is clear, Steve turns to Diane. "All right. I'm going to tell you something now that only a few people know, so I don't want you to overreact. I don't want to attract attention to our group."

Though Diane was smiling while her husband spoke, it wasn't because she was happy with what he was saying. As she looked at him, she saw the region's distinctive umbrella pine trees reflected in his mirrored sunglasses, and it struck her as funny. So when Steve finishes talking, he doesn't expect what comes next.

Diane lowers her voice to a frosty pitch. "I know you don't think I'm going to have a meltdown right here in front of you and the guys," she declares sarcastically. "Isn't that right, hon?"

"Um, well, yes... I don't think..." stammers Steve, flustered by his wife's conduct. "I'm just being cautious. This is pretty sensitive stuff, so I thought I'd—"

Diane knows Steve is confused by what she's trying to do, so she decides to let her frustration go. "Oh, just get on with it," she says with a wave of her hand. "No more stalling, okay? Just tell me what's going on."

"Okay, yeah," responds Steve clumsily. "Um, in a nutshell... The Mafia's angry that the pope excommunicated them, so they issued a hit and recruited ISIS to carry it out. And the Italian authorities commissioned us to help. That's what we've been doing, babe."

"Huh," replies Diane, staring at Steve with narrowed eyes. "Now I know why you've been so worried. I suppose this hit is going to happen soon, but you don't know when. That must be why you bribed me to come here for an unexpected shopping trip. You don't want to be alone, do you, babe?"

Sensing that he's in the clear, Steve grins and nods his head. But when he leans over to give Diane a kiss, she smacks him in the head again.

Reeling away, Steve rubs his sore spot. "What's this new shit?" he whines. "How come everyone's hitting me on the head?"

Diane sighs. "I guess we're just trying to knock some sense into that thick skull," she says. "I know you have experience with this kind of thing, but I don't want to hear later that you acted carelessly or without thinking things through first. I'm not ready to be a widow yet. You and I have too much to look forward to."

"Gotcha," responds Steve. "So, can we eat now?"

Steve picks up his fork and digs into his polenta. "Mmm, this is great!" he grunts happily, his face lighting up in delight. "Oh, wait," he says, looking at the others. "I just thought of something. Our meeting is only a few blocks from the Pantheon, so why don't we all walk over there when it's over? Dee, I can have a car pick you up so you can join us—"

"Wait a minute," interrupts Frank. "If there's a car available to us, why do we have to walk anywhere? If you can send a car here to pick up Diane, it can bring all of us to the Pantheon. I'd rather save my energy for the bad guys!"

CHAPTER TWENTY-TWO

While Diane shops in the Eternal City, the Americans talk in the AISI conference room as the rest of the team trickles in.

Steve is eager to get started, so he says, "Time is of the essence. Let's dispense with the usual chitchat." Turning to John and Kate, he asks, "What has the FBI turned up?"

"We've been lucky," reports John as he passes folders around the table. "We identified all four men and distributed photos to law enforcement. Look in your packets. The first two photos show Amid Tabul from Afghanistan and Josef Igmani from Iran. They're both munitions experts. Pay particular attention to Igmani. He doesn't look Middle Eastern. His mother was French, and he has light skin, blue eyes, and fair hair, which could be a problem. He can pass as European, so he probably won't be noticed in a crowd. The next photos are of Moammar Sanjoni and Azim Hassan. They're skilled Caliphate snipers from Syria — also not a good thing. We're pretty certain they'll be using at least one Barrett 82A1 .50 rifle and some Beretta ARX100s chambered with .556 NATO rounds."

"Why do you say that?" asks Steve.

"Those slots were empty in the weapons room in Cosenza. If these guys are already in Rome, they're most likely hiding out near Vatican City."

A scraping noise on the floor leads all eyes to Raphael, who grabs his folder and stands beside the table. "I do not need to hear any more," he says, focusing on Steve. "We do not know for sure when these men will be ready to mount the attack, so we need to plan as if it will occur next week, at the next public audience of Pope Urban. The Order of the Raven has decided to operate out of il Palazzo Cardinale Cesi, the hotel on the Via della Conciliazione. It is close to the basilica. Mr. Jackson, if you intend to continue as my shadow, I suggest that you get *il tuo culo* off your chair right now. As of this moment, we are both going underground."

"Raphael…wait," interrupts Vincenzo Bennini. "I have some news that may affect this operation: Interpol has issued statements revealing possible Al-Qaida threats to the G7 summit in Paris next week. They may move the conference, and Rome is their alternate venue. Our government is trying to confirm that information as we speak. But if it does move here, they will have to make changes to the public audience of the pope. I will share details with the group as soon as I receive them."

"All right, Vincenzo," says Steve. "Please give me daily updates on what's happening. If they move that summit here, our level of urgency will go up tenfold. Those fuckers may decide to take out some world leaders while they're at it!"

"This really complicates things," agrees Agent DeMaria, looking at Interpol officer Henri Franchi. "We'll have to rework our strategy. But depending on what happens with the pope's schedule, the mob will also have to make changes. I doubt they'll cancel their plans outright. They seem hell-bent on doing the deed as soon as possible."

"I agree," says Steve. "George, you'll be with the Ravens, so keep us informed about whatever information they discover. Raphael, I want to remind you that the Ravens agreed to do this together with us as a team. Do *not* go rogue on us again."

With a slight nod, Raphael dons his mirrored sunglasses and heads out of the room with George close behind.

Steve takes a couple of gulps from a bottle of water — *senza* gas — to settle his nerves.

"For some reason," he says after the door closes, "I still don't trust those Ravens, no matter what Raphael says. Colonel, you brought them into the group, so I'm holding you responsible for any hiccups on their end."

Steve reaches for his folder and leafs through it for a moment, then closes it. "Let's get back to business," he says. "Raphael is right. We have to assume the assassins are going to target next week's audience. Can someone get me a good map of the square and the surrounding area? I'm going to set up a perch there for myself. I want it to overlook the area where the pope will be."

"*Mi scusi*," interrupts Caputi. "The best places for snipers are on top of the basilica and the colonnades. Colonel, you can get Steve access to those areas, yes?"

"Sì. Yes, I can do that."

"I assume you will want to be close to Saint Peter's for the duration," Caputi continues to Steve, "so I recommend The Residenza Paolo VI Hotel. It has the only rooms that are directly on Saint Peter's Square."

"I guess that's the one, then. Can you book me a room there? And get one for Angie, too. He'll need to be close by as well."

"Va bene."

"Another thing," says Steve. "Can you place marksmen on as many rooftops as possible around Vatican City and near the mosques and any other places Muslims gather? It would be great if we could stop them before they do anything."

"The Grand Mosque of Rome is about six kilometers from *il Vaticano*. I will make sure to send some of my people there."

"Excellent. Now, Special Agents Samuels and DeMaria, I'd like you to pose as tourists. We'll need as many eyes on the ground as possible. Those goons will need to scope out the target area before they act, and I wouldn't put it past them to plant an IED somewhere in the square. They may even use a suicide bomber to distract everyone while they attack the pope and escape. So, watchers in the crowd are crucial."

"Done," declares Agent Samuels. "Anything else, boss?"

"I think we're good for now," Steve says, looking around the table. "Ah, don't ya love it when a plan comes together? We'll meet here again tomorrow afternoon."

Steve glances down at his watch. Moaning softly, he leaps out of his chair. "This took longer than I thought!" he frets. "I hope I can find my wife soon. If I know her, she's spending way too much money right now!"

The Moschea di Roma is the largest mosque in the western world — based upon the amount of land it occupies — but it's only one of a handful of mosques in Italy. It covers thirty-thousand-square-meters or three hundred-twenty-square-feet, and the entire complex can accommodate up to twelve thousand people. The main prayer hall alone, under the central dome, can hold two thousand five hundred people, including five hundred women, separated from the men.

But the Moschea di Roma is the only mosque in Rome. Most Muslims in the city gather in other types of large open spaces for daily worship, like warehouses and garages, so the team will not be able to monitor all the places where they get together.

The young killers are getting restless. They've been confined to one place or another for several months now, and they're itching to get out. They're tired of their restrictions. But the mob's instructions are strict: Only one person at a time is allowed outside of their apartment, and only to purchase necessities. Josef, Amid, Moammar, and Azim have been making do in their small quarters all this time, but their frustration is rising.

This morning, after more than the usual grumbling, Amid decides to do something about it. "It is such a lovely day outside," he says to the others. "It would be so nice to stroll around the plaza, would it not?"

"Oh, yes, it would be very nice," responds Josef. "Every day, I look outside and envy all the people who are walking around so freely."

"I feel the same," agrees Moammar wistfully.

"I think we all do," declares Amid. "But here we are, staring at each other all day long. Really, the only things keeping us cooped up inside this apartment are words from the mobster friends of the Caliph."

"Those are the rules we agreed to," says Moammar, stating the obvious.

"I know, but it is so boring! Are you not tired of watching Italian television?"

"We are all sick of it. But what can we do?"

"Look, there is no one monitoring us, so why can we not leave this stuffy place, even for a little while? What do you think about going out today, near sunset? I long to pray at a mosque again, and the Grand Mosque is not far away." Sensing flickers of hope, he adds, "We can pray Maghrib there."

The apartment fills with a tense silence while the young Muslims contemplate the notion of leaving the apartment.

"That would be wonderful," says Moammar. "But what about the rules?"

"What more can they do to us?" asks Amid mischievously. "We have already agreed to die for them, have we not?"

"Ha! That is true!"

At three o'clock that afternoon, the foursome drives to the Moschea di Roma in the van Cosa Nostra provided for them, each one looking forward to mingling with others of their faith. But they've been recognized. Members of AISI are in the crowd.

After the prayer service, the recruits return to their vehicle. However, Josef, the most unassuming of the group, isn't ready to go home yet. "Look," he says from the driver's seat. "We have been in Rome a long time, and yet, we have done nothing. Amid is right. Who knows how long it will be before we can do what we came for?"

"We are all tired of waiting, but what would you have us do?" asks Moammar, always the one to voice the doubts the rest will not. "We are not the ones in charge of our mission."

"We may not be in charge, but while we wait, we are visitors in this city. All of us can speak Italian, so for one night, let us be tourists."

Azim, the oldest of the four, is puzzled. "What do you mean, Josef? We are not tourists. We are only here because we are doing the work of Allah."

Josef narrows his eyes at his comrade. "Remember the plan, brother," he says sternly. "We must not stand out. Until now, only one of us has left our apartment at a time, so someone may have noticed that. If we are to remain inconspicuous, we should mingle with the populace, and the best way to do that is to get out and walk around — to tour Rome, to visit the infidels' decorated churches like everyone else, and to let the Carabinieri see us. If our faces become familiar, we will not draw attention when the time comes."

"Hmm... I do not know," reflects Azim. "What do you think, brothers?"

Before the others can debate the issue, Josef throws out a compromise. "Look, if it makes you feel better about going out, we can wear our disguises. We have them with us now."

"Well... We still need to purchase more maps of the area, so perhaps we can see some of Rome while we..."

"Yes!" exclaims Josef happily. "Come, brothers, let us see the sights of Rome tonight! We can begin at the Fountain of Trevi; I know where it is! Then we can have dinner out, at a real restaurant! I, for one, would love to eat something that we did not have to make for ourselves!"

"Can we get gelato for dessert?" asks Amid, excited now by the idea of even a brief taste of freedom.

Late that afternoon, Steve and Diane check out of the hotel. They're at the front desk, asking the clerk to send their luggage to the hotel Salvatore booked for them and Angie near Saint Peter's.

When George joins them to check out as well, he asks, "Aren't you going to take your bags with you?"

"No, we don't want to carry them around," says Diane. "The clerk is going to send them to the next hotel."

"But that means you'll have to wait for them to arrive," George says. "I'd rather take mine with me. I'll just catch a taxi to the address Raphael gave me. Should be interesting being around so many Ravens."

"Yeah, watch your step with them," says Steve. "Look, Angie's not ready to check out yet, so give me the address of your hotel. We'll meet you there later for a bite to eat."

The couple settles their belongings in their room at Residenza Paolo VI Hotel, then they take some time to relax and explore the hotel grounds. Soon, Steve gets hungry.

"You know, it's a nice evening, Dee, warm for November, and Piazza Navona is close by. Let's get Geo and find a restaurant; there are plenty near there. I can text Angie, so he'll know where we'll be." Looking at an app on his phone, he says, "It's only a twenty-minute walk to the piazza."

"Okay," agrees Diane. "Twenty minutes isn't too far to walk, especially when there must be lots of interesting things to see on the way. But it's good that Angie isn't with us yet. That man would complain the whole way there. What's up with him lately?"

"I don't know," shrugs Steve. "Maybe his bones are creaking. Listen, this app says George's hotel is just around the corner. Let's go."

In the lobby of George's hotel, the couple catches sight of Raphael exiting the elevator. They wave to him, but somehow, he slips out of sight before they know it.

"That man is a fox," says Steve. "I hope George knows

where he's going."

When George emerges from the next car down, he spots the couple with a small group of people, with Diane in the center. The former actress tends to stand out wherever she goes, so he's not surprised to see her signing an autograph for a fan.

"Hey, where did you park?" he asks Steve.

"Park?" queries Steve, raising a questioning brow to his pal. "I don't have a car, Geo. We walked from the hotel."

"Oh, so we're going back there to get your car?"

Steve shakes his head. "Watch my lips," he says as Diane joins them. "I...don't...have...a...car. We're walking to the restaurant, capeesh?"

George still looks confused, so Steve grabs his shoulder to make him listen. "Come on, old man. Let's take a leisurely stroll to Piazza Navona. It's a warm night, so this time, you can't say you're cold. And Angie's not here to complain with you. Let's enjoy some of the sights before everything gets crazy."

"Isn't Angie joining us for dinner?"

"Yeah, he said he'd meet us at the restaurant."

"Well, how's he gonna get there?"

Steve sighs in exasperation. "I don't give a flying fuck how that man's gonna get there! He's a big boy. Let him figure it out himself!"

"All right," says George. "But I better not be cold," he mumbles on the way to the door.

Piazza Navona is a large open area built on the site of the

Stadium of Domitian, commissioned by Emperor Domitian in the first century A.D. for festivals and sporting events. Though the stadium itself was removed in the fifteenth century, some of its remains can be seen underground. The ancient structure's curves are what give Piazza Navona its distinctive, oval shape.

The piazza's main attractions are three intricately carved fountains. The central and largest fountain, the Fontana dei Quattro Fiumi, or the Fountain of the Four Rivers, was designed by Gian Lorenzo Bernini at the request of Pope Innocent X. Constructed between 1647 and 1651, its carved images represent the rivers of the four continents that were under papal authority at the time.

At the southern end of the famous piazza, the Fontana del Moro, also known as the Moor Fountain, holds court. This fountain was built in two stages. It was initially constructed by Giacomo della Porta in 1575 merely as a large basin, and it existed in that unadorned stage until 1874, when Gian Lorenzo Bernini added the current, central statue of a Moor — an African-looking man — wrestling with a dolphin.

The piazza's northern end showcases the Fontana del Nettuno, Neptune's Fountain, featuring that mythical sea god surrounded by sea nymphs. Giacomo della Porta was also commissioned to build this fountain's basin, and it likewise stood unembellished until it was updated with a statue of Neptune fighting an octopus in 1878.

Today, the Piazza Navona is surrounded by buildings, including bars, restaurants, and the Baroque Church of Sant'Agnese in Agone.

While the group searches for a place to eat, they marvel at the beauty of this unique spot.

"This place is impressive!" gapes Diane. "Those statues are beautiful! It's amazing how lifelike they are!"

"I can't believe they're still here, and that they're in such good shape!" adds George. "But are we really going to eat around here, Steve? There are so many tourists that I bet the restaurants are pricey."

"They probably are," Steve replies. "But I don't care. The Italians gave me an expense account for this mission, so let's grab an outdoor table. We'll have a nice dinner, then walk to the Pantheon."

Several streets away, the "four horsemen of the apocalypse" are finishing their meal at a small, unassuming restaurant. Curiously, none of them are wearing the disguises they brought with them this evening.

The Caliphate loyalists are thankful to Josef for goading them into ditching their usual homecooked meal for what they all agree was wonderfully tasty food.

Amid sits back in his chair and pats his stomach contentedly. "I certainly enjoyed that!" he says happily. "But now we have to choose a gelateria. I have been thinking about which flavor I should order, but I cannot decide. The shops we passed have too many delicious options!"

"Yes, yes, we will find a gelateria," states Josef wearily. Amid has been talking nonstop about ice cream since they left the mosque, and he's tired of hearing it. "But before we leave this restaurant," he says, "let us talk once more about what we decided. After the gelateria, we agree that we will visit the Pantheon and the Trevi Fountain. Then, we will walk through Saint Peter's Square, making mental notes about its layout. Correct?"

"We have already agreed to all of that, Josef!" they reply. "Let us get started!"

Not far away from this small restaurant, Frank fidgets in a taxicab sitting motionless in traffic. There is an obstruction on the road ahead, and the cab hasn't moved in a while.

Frank knows that his friends are waiting for him, so he asks for directions to the restaurant that Steve texted him and tells the driver to let him out. Reluctantly, he sets off on foot on sidewalks as crowded as the streets.

As Frank weaves around another group of people, he decides that he better let Steve know that he's not far away. Pulling out his phone, he begins to compose a text message, but he immediately bumps into a man exiting a building and almost loses his balance.

"Oof!" says the man, grabbing Frank's arm to keep him from falling to the ground. "Are you all right, signore? You should look where you are going."

"Oh, yes. I'm terribly sorry," Frank responds. "But how did you know I speak English?"

"You dress like an American. Am I wrong?"

"No, you're right," smiles Frank, looking curiously at the stranger and the men around him. Something about them seems oddly familiar. "Please excuse me. I apologize for my clumsiness. I'm still getting used to my new phone."

"It is no problem, signore," the man assures him. Then he says something to his companions.

As the man walks away, something still tugs at the back of Frank's mind, so he snaps a quick photo, then continues typing his text message.

A few steps later, a lightbulb turns on, and Frank swivels around for another look. But the strangers are no longer visible; the crowd has swallowed them up.

Cursing, Frank runs the rest of the way to Piazza Navona.

At an outdoor table, Steve downs the last of his glass of wine and searches the crowd again, looking for Frank. Suddenly, he opens his eyes wide. Coming toward him is a highly unusual sight: Frank Angelo, the man who complains about walking anywhere, is running in their direction.

When Frank reaches the group, he's out of breath and panting. "Chic," he huffs, "I saw them!" He grabs Steve's arm and squeezes tightly. Then drops into an empty chair. "I saw them!" he repeats.

"Calm down!" Steve urges, alarmed by his friend's behavior. "Take a breath, will ya? Who did you see?"

Frank inhales and exhales rapidly, struggling to compose himself. "I saw the killers! My taxi got stuck in traffic, so I left it and walked here! I was texting you to say I was on the way when I literally ran right into Josef!" Pausing to catch his breath, he inhales again, deeply. "I wasn't looking where I was going, and he stopped me from falling on my ass! I didn't realize who he and the others were until they left, then I lost them!" He pauses again and takes another deep breath. "Here's my phone. I snapped a pic."

Steve clicks on the latest photo in Frank's gallery. "It's kinda fuzzy, and you only got a side view, but it sure looks like them," he states, passing the phone to George.

"I screwed up," Frank declares dejectedly. "Sorry, guys."

"Aw, don't say that," says George. "How could you know you'd bump into our assassins? At least you got them on camera, right? Here, have some wine. We'll get 'em in the end."

"Yeah, we will. But I better let Salvatore know I've seen them. Could you give me my phone back? I'll call him now."

While Frank shares his news with the AISI officer, George leans into the table. "So, our targets are doing the same thing we are tonight. They're enjoying Rome, too."

Steve sighs. "It's a fucking shame they got away. It would have saved us so much trouble if we caught them now."

Frank ends his call, then pours himself a glass of wine from the bottle on the table. "Josef speaks English with a mixed accent," he says. "Sounds Arabic, but there's some Italian there, too. That crew may have been in the country for a while. And he doesn't look Middle Eastern at all."

After dinner, the troop walks the cobblestone back-streets, past couples sitting at outdoor tables drinking "sexy" wine, a carbonated strawberry blend. Frank does his best to keep up, but he keeps lagging behind.

"What's wrong?" asks Diane.

"It's these shoes. They're giving me blisters that won't go away. I can't take much more of this."

"Angie, don't you know that Italy's known for their leather goods? You should buy some new shoes. You're gonna do a lot of walking here."

Close to the Pantheon, the group turns down Via della Rotunda, where traffic picks up noticeably — there's no shortage of people interested in this vaunted monument. Everywhere they look, pedestrians crowd the sidewalks, and tiny cars and scooters pass around each other in a weird ballet.

"Ooooh, there it is!" gushes Diane, pointing at the Pantheon's distinctive dome.

While they continue to walk, Frank glances casually at a van going in their direction, then stops dead in his tracks. "That's them!" he exclaims, pointing urgently. "Josef is driving!"

Turning to look, the group sees an unmarked vehicle traveling slowly toward the large piazza in front of the Pantheon.

"You sure?" asks Steve skeptically.

"Yeah, I'm sure! I just saw them, remember? Can we stop them?"

Steve surveys the scene. He'd love to nab their objectives now, but he doesn't know how they can stop the vehicle without hurting anyone in the thick crowd. But when traffic forces the van to a complete stop, he changes his mind quickly.

"George, stay with Diane!" he shouts. "Frank — let's roll!"

Steve and Frank rush toward the van, squeezing through sightseers. They hope they can reach it before it starts up again.

But without warning, the throng in front of them suddenly turns around and runs directly toward them, screaming and yelling as they go.

Confused by the panicked looks on their faces, the pair looks ahead to see a black BMW sedan barreling through the crowd directly toward the van.

In the driver's seat, Josef also sees the BMW, and panics. To avoid a collision, he steers maniacally through the crowd, sending people and cars onto narrow sidewalks to avoid getting run over.

"Who the hell is that?" shouts Steve, as confused as everyone else. Then he spots the BMW's driver. Screaming at the top of his lungs, he shouts, "GODDAMN IT, RAPHAEL! WHAT DO YOU THINK YOU'RE DOING?"

The very next minute, he and everyone else ducks when shots ring out from the black sedan. While they're still down, the two vehicles disappear into Rome's side streets, followed by a caravan of blaring Carabinieri Alpha Romeos.

"Those fucking Ravens!" fumes Steve through gritted teeth. "No more Mister Nice Guy! I'm not gonna be politically correct with those assholes anymore!"

Clicking a number in his cell phone, he shouts a demand

as soon as the call is answered. "Here's what you and the colonel are gonna do!" he yells into the phone. "You're both gonna bring those fucking ghosts into line! No more excuses! I'm tired of their macho bullshit!"

Salvatore Caputi tries to make sense of what Steve is saying. "What is going on, Steve?"

"You'll get my report soon enough!" Steve shouts, cutting Salvatore off. "And you'll also see it on tonight's news! I want a meeting with Accola and those ghosts at eight o'clock tomorrow morning, Sal! That's eight a.m., SHARP!"

Steve clicks End Call, then glances at Diane, who is pretty upset. "It's times like this when I *really* miss slamming down a phone receiver!"

Steve sighs heavily and looks across the piazza at clusters of people discussing what happened. "Anyone know where we can get a taxi?" he mumbles.

"Um, I think I saw a taxi stand near Piazza Navona," offers Frank.

"All right, let's go back in that direction. We need to get the hell away from here!"

While the crew grabs a taxi back to their hotels, the pursued and pursuers play cat and mouse through the narrow streets of Rome. At the rear, police vehicles with blaring sirens try to keep up.

Though Raphael drives as fast as he can, he can only occasionally narrow the gap on his target, which sends him into waves of fury. Somehow, Josef consistently manages to outmaneuver the more experienced driver, even though he's driving a much larger vehicle.

As the unlikely convoy speeds through traffic, Raphael regularly leans out of his window to fire at the van. The Raven is unwaveringly focused on his target. He's unconcerned about anything but his mission, even though pedestrians and other vehicles scatter in all directions to avoid his shots.

Behind the van, Raphael keeps one eye on the prize in front of him and one eye on his rearview mirror. It would be disastrous for his cause if the police catch him. When the Carabinieri's lead car collides with a taxi on Via del Somaschi and the others behind it skid out of control, he's enormously relieved. *One less thing to worry about,* he smiles.

With the police out of the picture — for now — Raphael concentrates all his attention on the van. But at Lungotevere Marzio, a tree-lined thoroughfare along the Tiber River, he takes the turn a little too fast and clips the curb.

Cursing at his carelessness, he regains control quickly. However, when a teenaged couple on a scooter suddenly appears out of nowhere, he oversteers to avoid hitting them and crashes headlong into a lamp post. Ahead of him, the van disappears into the night.

Slumped inside his crumpled car, Raphael curses again. Blood is streaming out of his nose, but the airbag has done its job. However, the Raven is not happy.

Concerned that he could be found out, he pushes the helping hands of onlookers away and crawls out of the wreckage on his own. With sirens blaring in his direction, he insists to the growing crowd of gawkers that he's all right. And as inconspicuously as possible, he inches farther and farther away from his disabled car, until none in the crowd can see him anymore.

Near midnight, Josef is finally convinced that he's eluded his pursuers. At Ponte del Risorgimento, he drives his bullet-riddled van over the Tiber, then turns left onto Lungotevere delle Armi, where a fence borders the street along the river. When he comes upon a gap in the fencing, he slows down and stops.

"We should get rid of this van," he says to the others.

Obscured by the darkness, the four men exit the vehicle and push it into the Tiber. Then they walk through the neighborhood to find a taxi stand.

While they wait for a cab at Piazza Mazzini, Azim puts a hand on Josef's shoulder. "Allah drives with you," he says gratefully.

"Allahu Akbar," smiles Josef. "Allah drives with all of us. But now we need another van. And we still need to go to the infidel church."

CHAPTER TWENTY-THREE

It is well into the early morning hours when the potential pope-killers finally make it back to their apartment. However, they can't sleep. All of them are deeply troubled by the evening's turn of events. They are anxious and worried; they pace their small rooms, talking for hours.

On the one hand, the Caliph's men are relieved that they made it back safely. On the other hand, they know that the authorities will now significantly increase security at key points, and that will make it much harder for them to fulfill their mission.

Even so, all of them are determined to continue. They still need to explore the target area, so they decide that it will be better if only two of them go to Saint Peter's for that task. They also agree that the ones to go should wear disguises in case someone recognizes them from the chase.

When there is nothing left to discuss, they pray and choose Josef and Azim to make the trip. Then, they try to get some sleep.

A few hours later, daylight streams into their rooms much too soon, but they all rise. Years of discipline compels them to pray Fajr, the dawn prayer, despite knowing they will be groggy from too little sleep.

After the prayer, they share a light breakfast, then Josef and Azim gather their supplies to begin their transformations. To stop worrying, the two who will remain home fall back into regular activities: Moammar oils rifles at the table and Amid watches porn in the living room.

At mid-morning, Josef and Azim are still taking turns using the mirror in the apartment's only bathroom. Azim is shaving his head and beard while Josef is watching the time. The directions on the hair dye box says he needs to let the chemicals do their work before he can wash them out and change his light-colored hair to a dark auburn.

When Josef's hair is dry, they dress in the U.S.-style clothing and accessories the Mafia gave them — new jeans and t-shirts for both, and a backpack and Toronto Blue Jays cap for Azim, and sneakers and a fanny pack for Josef. Then they pocket burner phones and forged Canadian passports.

Moammar and Amid are happy that their companions look more "touristy" now, but they're still jittery from last night's chase. Before they send them off to Saint Peter's Square, they offer prayers that they won't be recognized.

"The Ravens were involved in another clusterfuck last night!" announces Special Agent John DeMaria when he enters the conference room.

"I saw some of it myself, and Caputi briefed me about the rest," states Steve grimly. "I've had it with them!"

When others file in, Colonel Accola hopes to slip among them unnoticed, but Steve sees him and won't let him get away with it. He's still angry after the fiasco he witnessed the previous evening. "Where's your *paesano* today?" he asks, staring hard at the man who keeps assuring him that the Ravens are just doing their jobs. "Is that *pezzo di merda* sleeping in?"

"He has a broken nose and is having it looked at this morning," Accola replies. "He will contact George Jackson later today. Look, I know the Ravens are running loose. I told you that it would be difficult to reign them in. However, I did what I could. Last night, I spoke with the cardinals and Pope Urban. They assured me that this will not happen again."

Steve looks at each man around the table, then points an accusing finger at Accola. "It doesn't look like anyone can control them, not even the Church," he growls crossly. Raphael managed to ditch Geo yesterday, so I ordered him to use whatever force is necessary to stop Raphael or any other Raven from going rogue again. Do you understand me?"

Colonel Accola has begun to chafe under Steve's authority. However, he knows he's right, so he doesn't contradict him.

"Let's move on," says Steve. "Because of yesterday's fiasco, those fuckers know we're onto them. So we should expect them to attack at any time."

"But we do not know where they are now or where they went yesterday," frets Interpol officer Henri Franchi.

"We did pick them up on traffic cameras," announces Salvatore. "We recorded their vehicle throughout the entire chase, until it turned left at Ponte Risorgimento. We did not see it after that, but four men fitting their descriptions were picked up walking on a street close to Piazza Mazzini."

Steve cracks his neck. "So the last time you saw the van was at Ponte Risorgi...? Whatever you said."

"Yes. That bridge is not far from il Vaticano. It goes over the Tiber River."

"Hmm. If you didn't see the van after the bridge, they could have ditched it in the river. What about video from that piazza? Don't you have cameras at your town squares?"

Caputi looks uncomfortable. "Our cameras are not functioning there."

Heavy sighs around the table make Henri Franchi ask, "Are we at another dead end, then?"

Theodore Accola shakes his head. "Not necessarily," he says. "There is a taxi stand at the piazza. We can check with the drivers. If they no longer had the van at that point, one of them may have seen the men or even driven them somewhere."

"Well!" grins Steve. "That's a great idea! Get on that right away, Captain. Now for the rest of us... Geo, find Raphael and stick with those blasted ghosts. Try like hell to get them to start patrolling Saint Peter's Square. Angie, DeMaria, and Samuels, you guys make like tourists; mingle with the crowd. Caputi, you and I are going to the river. You have a dive team, right?"

"Yes."

"Thank God." Steve turns to Accola. "Call me after you talk to the drivers. And you had better have a good talk with Raphael, too, or whatever his real name is. If his group fucks up one more time, I'll have no problem breaking his nose again, just for shits and giggles."

"Why do you give that man so many chances, Steve?" asks Henri. "You have said over and over again that that group cannot be trusted."

"I know, but we need them. And if you tell him that, I'll break your nose, too."

It took a while before Salvatore could leave with Steve for the Tiber River. He had a few things to take care of, so he sent a patrol ahead of him to check it out before he got there.

When he and Steve arrive at the fence along the river, Steve is surprised to see divers scouring the water near the bank. "The dive team's here already?"

"Sì. My men found several holes in the fence near the last

place the cameras spotted the van, so they requested the team."

"Wonderful! I'm happy to see that your agency can do something right!"

Salvatore isn't pleased that Steve is always making digs about his department's ability to do its job, but he lets Steve's comment go — again — and parks his Fiat along the bank. "I am going to talk to my men," he says stiffly.

"All right. I'll look around here."

Almost immediately, Steve sees something interesting on the curb. "Hey, Sal!" he calls to the AISI officer. "Tell the divers to search the area around here! Looks like something jumped the curb!"

Salvatore shouts a command in Italian, then comes over to where Steve is pointing. "What did you find?"

"These look like fresh scrape marks on the curb."

"*Si, sono d'accordo,*" agrees Salvatore. The divers will come this way."

A few minutes later, a frogman emerges from the water and lifts his mask. "*C'è un furgone in acqua qui,*" he tells Salvatore. "*Diremo al quartier generale di inviare una gru.*"

"What did he say?"

"He found a van and will tell headquarters to send a crane to lift it out."

"That's great!" replies Steve. "But I bet there's nothing in it that'll help us. Maybe we can at least find out who owns it."

"It could have been rented."

"Yeah, that's possible. Look, I'm gonna check on the taxis now. Let me have the keys to your car."

Steve's demand for his keys is the last straw for Salvatore. The brash American's irritating behavior has finally pierced the Italian's hide. Salvatore throws up his hands in frustration and shouts, "Stefano! If you take my car, how do I get back to my office?"

Steve merely holds his hand out for the keys. "I bet you can hitch a ride with your crew," he replies.

George nurses a caffè macchiato and a large, cream-filled pastry while scrutinizing the scene out of the window of a small café. He chose this establishment because it has a good view of Saint Peter's Square, and he's searching for anything unusual among the throngs of people walking by. When there's a break in the crowd, he spots Frank posing as a tourist taking pictures of one of the square's enormous fountains.

In another area, FBI Special Agents John and Kathryn are also acting like tourists today. They're also photographing the usual sights while keeping watchful eyes on everything.

"You know, we should ask someone to take a photo of us," John says. "That's what visitors do, right?"

"That's a good idea," replies Kathryn. "Ask that guy over there; he looks American."

John approaches a man wearing a New York Yankees baseball cap. "Hey, there. Can you take a photo of my wife and me?"

"Sure!" replies the American, happy to help. Taking John's phone, he snaps several photos, one of which captures Josef walking alone in the background. Earlier in the day, the Caliphate recruits agreed to split up to explore the area where they planned to kill the pope.

At the café, George finishes his morning snack and starts walking toward the basilica. Down the block, he spots a man pointing his camera at the rooftops of the buildings running down the Via della Conciliazione. "That's odd," he mutters under his breath. "What's so special about the tops of those buildings?"

George feels that he should investigate, so he heads in the photographer's direction. However, the man sees him coming and turns around in a hurry.

"Could be something up with that guy," George mutters again and starts following him. But after walking a few steps, a hulking mass of flesh blocks his way.

"Come with me," commands a familiar voice. "I need to talk to you."

George cranes his neck around the intruder's bulk, but he can no longer see the photographer. "Dammit!" he scolds, looking up into a pair of familiar sunglasses. "There was a suspicious character here a minute ago, but now he's gone!"

Suddenly, George notices a large bruise on the Raven's face. "What happened to your nose? Did a jealous husband finally catch you in the act?"

Raphael sets his mouth into a thin line. "Follow me," he declares tonelessly.

The pair walk down a side street into a narrow alley between two buildings, where Raphael pulls George into the shadows. "There is an informant inside our operation, so we must be careful about being seen together," he states quietly.

This shocks George, and he widens his eyes at the stoic papal defender. "You must be kidding!" he splutters. "An informant? Inside the Ravens? How could that happen? Your group is supposed to be so tightly-knit!"

Raphael gazes down at George with such anger that George prepares to duck in case the Raven takes a swing at him.

"It is someone within *your* organization, not mine," replies Raphael, his voice held steady through sheer force of will. "Now, listen. I have no time to waste. I have important information for you. First, the G7 summit will be moved here, so there will be much more that we will need to prepare for. Second, we discovered where the terrorists are hiding. That is what I came to say."

At that, the man of few words turns on his heel and heads out of the alley.

George has become accustomed to Raphael's abruptness and quick movements, so he stays right behind him, determined not to be left behind. "Hey!" he calls out. "I'm coming with you! I have a few things to tell you, too!"

While Steve drives to the AISI building in Salvatore's Fiat, he recalls how Salvatore practically threw the car's keys at him.

Steve knows that he's been pissing Salvatore off, but he can't help it; it's just his way. Most people know that he's a good-hearted person and forgive him for it, but there are always a few who let it fester. "I hope Sal doesn't kill me before this is over," he mumbles while stopped at a light. "He's a nice guy."

Inside the AISI building, it takes Steve a while to make the clerk understand who he is and why he's there. He has to try several times before the clerk permits him to pass through to Vincenzo Bennini's office.

The clerk gives Steve directions that he thinks he understands, but he quickly gets lost in the maze of hallways. He wanders around the corridors until he finally finds a sign with the AISI official's name on it.

Relieved, he knocks lightly and enters Bennini's office. "I

really need to learn more Italian," he says.

"That would be helpful," agrees the AISI agent dryly.

"Did you get anything from the taxi drivers?"

"Sì. One of them picked up four men and took them to Piazza del Risorgimento."

"There's that word again. Where's this piazza?"

"It is a few blocks north of *la basilica*. I told Caputi to go there."

"Do we know if they're our guys?"

"Sì. Security footage shows them entering an apartment building at the piazza. A SWAT team is going there now."

"Great!" says Steve. "Can you tell me where it is? I drove Salvatore's car here, and I want to be there when they go in."

To the team's great disappointment, the apartment at Piazza del Risorgimento is empty when the Carabinieri SWAT unit storms it.

But that doesn't surprise George. Grabbing Steve's arm, he pulls him aside to talk privately. "Raphael says our team's been infiltrated," he whispers.

Steve inhales sharply at this distressing news. "Now ain't that fucking dandy," he mutters through gritted teeth.

"He also said the G7 meeting's coming to Rome."

Over George's shoulder, Steve spots Vincenzo Bennini and Salvatore Caputi talking to Raphael. "I hope that Raven isn't telling the AISI guys that the team is compromised. Until we find out what's going on, we shouldn't trust anyone but the Ravens."

Startled, Steve realizes what he just said. "And what a fucking turn of events *that* is! This is such a shit show! Don't tell the FBI about this, either. Not yet, anyway. I gotta think about this."

Steve glances over at the two government officials. "I need to talk to Sal about something else, so let's join that group."

When the three Italians see Steve and George coming, they stop talking. "What are you guys talking about?" asks Steve, suspecting they were talking about them.

"Ah... We are frustrated that no one was in the apartment when we arrived," replies Vincenzo, a little too quickly for Steve's taste.

"So are we," says Steve, looking at Salvatore. "Any news from the river?"

"We are pulling the van out now. When we get *la targa*... the license plate number...we will check our records for ownership."

George leans close to Steve. "I forgot to tell you," he whispers. "I may have spotted one part of our package outside Saint Peter's, but I lost it in the crowd. Fucking Raphael interrupted me with the news about the mole."

Now Salvatore is annoyed by the Americans' hushed conversation. "Is there anything we need to know?" he asks icily.

"Nothing important," replies Steve with a wave of his hand.

Vincenzo's phone buzzes, so he looks down, then gestures for everyone to follow. "We can go into the building now," he says.

Inside the main entrance, the men climb one flight up and enter a small unit, where SWAT officers are holding trained dogs on a tight leash. The animals have sniffed bomb residue, and they're agitated.

There's nothing much in the place, though; it seems empty of anything important. Even so, the forensic team is conducting a meticulous search, so Steve takes the opportunity to peek around.

"Looks like they left in a hurry; there's food on the stove," he says, raising a questioning brow at Salvatore. "Do you know anyone who could have tipped them off?"

"*Che diavolo?*" seethes Caputi, offended by Steve's supposition that he knows more than he should. "Do you think I am working with the mob? *Sei pazzo?* Are you crazy?"

Steve narrows his eyes and says, "Someone told them what we were up to. If it wasn't you or someone from your office, then who else in your organization could be in bed with the mob or the Caliphate? You didn't seem too surprised about the van in the river, the taxi driver, or the security cameras!"

Salvatore is outraged. "Many people knew about this operation! *La polizia*, Interpol, il Vaticano, your FBI, you and your friends... Why do you think I had something to do with this?"

Salvatore stops his tirade only because his cell phone buzzes with a text message. *"Mannaggia!"* he fumes. "The van is a dead end! A florist in Cosenza reported it stolen!"

Hearing the heated voices, Vincenzo Bennini hurries over to find out what's going on. "What the hell is wrong?" he asks.

Steve pins Bennini down with his sniper stare. "The fucking terrorists were tipped off by someone inside our operation! Those assholes are long gone by now! And fuck it all, we're back at square one... Again! Unless we get very lucky, we better prepare for this attack to happen much sooner than we thought!"

Steve pokes his finger into Caputi's chest. "I'm calling a meeting for this afternoon! Get your shit together by three o'clock, or my friends and I are done with this fiasco. I can't work like this anymore! You brought me in to help with this mess, but nothing is working right! Jackson, let's get the fuck out of here!"

On the way out of the apartment, Steve catches sight of a crumpled piece of paper in a trash can near the door. Stopping near the can, he pretends to bend down to tie his shoe and reaches in to grab it.

When Steve and George are back on the street, he opens the paper ball. "This looks like a phone number," he mutters.

"Where'd you get that?" George asks.

Steve smiles and winks. Taking out his phone, he dials the number on the paper and listens wide-eyed, then hangs up quickly. "Ha! I got the bastard!"

"Who?"

"The mole! Contact the Ravens and tell them about the three o'clock! I'm going to call Angie and the FBI!"

CHAPTER TWENTY-FOUR

When the Americans arrive at AISI, they walk into the conference room to curious stares from the rest of the team. Steve's buddies make themselves comfortable, but Steve remains standing.

"I know you're wondering why I called this rush meeting," the team leader begins. "And you're not gonna like the reason." Steve stares hard at each face. "There's a mole inside this group. Someone tipped the Muslims off about our plans to raid their hideout." He turns to Sal and says, "Tell the group about the van, and what else you found."

Salvatore squirms uncomfortably. "We found the van in the Tiber River, but it was stolen in Cosenza, so no surprise there. But in the apartment, we found traces of plastic explosives and a .556 cartridge. The apartment was rented for three months, cash in advance. Footage from a traffic camera shows a vehicle with occupants fitting the descriptions of our assets heading south toward Saint Peter's Square. The timestamp is a few minutes before we arrived at the building. Fifty minutes after that, another camera in Vatican City picks up the same vehicle with the identical individuals near the Sistine Chapel entrance."

"This is not good, people," Steve declares. "As of right now, we are increasing our presence around the entire basilica. Sal and Vincenzo, this one is on both of you. Now, everyone but Raphael and the colonel can leave. I need to talk to them alone."

Once again, Salvatore gets upset by something Steve

does. "I protest!" he shouts. "You will talk to them without the rest of us? Why will you have a separate meeting? We need to work together...as a team! You have said this thing one hundred times!"

Steve rubs his eyes. "We have a snitch," he says tiredly. "The only people I trust right now are my guys, and surprisingly, the Ravens. Kate and John, do you have the info I requested?"

"Yes, it's right here," replies John.

"All right. The two of you can stay as well."

Steve motions to the door, prompting Caputi and Bennini to leave the room, each of them complaining in loud voices the entire way out.

Steve turns to Agent DeMaria. "What did you find out?" he asks.

John opens a large folder to read from a typed sheet. "Henri Franchi is Italian by birth; born in Cefalù. His family moved to Paris when he was eight years old. He's now a French national and has been working with Interpol for the last ten years."

"Why are we talking about our Interpol liaison officer?" asks Colonel Accola.

"Give them the kicker, John," instructs Steve.

"His mother's maiden name is Scarapelli."

Raphael clears his throat to speak, surprising everyone. The Raven isn't in the habit of volunteering information without a direct question, so no one expected him to say anything.

"Yes, she is part of the crime family," he affirms.

Steve looks at Raphael curiously but continues. "Franchi's our mole," he says. "I found a discarded piece of paper at the apartment with his phone number on it. Bennini or Caputi must have called him to update Interpol about our investigation. Do we know where this asshole is now? I haven't seen him since our last meeting."

John replies, "He's at Interpol headquarters in Paris."

"I guess we're going to France," says Steve, glancing sideways at Frank and George.

Across the table, Raphael leans toward Colonel Accola to tell him something the others can't hear.

Accola nods. "Steve, you and your friends have no authority in France. The Ravens will oversee this. Their operatives in Paris will convince Mr. Franchi to return to Rome."

Steve laughs at the comment, but his smile is grim. "Yeah? Well, you better make sure he gets here vertically, not horizontally."

Steve looks directly at Raphael to issue a command. "You got twenty-four hours to get him here before I notify the Italian government, Paris, and our State Department."

Raphael is not disturbed. "I will have no trouble meeting your deadline," he states calmly.

Steve tells the others, "I don't want to include our AISI buddies in what we're doing until after we speak with Franchi. We can't trust them right now."

"We understand," replies Accola.

Steve continues, "Just be careful, Raphael. If Franchi ends up dead, it's on your head and the colonel's. Give your ghosts our info on this Interpol agent. Just make sure they tamp down their 'enthusiasm' for doing their job. Now, let's get back to the Vatican. We need to keep our eyes out in case our friends show up again."

On the way out of the room, Colonel Accola mumbles something in a low voice, which Frank overhears. Hanging back a bit, he walks alongside Steve and says, "I think he just uttered something about you not knowing who your father is."

At 6:15 that evening, an Embraer Legacy 500 Executive business jet taxis to a small hanger at Paris-Le Bourget Airport. Nearby, a black Bentley waits for Raphael and George to deplane with two Ravens.

At the same time, a waiter with a concealed tattoo pours another glass of Burgundy wine for Henri Franchi at a café across from the Fontaine Saint-Michel.

Whenever Henri is in town, he likes to eat at this popular restaurant. It's across the street from the tallest fountain in Paris, a monument to Saint Michael the Archangel's original battle against the devil. Henri likes the statue because it reminds him of his job at Interpol. He imagines that fighting criminals around the world is a little like battling Satan.

The fountain is just a few blocks from Notre Dame Cathedral, but it's not on the radar of many tourists, and that suits Henri just fine. Each foreign visitor who stops by annoys him. He knows the city depends on the travel industry, but the stream of curious sightseers wears on him. He would much prefer to keep Paris for the French.

As Henri eats, he stares with repugnance at the passing throng of people ruining his early evening respite. His thoughts go as they always do: *These vacationers have no regard for the people who live here. They enjoy themselves for a little while, then leave the cleanup to us.*

Henri takes a few more bites of his meal, then washes it down with another long gulp of wine. When he tries to pick up his fork again, he finds his eyesight blurring, and he begins to feel lightheaded. Alarmed, he pushes back his chair and stands as tunnel vision slowly restricts his ability to see.

At that moment, a black Bentley stops near Franchi's table, and two men pop out. At an imperceptible nod from the tattooed waiter, the men walk up to the impaired Interpol officer and grab his arms. With no struggle from Henri, they lead him away from his table — right into the back seat of their car.

As the car merges into traffic, the waiter removes all evidence of Henri's presence from the table. When his job is complete, he takes his apron off and retreats into the crowd inside the busy restaurant.

The moment the mob was tipped off to the law enforcement raid, they sent someone to the Risorgimento building and moved their lackeys to a different apartment in Rome. The assassins had to pack quickly; there was no time to do anything else. But they didn't treat it as a hardship. They don't have much, and the process was actually a welcome break in their boring routines.

Things settled down fast, however, and familiar patterns returned. To keep themselves from going crazy, they quickly resumed their schedule of tasks, the most popular being kitchen duties.

When it's each man's turn, he usually shops for what he needs and makes something he's familiar with. Tonight, it's Amid's turn.

That afternoon, Amid checks the cupboard, then makes a quick trip to a local Mediterranean market for a few staples for the evening meal.

When he returns, he busies himself in the kitchen while his comrades pass the time in the usual way: watching pornography on their cell phones.

After a while, tantalizing odors begin to waft through the apartment.

"That smells delicious," says Moammar, tearing himself away from his phone. "What are you cooking?"

"It is called Tepsi Baytinijan."

"Huh? Never heard of it."

"It is a casserole made with eggplants, potatoes, meatballs, onions, and garlic, baked in a tomato sauce," replies Amid proudly. "I learned how to make it when I was training in Iraq."

Amid waits for a reaction to his recipe, but Moammar is no longer listening; he's back on his phone. Disappointed, he goes back to cooking. A moment later, a sharp knock at the door startles everyone, and they all freeze in place.

"Shh," mouths Josef. Grabbing a Beretta, he holds the gun tight and backs up to the wall next to the door. Slowly and carefully, he releases the bolt and opens the door a crack.

"Ahh," he says, breathing in a sigh of relief. "Come in."

Josef drops the gun and opens the door wider to allow Giuseppe Sarducci to enter the apartment with a large, wheeled suitcase.

"I have news," Sarducci announces grimly. "The mission has been moved up to Monday."

The men are surprised by this unexpected change in their carefully crafted plans, and they glance at each other uneasily. They are itching to act, but they know what will happen to them when they do.

"I have arranged for all of you, except Josef, to work at one of the street vendors lining Saint Peter's Square," says Sarducci. "Tomorrow morning, three of you will learn how to sell bottled drinks and cheap souvenirs. My men will explain the pricing and teach you how to use the equipment. Learn fast, and live. I have brought more hair dye, cosmetics, and other items, so you can change your appearances again."

"Wait... Why am I not going?" asks Josef warily. "What will I do while the others are at the booth?"

Sarducci directs a cross look in Josef's direction. "You will remain here until we tell you otherwise!" he barks. "The Italian government has partnered with Americans, so now, there are even more people looking for you. Keep your escape bags ready at all times!"

Another cross look silences further questions. However, Amid needs to risk a rebuke. "What if they come for us again?" he asks quietly.

Sarducci frowns at the future martyr but says, "If they do, leave at once. We cannot risk having you captured. Find a place to hide and contact us the way we arranged."

Sarducci knows his capo has high hopes for each of the men in front of him, so he adds, "However, if the way seems clear, you can complete the task as planned. But if someone has already seen you, you will be on your own. My organization will not come to your aid."

The men are silent as they ponder the words of Vito's first lieutenant.

"Today is the last time you will see me," continues Sarducci. "My boss cannot take the chance of being implicated in our arrangement, so we will have no further contact from this day forward. You are not to call me ever again."

Giuseppe wheels the suitcase into the middle of the floor and drops it there. *"Mi capite tutti?"*

Henri Franchi opens his eyes aboard the Legacy 500 on

its final approach to Roma Urbe Airport, a small airfield in the northern part of the city. He senses that someone is standing over him, so he tries to focus and say something, but he can't, and realizes that he's bound and gagged.

"Welcome back to Rome," says Raphael, holding a hypodermic needle in one hand. "I hope you enjoyed your little nap. Now, you will enjoy another one, and tonight, you will tell us what we want to know. Or," he adds ominously, "I will cut your balls off and ship them to Paris in a jar."

The poker-faced Raven leans over his captive and doses him with a shot of sodium pentothal, then watches with disinterest as he fades back into unconsciousness.

Steve sighs and rolls off Diane. "Sorry, babe, my mind tells me I can do things my body can't keep up with. Guess that old saying's true: Once a king always a king, but once a night's enough."

"There's always the morning—" begins Diane, until a sudden knock on their hotel door startles her into silence.

The couple looks at each other. Then Steve turns to the clock on the night table, which only reads a little past midnight.

They hear another knock, and then a muffled voice drifts through the door. "Chic, it's Geo. Are you guys decent?"

"What the hell does he think?" mumbles Steve.

Diane hides under the covers as Steve flips on the light and fumbles for his pajama bottoms.

"What the fuck do you want?" Steve grumbles, opening the door a little. "You know it's sleepy time, right?"

George shrugs one shoulder and turns both palms upward. "I know it's late, but this can't wait. Raphael called a few minutes ago. The Ravens snatched Franchi, and they're going to interrogate him within the hour. I told him we'd be there. Sorry, bro. I'll wait in the lobby."

Steve closes the door and looks back at Diane sitting up in bed with the sheet covering her good parts. "Seriously, Chic?" she whines. "It's midnight, for cryin' out loud!"

Uh, oh, thinks Steve, knowing he's in trouble. Diane never calls him Chic unless she's truly pissed. "I'll make it up to you, Dee, I swear."

Diane sighs, then smiles coquettishly and lowers the sheet. "Here's a reminder of what you're leaving behind," she winks. "Have fun, stud. And shut that damn light." Turning over, she snuggles under the covers and hides her head under the pillow.

Steve groans softly. Cursing under his breath, he turns off the light and fumbles in the dark to get dressed. He knows he's going to have to spend a bunch of Euros to make Diane forgive him for leaving her right now.

Rome is a different city in the dead of night. Without the throngs of people and vehicles that usually plague the famous streets, Steve and George are free to wander about unhindered, and they couldn't be more delighted.

As they stroll past one of the city's many ancient structures, Steve stops to admire the old stones. "Just look at this thing!" he says, studying the carvings by moonlight. "It's hard to believe this has been here for centuries." Acting like a regular tourist, Steve reaches out and fingers the rocks lightly, genuinely touched by the skill and ingenuity of ancient

Romans.

When the pair reaches Saint Peter's Square, they come upon a yellow- and blue-striped Swiss Guardsman standing stiffly in front of a small guardhouse.

"Hello," says Steve, "I know it's late. Or maybe it's early, depending on your point of view. But Colonel Accola asked us to meet him here. My name is Steve Ciccone, and this is my friend, George Jackson."

The men wait for a reply, but the six-foot-six guard remains silent and impassive, and they wonder if he heard Steve's greeting.

"Um, we have a meeting," Steve repeats.

The tall guard heard what Steve said. He's deciding whether these night owls are genuine or if they're pulling a prank on him, as it wouldn't be the first time someone tried to disturb the outward calm of a Vatican guard.

When the visitors don't go away, the guard confers with a companion inside the guardhouse, and the inside guard picks up a phone.

"Wait here," the outside man says to Steve. "Colonel Accola will come out to meet you."

With nothing more to say, the guards return to their positions. Standing tall and erect, they stare out at Rome, ignoring the men still in front of them.

George looks at the taciturn guard and shrugs. "Guess we just wait," he says.

Five minutes later, footsteps echo off the cobblestones from the quiet of an inner courtyard, and Colonel Accola appears through the gloom.

"Come with me," he motions to the Americans. "Raphael told me what is going on. I know you want to interrogate Franchi before the Ravens have a turn at him, but they are impatient; they do not like delay. I did manage to convince them to wait until you could get here, but you need to understand that if Franchi does not cooperate with you, they will ask both of you to leave, and they will continue with their own methods of persuasion."

Steve suspects that the Ravens have already begun to apply their own "methods," but he knows there's nothing he can do about it at this point. So he stuffs his usual bluster down his throat and instead uses sarcasm to get his point across. "I'm so glad they're 'letting' me speak with him," he replies to Accola dryly.

The colonel picks up on Steve's disdain and shoots Steve a hostile look. But he also holds himself in check.

The men's destination is the Palace of the Governate of the Vatican State, a majestic-looking building bathed in nighttime shadows. Constructed from 1927-1931, the palace consists of three massive buildings connected to the church of Santa Maria Regina della Famiglia in the Vatican Gardens behind Saint Peter's Basilica.

Accola leads them inside the main building, to a small elevator that brings them down to a sub-basement floor. At their floor, he heads for an elaborate video communications center, where he wordlessly points to a large monitor.

Figured prominently on the screen is Henri Franchi, gagged and shackled to a hard wooden chair in a bare concrete room. The room could easily pass for a tomb, except for the four comfortable-looking chairs directly in front of Franchi and the eerie yellow glow cast by a series of bare light bulbs hanging from the ceiling.

While the group watches the screen, Raphael appears beside them. "You have ten minutes to speak with our guest," he declares in his characteristically aggressive manner.

"Uh, uh!" declares Steve, shaking his head forcefully and rising on his toes to go nose to nose with the taller man. "This is *my* show, not yours, so I'll take as long as I want. This meeting was supposed to happen later today, not at such an ungodly hour. Now behave, or you can leave us to handle this alone. GOT IT?"

Raphael peers down at Steve and scowls but presses a red button under the com center's desk. When a buzzing sound answers in the distance, he leads the men to the concrete room.

When the door opens, Henri looks up expectantly, only to be dismayed when he sees Steve and George. He dreads the questions he knows are coming and watches unhappily as the anti-assassination team leader and his close friend choose seats in the comfy chairs. Henri doesn't know what will happen next, but he has a good idea that it won't be pleasant.

Sweat starts to bead on Henri's forehead, but the men just sit there, staring at him with unblinking eyes. They don't ask questions; they just glare at him coldly, which makes Henri more tense than if they had already begun their interrogation.

Steve is counting on making Henri nervous. He wants the informant to squirm before he gets down to business, so he stays silent for five, then ten, then fifteen long minutes.

When Steve finally removes Henri's gag, Henri wastes no time; he starts complaining as soon as his mouth is free. "I am an officer with Interpol!" he shouts angrily. "And a resident of France! You have no authority over me! You cannot keep me —"

"Shut the fuck up!" shouts Steve. "You're an informant for Cosa Nostra, you shithole! I found your number at the terrorists' apartment, and we know about your mother's connection to the mob!"

Henri's face goes pale, and he looks from one man to the other.

"I'm going to ask you a few questions...civilly..." continues Steve, "and you better answer them all. If you don't, our companion here will question you instead. And just to let you know, he won't be as nice as me."

"Ohhh, you do not understand," moans Henri, perspiring profusely. "They will kill my father, my sister...my entire family! And they will kill me!"

"You're worried about the mob? What do you think the Ravens will do if they get the chance? Take you out to dinner?"

Henri lowers his head. "If I talk to you, I will need a new identity, and you must make my family think I am dead. That is the only way they will survive."

"*Iam mortuus es*," Raphael blurts out menacingly. It's Latin, but the Americans don't need a translation.

"Let's talk, Mr. Franchi," Steve urges.

Henri looks around the room, but there's no escape, so he resigns himself to whatever's coming. "You will do as I ask?" he inquires hopefully.

"Yes."

Henri exhales, letting his breath out slowly. "Vito Scarapelli recruited me," he states bitterly. "He made me an offer I could not refuse, as they say in your movies."

"Oh, great; we have a movie critic here," chides George. "What does Vito want you to do?"

"He told me to keep him informed of your team's progress and warn him if you get too close. That is all."

"Yeah? How do you know what's going on? You don't attend all our meetings."

"Salvatore Caputi is very thorough. He tells me everything I miss when I am not there."

"Salvatore? Is he involved with the mob, too?"

"Oh, no, only me! Poor Salvatore, he knows nothing about what I am doing!"

Steve glances at George, then turns back to Henri. "Does the mob know you left Rome?"

"No, I went to Paris to visit my sister. She is dying of cancer. Ohhh, Monsieur Ciccone!" Henri wails in despair. "My parents live in Cefalù! They will not hesitate to kill all of my family if they know I am talking to you!"

Steve looks at Henri thoughtfully. "I don't think they'll hurt your sister or your mother," he says. "But your dad and others, well, that's another story. Give us the names of the mobsters in Rome. Tell us where they live and what they're doing."

Henri looks down at the floor. "I do not know anything about that. I told you everything I know."

"Are you sure you don't know anything else?" prods Steve. "If you're holding back…"

"I do not know anything else! I swear it!"

Steve doubts that Franchi is telling the truth. "Right," he says. "Civility is over. There's nothing more I can do for you."

Just then, a loud buzzer sounds, and the door swings open to admit another Raven. This one is shorter than Raphael, and he's covered head to toe, like a ninja. He's also carrying a large metal case.

Henri suspects that he's now in for a very rough time. He shudders and wets himself, begging for mercy in every language he knows.

But Steve, George, and the colonel leave him to the secretive Vatican organization.

Outside the room, the trio passes the com-center to get

to the elevator, but none of them have the heart to look at the monitor again. They reenter the elevator in silence for the ride back to ground level.

On the main floor, Steve says, "It's now two a.m. We'll meet at AISI at nine. We need to give everyone a heads-up about what's going on. And Raphael may have something to tell us by then."

George looks grim. "If I know the Ravens, I don't think we'll need to worry about new IDs for Franchi."

Steve groans and runs a hand through his hair. "Monitor them closely," he orders Colonel Accola. "I don't want that man dead."

CHAPTER TWENTY-FIVE

Two hours of sleep just doesn't cut it anymore. With an espresso in one hand and a coke in the other, Steve wanders slowly into the now all-too-familiar AISI conference room, where nearly all of the familiar faces are present and waiting. "The Raven and his scoutmaster are running a little late," he says, "but they should be here momentarily."

"Why are we meeting so early again?" asks a peeved Salvatore. "I am not used to rising at this time of day."

"So sorry that I interrupted your daily routine," Steve responds caustically. "I called an early meeting because we talked to Henri Franchi, and he told us who was leaking information to him. I thought you'd like to know who it is."

"Oh? Who is it? I know it is not me!"

"It's not you directly, Sal. But you're heavily involved."

Around the room, surprised eyes turn to Salvatore.

"You've been diligent in keeping him up-to-date on what we're doing, which is what we wanted you to do," explains Steve. "But... He used you to pass that info on to his crime boss."

"*Madonna!* He is a Mafiosi?" questions Salvatore, stunned by the news, along with the rest of the group. "I... I did not know! He works for a respected agency! How could I know?"

"Calm down, Sal. I don't think you knew what he was up

to. But we can't take chances like that anymore. From now on, we're going to have to keep a tight lid on everything we do and say."

"Where is Henri now?" asks Salvatore. *"Gli torcerò il collo!"*

"What?"

"I will strangle him with my bare hands!"

"No, you won't. He's in a holding cell here in the city. That's why Raphael and the colonel are late."

"But how do you know he is connected with the Mafia?"

"His mother's maiden name is Scarapelli; Vito is her uncle. That Sicilian crime boss must have a good amount of control over her family."

"This explains why our raids at the villa and the apartment failed," remarks Vincenzo, with a pained look at Salvatore.

"Yes," replies Steve. "Henri tipped them off before we got to both of those places, so here we are again."

When the door swings open, the team watches intently as Raphael, Colonel Accola, and George make their way to empty seats. Their stares are intense, but they're nothing compared to Steve's.

Sensing the tension in the room, Raphael displays a welcome willingness to share what he knows.

"I know you are curious," he says, "so I will tell you what has happened since yesterday. We found Henri Franchi at a restaurant in Paris and brought him here late last night. Early this morning, Steve had a chance to question him, but Franchi wasn't very forthcoming. So Steve left him to us. We continued the interrogation until we felt there was nothing more he could contribute."

Steve doesn't like the way the Raven phrased his statement. With narrowed eyes, he asks, "Is he still among the living?"

"I will answer that," says Colonel Accola with a restraining hand on Raphael's arm. "To clarify, I will use one of your amusing American terms: Franchi is now a little 'wet around the collar.' But he will be fine."

Raphael is dissatisfied by the colonel's explanation, so he jumps back into the conversation. "The term *we* use is tactical baptism," he states condescendingly.

"Whatever," replies Steve. "What did Franchi tell you?"

"He gave us the name of Vito Scarapelli's main officer, a man called Giuseppe Sarducci. He said Sarducci negotiated the Mafia's scheme with the Muslims and that he arranged for the assassins to enter Rome undetected."

"Then Franchi knows where they're hiding?"

"No, Henri only knows that Sarducci set the men up somewhere close to the basilica."

Steve sighs disappointingly. "No rest for the weary," he says sadly. Reaching for his beverages, he takes alternating sips of coke and espresso to try to wake up.

Salvatore asks, "What will become of Henri now that he talked? He's with Interpol, so they're going to look for him."

"We will arrange for him to appear to die in a fiery auto accident, and then we will give him a new identity," says Raphael. "Those were his terms for speaking to us. But Henri did tell us something interesting. He said the murderers were set to put their plan into motion on Wednesday, during the regular papal audience. But now that the G7 officials have moved their summit to Rome, the general audience will occur on Monday, not Wednesday. And the new schedule of activities calls for the G7 leaders to have their audience with Pope Urban on Monday as well."

"The Secret Service and the U.S. State Department persuaded our president not to attend that audience on Monday," interjects Agent DeMaria with more information for the team. "France and Germany will still be there, but all the other leaders have backed out."

"Oh, no," moans Colonel Accola. "The date for Monday is November 27."

"So? What happened on November 27?" asks Agent Samuels.

"Pope Urban II called for the Crusades on that date in 1095."

With loud gasps around the table, everyone turns to Steve.

"I know, I know," Steve says. "That's not good. It'll give the assassins an added reason to make the hit that day. So now, all bets are on Monday. This is it, team. If we're gonna keep the pope safe, we have only a few days to get our shit together."

"There is a little more," declares Raphael. "Franchi also revealed the names of some of the others who set up apartments for Vito's criminal associates in Rome. But we think Sarducci was the one who arranged most of the details."

Raphael says nothing more, but the team members don't look satisfied. This was the first time he shared so much information, so the group is waiting for him to speak again, and that irritates him.

The intimidating Raven looks crossly at the expectant faces. "What more do you want from us?" he declares reproachfully. "You told me that you want us to behave and follow. But now what? You want more? You want us to lead because of the information we collected? Very well, then. Here is what we will do. Give me a list of all the apartments bought or leased in the last few months around Saint Peter's Basilica. I will direct the Ravens to find out where the Muslims are living now. And we will give you Sarducci as well!"

"Whoa! Hold on just a minute!" interrupts Steve, waving his hand around the room. "I know the Ravens got some useful intel, but we still can't give them free rein! That is, unless no one here cares about collateral damage anymore!"

"Then what do you propose?" challenges Accola.

"Well, I have no problem with the Ravens looking for Sarducci and the Muslims. They can do what they want with the assassins, but if they find Sarducci before this ends, I think they should bring him here so we can question him ourselves."

"That sounds fair," replies Accola. "Vincenzo, can you get the info the Ravens need from city records?"

"Sì. It will not be easy, but I will do it."

"When we have addresses," says Steve, "we can decide whether we should let the hounds loose on the assassins. As far as I'm concerned, those killers don't deserve any special treatment from us, so I'd be okay with it at that point. Does everyone agree?"

At nods and murmurs of assent, Steve uses an old Mafia saying about going to war: "To the mattresses, everyone!" he orders. "Anyone have questions?"

Vincenzo raises a finger. "What if Cosa Nostra is tipped off even further by the Ravens snooping around for Sarducci? And what if the Ravens find Sarducci, but he will not talk to them? Can we really trust the Ravens to do the right thing with him?"

Raphael scrapes his chair along the floor and rises from the table. Then he walks over to Vincenzo and leans close to whisper something into his ear. When he's done, he turns for the door.

"Hey!" shouts George, knowing the Raven is about to leave abruptly. "You're not going anywhere without your shadow!"

At the conference table, Vincenzo is as pale as a ghost. He crosses himself, then says to Colonel Accola, "Please apologize to the cardinals, the pope, and the Ravens for my lack of respect." Looking at the others, he says mysteriously, "Please excuse me. I must leave you now." Then he rushes out of the room.

Colonel Accola is left to explain what happened. "The Ravens are everywhere and nowhere," he says cryptically. "They can be your best friend, or your worst nightmare. I think Vincenzo just had his nightmare. I pray that none of you have yours."

Steve nods toward Frank. "Happy Thanksgiving, pal," he says. "This reminds me of the time we dealt with Muslim terrorists in Miami. Only it's worse this time. Come on; let's leave as well. I still have some jewelry to buy so Diane won't kill me."

Outside the room, the friends encounter Salvatore Caputi at the elevator, so Steve asks, "What really happened to Vincenzo? Accola didn't say anything substantive."

"No, he did not. But we have had run-ins with the Ravens before. Raphael did not appreciate being chastised. Bennini must have certain things he is hiding, so I suppose the Ravens discovered them. Tell Mr. Jackson to be careful while he is with those snakes. He can get bitten very severely."

The Italian drama that Steve seems to run into at every turn is getting exasperating. "It never ends over here," he sighs. "This situation is FUBAR. I never thought I'd be searching for terrorists in Italy."

Salvatore is confused. "What is FUBAR?" he asks Frank.

"It means, *fottuto oltre ogni riconoscimento*."

"Ah, sì," agrees Salvatore. "*È davvero fottuto!*"

"What did you say to him?" asks Steve.

"I said it means this thing is fucked up beyond recognition."

"Ha! That's about right!"

The cobblestone street in front of Vito Scarapelli's restaurant in Cefalù is quiet today, as an afternoon thunderstorm is keeping many of the townsfolk indoors. It's having no effect on the Ravens, though. They're still watching the restaurant as closely as ever.

For several weeks now, three Ravens have been continuously holed up in an apartment with line-of-sight views of Vito's business. For efficiency, they worked out a schedule: while one of them naps or grabs something, the other two peer through the unit's dirty windows.

Now and then, the men capture suspicious actions. Their equipment records everything, so when they get something worthy of further investigation, they flag it and send it to their superiors. At this moment, their equipment photographs Giuseppe Sarducci entering the restaurant.

Several miles away, Raphael is turning his car off the highway. The streets of Vito's city are familiar to him, so his mind wanders as he drives. Almost by instinct, he parks his Mercedes Benz Minivan in his usual spot around the corner from the Ravens' location, where Vito and his goons can't see it.

Raphael kills the engine, then takes a minute to survey his surroundings. When he believes the way is clear, he directs George to follow him closely.

The pair scampers over worn cobblestones toward the building that houses the Ravens' lookout post, just as another rain shower begins. Raphael moves quickly, but George takes his time. The rain is making the ancient stones shine like ice, so he doesn't want to slip.

Inside the building, Raphael tells George that they need to use the stairs to get to the third floor because there is no elevator.

George is skeptical; the staircase looks dilapidated. However, he has no choice but to follow the Raven. Three flights of creaky boards later, the men tread over worn carpeting to the last door on the floor, where Raphael knocks in a prearranged signal. When the signal is accepted, they're admitted into a sparse area with a small kitchenette, a bathroom off to the side, and another room with a closed door.

Though George knows the Ravens are all business, he's surprised that these men have been here 24/7 with no comfort. All he sees are two folding chairs, a couple of cots, and one small table. But there are also two sets of high-powered binoculars on tripods and a second tripod with a professional camera and a large telephoto lens.

Raphael moves his companions some distance away so they can speak to each other out of George's earshot, but he needn't have bothered. George thinks it sounds like they're conversing in rapid German, and he doesn't understand a word of it.

After a while of talking, Raphael finally remembers his shadow. "Sarducci is inside the restaurant," he explains to George. "When he leaves, we will follow him. It is not advisable to capture him in this city."

"Oh, no? I wonder why?" responds George with a sneer. The notion that they would make a move to nab Vito's right-hand man in front of the Mafia boss and his underlings is ludicrous.

Raphael stares silently at George with a slightly furrowed brow and narrowed eyes. Then he turns away and resumes his conversation with the Ravens. They talk more urgently now, then Raphael points one of the men out to George. "This is Aldo," he says. "He will accompany us while we follow Sarducci. Now, we will all go downstairs to wait."

On the way out, Raphael grabs one of several handheld radios lying on a table.

Back on the street, the trio piles into the minivan, then Raphael moves the car to a place where they can see the restaurant. The men settle back for however long it takes for Sarducci to appear.

Steve arrives back at his hotel with two surprises for Diane. The first is an extravagant gift he hopes to present as a peace offering. The second concerns dinner.

In front of their door, he pats his pocket to make sure the gift is still there, then enters, excited to see the look on Diane's face.

But Diane's not there.

Disappointed, he picks up a note on the bed, which reads, *Meet me in the restaurant downstairs. I'm spending the afternoon* riposo *there. They cater to tourists, so they're open during the extended lunch break.* At the bottom of the note, an imprint of red lips makes him even more upset by this kink in his plans.

Down in the lobby, Steve passes through the stone archway marking the entrance to the restaurant's bar and stops to look for Diane. Gazing around, he spots his attractive wife sitting on a barstool, looking as captivating as always in an unfamiliar black cocktail dress.

With a mischievous grin, Steve saunters over and kisses Diane on the cheek. "You know, you still got it, babe. If you ever wanted to work again, you could still rock the silver screen."

Diane cocks her head at her husband, knowing he's biased. "That would only be true if they don't take closeups," she replies sensibly. "Hey, you like this dress? I bought it when you left me to shop for myself in Rome."

"Yeah, it's cute, like you. Look, I was kinda hoping you'd be upstairs, but no matter. Here, this is for you." Steve retrieves a small, gaily wrapped box from his pocket and hands it to Diane.

Diane eyes her husband suspiciously. "You're sweet," she says. "But before I open this, shouldn't you just go ahead and tell me what I probably don't want to hear?"

"I'm not trying to keep anything from you, Dee. I'm just sorry that I've been leaving you alone so much in an unfamiliar city. Now go on, open it."

Diane fumbles with an elaborately tied bow on the elegant-looking box and lays it aside. Then she lifts the lid partway and peeks inside. What she sees renders her speechless.

Sparkling up at her is a gold rosary with diamond and ruby prayer beads.

"Steve! This is absolutely beautiful!" she gushes.

"I thought you'd like it," Steve replies happily.

Diane holds the prayer beads up to the light to admire how they sparkle and shine. "Come here, you wonderful man," she says, pulling Steve close.

When Steve is near, Diane whispers against his neck, "Now tell me why you spent so much money. It can't be just because you've been leaving me alone. Whatever it is, it must be big."

But Steve just says, "I have another surprise for you."

Diane pulls back to look Steve in the eye. "Another surprise? Um, what's going on, Steve? Should I be worried?"

"Nah. I spoke to the concierge this morning about a traditional American Thanksgiving meal, and he agreed to ask the chef to prepare something for us. Let's have some drinks until it's ready."

"We're going to have a Thanksgiving turkey dinner in Italy?"

"Yeah, but there's gonna be one thing missing. He can't make pumpkin pie."

George and the two Ravens have been waiting in the car for hours now. Giuseppe Sarducci still hasn't appeared, and George is getting hungry. "What are we going to do about eating?" he asks. "I'm starving, and I bet you are, too."

"We are here for a reason," responds Raphael coldly. "If you are not up to the task, you can leave."

"I'm just saying I'm hungry," says George. "Can't you move the car to a different place where we can still see the restaurant? One of us can get takeout and bring it back."

"No," responds Raphael firmly.

George sighs in the back seat and returns to staring out of the window, getting hungrier by the minute. "Well, if we can't eat, can we at least have some conversation? I don't know how you two can stay quiet for so long."

"George..." begins Raphael, intending to reprimand him again.

"There he is," announces Aldo.

"Oh, thank God," mumbles George.

Giuseppe Sarducci is standing on the sidewalk, taking long drags of a cigarette; he looks like he's waiting for something. Soon, a Maserati Quattroporte pulls up, and the Mafia hitman puts the cigarette out and slips into the car.

"All right!" George exclaims. "It's go-time!"

Raphael edges his minivan into traffic a few car lengths behind the mob car. Maintaining his distance, he follows it onto SS113, a two-lane road along the coast, then onto narrow SP54 bis/Via del Giubileo Magno. Eventually, the two cars turn off onto an unnamed country road in the quiet Sicilian countryside.

George wonders what Raphael is up to. "There's no one else on this road but us," he comments from the back seat. "Are you going to take him soon? They must have spotted us by now."

"Look," says Raphael.

Up ahead, a fork in the road appears, and Raphael motions for Aldo to lower his window. As the window drops, Raphael reaches into his shoulder holster, fingers a silenced Beretta, and steps on the gas.

With masterful skill, Raphael steers his car alongside the Maserati while he aims his weapon out of the window, just past Aldo's head.

Two quick shots later, the Maserati's driver is dead from a bullet to the temple, and the Quattroporte is jolting to the right and climbing up a dirt embankment.

Raphael knows that if he wants to take Sarducci alive, he's going to have to do something to stop the driverless car. So he turns his wheel toward the other car. As the cars continue down the road, he eases the minivan closer and closer to the other vehicle until they rub against each other. Then he applies pressure to his brakes, and both cars stop.

Jumping into action, George slides the minivan door open and slips into the small space between the two cars. With mighty curses, he reaches through the shattered back seat window for Vito's lieutenant, but the mobster has moved to the other side of the car.

. With Aldo's help, both men lean in far enough to grab Sarducci's arms while he fights back tooth and nail, squirming and kicking at anything he can. Despite Sarducci's struggles, George and Aldo manage to wrestle him through the window and into the minivan.

Sarducci knows he's in a bad position; he continues to fight to get out of the van. However, Aldo has had enough. Without warning, he knocks the mobster out with the butt of his pistol and slides the side door closed on him.

Aldo shrugs when he catches George's raised brows. "I am tired of him," he says. Then he climbs into the front of the van with Raphael.

Having completed the first part of their mission, Raphael turns the car around at the fork and heads back to Palermo. There, another Legacy 500 business jet waits to bring them to Rome.

The Thanksgiving meal didn't turn out as well as Steve had hoped. The chef tried his best, but with so little time to prepare, it looked and tasted more like roasted chicken than turkey. It was good, but Steve was hoping for the classic American meal.

Diane continues to eat while Steve finishes his Lambrusco. The restaurant is quiet and cloaked in a romantic, dusky light, and Diane's long blonde hair frames her face like a magazine cover. Sensing that she's being stared at, she raises her head to see her husband looking at her with a strange expression. "What's wrong?" she asks. "You're making me nervous."

Steve sighs. "I better tell you what's going on."

"It's about time," says Diane.

"Yeah, well, starting tomorrow, I'm going to have to leave the hotel. I'll be working exclusively out of AISI headquarters, and I don't know how long I'll be there."

"So you're going to leave me alone again," Diane concludes. "Ooooh, wonder what I'll get this time!"

"Funny. We expect everything to hit the fan on Monday, after the G7 talks. That's when the participants are going to have a special papal audience at Saint Peter's. Of course, we hope we'll be able to end it all before then, but who knows? Anything can happen."

"That doesn't sound good. Do you have any leads?"

"I can't say any more. I just want you to know that you need to go home tomorrow morning. If we can't stop the terrorists, it'll be safer if you're nowhere near Rome."

"No! I'm not leaving here without you!" retorts Diane, shaking her head firmly.

"Hon, please. These guys are going to blow stuff up. I beg you—"

Diane purses her lips in the way he knows too well. "Okay, okay," he says, backing down in the face of his wife's wrath. "But I'm not gonna change my mind about this: I insist that you do not, under any circumstances, leave the hotel while you're here. And I want you to stay far away from the windows at all times. You think you can do that?"

"I'm a big girl, Steve. I'll find something to keep me busy while you're saving the world. Besides, I have my new rosary. Guess this will be a great time to use it."

Steve grabs Diane's hand and looks deep into her eyes. "This is the last time I'm going to do anything like this," he declares solemnly.

Diane laughs, then swallows a forkful of food. "How many times have I heard that before? You know you can't resist this kind of stuff! You said you retired a year ago, and yet, here you are. You love the thrill of the hunt way too much!"

Diane picks up another forkful of food but notices that Steve still has that unusual expression on his face. "Wait...do you mean it?" she asks cautiously. "Would you really be able to turn it all off?"

"I'm going to try my damnedest, Dee. You have my word on that — no more hero shit. I'm not getting any younger, as you keep reminding me. And...and this is a big one... I'm too much in love with you to take a chance on leaving you early."

Diane looks at Steve and realizes that this time, he's telling the truth. "Well, well, well," she says, stunned by the possibility that maybe, she won't have to worry about what her husband's doing anymore. "I'm *certainly* glad to hear *that*," she declares, covering Steve's hand with hers. "Let's finish dessert. Then we can go upstairs, and you can show me how much you'd miss me."

Vito Scarapelli has nothing else on his mind but what he's doing right now. Fifteen minutes ago, the mob capo felt frisky, so he enticed his wife into the bedroom of their expansive Sicilian villa. Now, with single-minded concentration, he's grunting and moaning while the bed is shaking beneath him.

Just outside the bedroom door, two of Vito's trusted soldiers are looking at each other nervously. They have strict orders to bring their boss important news whenever they hear it, but the cries of passion coming from the room are making them hesitate.

"What the hell we gonna do?" one of them whispers. "The don needs to know what happened. If we do not tell him soon, we are dead."

"Sì," replies the other. "But if we interrupt him now, he will cut our balls off."

The men shift foot to foot, trying not to listen as they wait for the passion song to end.

When all is finally quiet, the older man puts his ear to the door. He hears nothing more from the inner sanctum, so he knocks gingerly and puts his mouth up to where the door meets the jamb. "*Scusa!*" he calls loudly. "Don Vito? We have urgent news!"

An answering stream of obscenities makes him jump back anxiously.

Inside, Don Vito stomps to the door without bothering to cover himself up. Flinging the door open, he stares daggers at his men. The soldiers know they've interrupted something, so they cower in fear.

"Well?" Vito bellows, daring the older man to explain the intrusion. "Speak up! What is it?"

The soldier's mouth is suddenly dry. Looking down, he clears his throat, then looks up at his boss. "Don Vito," he says hesitantly, "we have come here... We heard... We want to tell you—"

"*Imbecille!* What am I paying you for? Tell me right now!"

"It is Giuseppe Sarducci! He was kidnapped! By the Ravens!"

Vito's eyes widen, then he turns beet red as his blood pressure rises to match his ire. The don is beyond furious that one of his trusted officers is now in the hands of an arch enemy. *"Quei fottuti bastardi Vaticani!"* he explodes, spitting on the expensively carpeted floor in disgust. "I will not let those fucking bastards get away with this!"

Vito curses up a storm and holds his hands to his throbbing temples as he paces back and forth in front of the door, not caring that he's still naked as a jaybird. Behind him, his wife grabs a robe and tries to get him to put it on, but he pushes her away.

"Call that *bastardo, Cardinale Carlotta, subito!*" he shrieks to his men with eyes full of hate. *"Figlio di puttana!* He needs to remind his Raven *amici* who they are dealing with!"

While Vito screams and yells on the Sicilian coast, Giuseppe Sarducci regains consciousness twenty thousand feet over the Bay of Naples. He looks out of the window, then at the men sitting in front of him. Spotting George, he purses his lips and narrows his eyes. Then he speaks to the Ravens in Italian. "I know who *you* are, but who the hell is this black bastard?"

George doesn't understand much Italian, but he does know what *bastardo nero* means. Incensed by the insult, he jumps out of his seat and gets up into Sarducci's face. "This nigga is your worst nightmare!" he shouts angrily.

Next to him, Raphael grins admiringly.

Ten minutes ago, Steve was acting like a twenty-five-year-old, and Diane is now resting comfortably at his chest.

Steve is happy tonight. He absently strokes Diane's hair and lets his mind wander. As he does, his favorite people pop into his mind: his kids, his grandkids, his wife, and his friends. He pictures all of them clearly. But when he thinks of his late wife, the picture is fuzzy. Steve knows that he's lucky to have found happiness twice, but lately, his first wife's image is becoming more and more blurry, and he's afraid he's going to lose it altogether.

When Steve's cell phone rings, it's a welcome intrusion for once. "Hey, Geo. What's up?" he asks.

Beside him, Diane rises from the bed, shaking her head at Steve's constant cell phone use.

"We got Sarducci," George says. "The Ravens are taking him to that little room in Vatican City. I wanted to go there with them, but, well, that didn't happen."

"Why not?" asks Steve. Then he decides he'd rather not spoil the mood. "Never mind," he says. "I'll catch up with you in the morning. Thanks for letting me know, bro."

CHAPTER TWENTY-SIX

Early Friday morning, the Swiss Guards help law enforcement set up barricades. Fencing is going up at the perimeter of Saint Peter's Square, and alongside Largo del Colonnato and Largo degli Alicorni, the two famous colonnades jutting out from the basilica. Barriers are also going up in the outlying piazza known as Papa Pio XII and down the Via della Conciliazione, the main boulevard in front of the church.

The crowd restraints are going up well before the pope's general audience on Monday. The city ordered them to be put up early because they don't want to be caught unprepared, especially since some G7 leaders will be at the audience.

In the small apartment, the pope's aspiring assassins have said their morning prayers and are now coming together for one last meeting. Today is the day they have waited for; they will decide which of them will wear the suicide vest. All of them know the stakes, and each is ready to make the fateful decision.

However, their meeting ends before it begins. Josef tells his companions that he's thought long and hard about why he's there and has come to a decision. "I will make this easy on you, brothers," he says, right at the outset. "There is no need to talk about this. I am willing to wear the vest and get close to the pope — to sacrifice myself for Allah."

The others are pleased. They readily accept Josef's decision, happy that there is no need for one of their lengthy discussions, and that they've been saved from having to wear the dreaded explosives themselves. To support their comrade, they vow to do everything they can to back him up from the souvenir booth. They know they won't escape the day unscathed; they're all prepared to die for Allah.

When it's time for the booth workers to head for Saint Peter's Square, they thank Josef again for his bravery. Today and tomorrow, Amid, Moammar, and Azim will man the booth all day, and Josef will take Azim's place on Sunday. The day before the big event, the weapons guy will need to remain at home to recheck all their firearms.

When the gunmen arrive at the booth, they get busy setting out their cheap souvenirs and inexpensive snacks. They want to make sure they are seen arranging their wares, so they'll be overlooked on Monday.

While they work, law enforcement officers crisscross the area, but they're not concerned. Even though they're in the open again soon after their recent vehicle chase, each of them looks quite different. With the supplies Giuseppe Sarducci left, they dyed their hair again and applied various facial features in the off chance that someone might remember them from the chase.

As the aspiring assassins get things ready for another full day of tending the booth, a vehicle drives past — an AISI van occupied by Steve and Frank. Regrettably, neither man on the papal anti-terrorism team pays any attention to the souvenir vendors.

The vehicle transporting Steve and Frank is on its way

to pick up the other Americans on the team. AISI has arranged for them and the others to stay at their headquarters building as long as the mission is in effect. They've set up a couple of empty offices with food, cots, computer terminals, and everything else the team requested. All team members will remain in these few rooms indefinitely, even bunking there at night. The only exception is FBI Special Agent Kathryn Samuels, who will sleep in a different part of the building.

Salvatore and Vincenzo are already in the conference room when the three musketeers and the FBI agents arrive. They're helping themselves to a cold breakfast buffet of lunch meat, cheese, yogurt, and cappuccino.

Steve asks, "Has anyone heard from Accola?"

"Nothing yet," responds Salvatore. "As far as we know, they are still interrogating Sarducci."

"I hope they're getting something useful," says George.

"We will just have to wait and see. However, Henri Franchi is now officially 'dead.' My office was able to stage his 'auto accident' in Paris."

Steve looks relieved at that bit of good news. "All right, at least that's done," he says. "Now, what about the apartment rentals? Any information about that?"

"I expect to receive a list later today. I directed my team to look for units that changed hands in the past six months."

Behind them, the door swings open to admit Colonel Accola. "Buon giorno," he announces tiredly. "I am sorry to be late, but I was detained unexpectedly. I have an update, but please let me get something to eat first. I have been awake since three."

Steve waits until the colonel sits down with a full plate. "What do you have for us?" he asks.

"Sarducci has not been very cooperative, so the Ravens

have begun to use their enhanced interrogation techniques. They hope to have answers to their questions sometime today."

Frank raises his brows and gives George a sideways glance. "Enhanced techniques, huh? After they're done with him, his capo will probably have to call him 'Three Fingers' Sarducci."

Steve hears the comment and smirks but gets down to business. "If we're going to have a chance at spotting the assailants, we're going to need a heavy presence in the streets around Saint Peter's. I want surveillance in the air as well. And make sure we have eyes on the rooftops."

"Everything is arranged," responds Vincenzo Bennini, taking a bite of cheese. "We are coordinating across multiple agencies."

"Good to hear that," says Steve. "Colonel, I know you're probably tired, but if they're still questioning Sarducci, I'd like to be there. Will you go with me? We can leave after you finish eating."

Deep underground, Giuseppe is woozy from a significant amount of blood loss. The Ravens bandaged his hand after their last session, but the dressing is full of blood again and needs to be changed. Along with that, the coldness of the room is making him shiver.

Sarducci is extremely tired. He hasn't been allowed to sleep or eat since he got there, so despite his pain and discomfort, he's nodding off in the stiff wooden chair the Ravens strapped him to.

Though Raphael and his colleagues have left him alone for a while, they're still keeping tabs on him through the room's camera. When they see his head fall to his chest, Raphael tells the others to give him five minutes to rest. "Va bene," responds one of the Ravens. "Let us get some coffee before we go in again."

Twenty minutes later, Steve and Colonel Accola arrive to find another "tactical baptism" in progress.

"How long has that been going on?" Steve wonders aloud, pointing an angry finger at the communications center monitor. "If they keep that up, he's gonna be dead before he has a chance to say anything! You gonna go in there or should I?" he asks the colonel.

But Colonel Accola shows no willingness to enter the chamber. "What they're doing is unacceptable!" Steve shouts. "If you're not gonna stop it, I will! We need that man alive!"

Without further delay, Steve moves toward the interrogation room, but the colonel won't have it. He reaches out to grab Steve's arm to stop him. However, the impetuous American is already too far away. Steve is sprinting down the hall, anxious to help the struggling man.

Determined to stop the madness, Steve flings the door open and hurries over to Raphael. "Enough!" he growls while pulling a water hose out of Raphael's hand and throwing it aside. "He's no use to us if he's dead!"

The towering Raven is infuriated by the interference. Seething with anger, he grabs Steve by the shirt and jams him up against a concrete wall. Through sheer force of will, he holds Steve in place several inches off the ground while he eyes the shorter man aggressively.

Several feet away, the colonel watches the exchange with alarm. He knows what Raphael is capable of, especially when he's offended, so he runs toward the Raven to try to keep him in check. "Stop! Let him go!" he shouts at the top of his lungs while he desperately yanks on Raphael's arm.

When Raphael releases his grip on Steve's shirt, Steve slides slowly down the wall. As he goes, his adrenaline kicks in, and his twenty-five-year-old psyche unwisely overrides his sixty-nine-year-old body. Without thinking it through, he swears to take his best shot at the younger man who's been causing him problems. *I'm gonna have only one chance to set this guy straight*, he snarls to himself.

Rising to his full height, Steve throws a sweeping overhand punch that connects with Raphael's nose and breaks it with a satisfying crunch.

As blood drips onto the floor, the Raven roars in pain, and Colonel Accola rushes forward to part the two men again. Pushing hard, he forces the stronger man further and further away from Steve, while keeping an eye on him, afraid of what he might do now.

But the Raven surprises them all. He touches his bleeding nose gingerly, then laughs loudly and calmly picks up the hose. In silence, he cleans the blood from his face, and when the water no longer runs red, turns the hose on Steve.

The unexpected blast of icy water dissipates Steve's anger as quickly as it rose. He wipes his eyes and joins his adversary in loud, unrestrained laughter. The Raven's unpredictable behavior amuses and impresses him in equal measure.

Standing a few feet from each other, the rivals size each other up, one man with a broken nose and the other soaking wet, and they realize the futility of their hostilities. With broad smiles, they reach out and embrace each other in a testosterone-filled man-hug.

"You're a mess, brother!" laughs Steve.

"And you're soaking wet!" retorts Raphael as he grabs a towel to wipe his nose. "I like you, Mr. Ciccone," he declares nasally. "You should get one of our tattoos. You're like me, but much older, of course."

Nearby, Sarducci begins to moan, which makes the colonel show some backbone. Shouting commands, he orders the Ravens who have been looking on to take him to his cell and get him dry clothes and hot food. Then, he turns around to Steve and Raphael. "Are you two finished?" he asks somberly.

"Yeah, we're done," replies Steve, grabbing a towel. "But you should also make them get medical attention for Sarducci's hand. And can you tell them to get me a hot coffee? It's fucking freezing in here!"

When Josef's comrades left for the souvenir booth, he turned the television on to keep himself occupied. But its nonsense didn't hold his interest for long. He was too restless; the thrill of the recent outing with his companions kept popping into his mind. For him, the entire night was exciting, even the frantic race through the city. Josef desperately wants to leave the apartment again. He knows he should stay put, but he's much too fidgety.

When he finally tires of the noise of the television, he turns it off and wanders from room to room. Eventually, a craving for a snack sends him into the kitchen, where he finds their supplies low. "No food?" he mumbles. "This is perfect! I will have to go out, no matter what that mobster says!"

Josef is happy that he now has a compelling reason to circumvent the rules. Humming a tune, he picks through the suitcase Sarducci left to find a suitable disguise.

An hour later, Josef leaves the apartment wearing brown contacts and a baseball cap. *I will not be gone long*, he tells himself. *I am just going out to get some food.* But on the way to the store, he sees a coffee bar and goes in. *Might as well enjoy myself while I am out*, he reasons.

While Josef waits for his order to be ready, he hears a reporter on an overhead TV commenting on the upcoming G7 meeting in Rome. *This is interesting*, he thinks. *It may be good for us. Perhaps we can catch some world leaders in our papal net!*

While Josef eats, he decides that instead of shopping at the Arabian market near the apartment, he will go to an Italian *supermercato*. His Italian is good, and with his European DNA and Persian ancestry, he looks Sicilian.

Josef takes a winding route to the supermarket. He strolls down the Via dei Corridori, then passes under the Passetto di Borgo near the garage where the Mafia left another van to replace the one he dumped in the Tiber. "I do not know if we will need that car, but it may be useful," he mutters.

At the supermarket, Josef grabs a wire basket and heads for the vegetables, where a young woman is staring at the produce with unsure eyes. As Josef picks out a few ripe tomatoes, the woman says, "I can never tell which ones are best. I should know how to do this, but I was never interested in learning. You seem to have no problem knowing which ones are good. Can you help me?"

Josef is startled that someone who is obviously Italian is speaking to him so casually. He smiles — not at the Italian beauty, but at the fact that he is blending in. "Oh, it is simple," he replies in Italian. "Just give them a slight caress. If they feel firm, they are not ready." Josef hands her a perfect specimen. "Here. Like this one."

"Oh, I see," says the young woman, taking the tomato. "Um, my name is Regina."

"Ah... Hello. I am Josef."

Regina leans close. "You were nice to help me," she says, looking around to see if anyone is listening. "I have been in Rome for a while now, but I have not made many friends here. Um... This is going to sound forward, but... Would you like to share a meal with me? Or maybe get some coffee?"

Josef is taken aback by the woman's request. It's only a few days before the attack, and he doesn't want to get involved with anyone. But the woman is pleasant to look at, and he doesn't want to appear rude. "Um… Okay," he replies. "That would be nice. There is a gelateria across the street. Do you want to go there now?"

Curiously, Regina flushes with embarrassment. She has never been the aggressor before, so now that Josef has accepted, she suddenly hesitates. "Uh, I have a few things to do today," she states cautiously. "How about tomorrow evening? Are you available then?"

Now, Josef must make a decision. He's tired of being locked up with only a few men for company, and Regina is piquing his interest. He will have to find an excuse to leave the apartment again tomorrow. However, he is very interested in spending some time with a woman before going to his reward. "Tomorrow evening is fine for me," he replies. "We can still meet at the gelateria. Is eight o'clock a good time?"

"Yes, eight is good," says Regina, smiling broadly. "I will see you then."

As Josef watches the brash Italian retreat down the aisle, he immediately begins to have doubts. *What am I doing?* he argues within himself. *Should I be with a woman right before the attack? What will the others say? Ah, but they are weak. None of them complained when I told them I wanted to wear the vest. If I am going to leave this world soon, I deserve a pleasant diversion before I go!*

While Sarducci is getting cleaned up, Steve and Raphael sip espressos and chat with Colonel Accola at the computer console outside the interrogation room.

When the monitor shows the prisoner being escorted back to his chair, they're pleased to see that he's clean-shaven, is wearing dry clothes, and his bandages are new.

"All right. Let's continue this," says Steve.

Though Sarducci feels better than he did before, he's still suspicious about what will happen next. So when the door opens, he flinches.

In silence, the trio takes the same tufted leather chairs they used when Henri Franchi was in Sarducci's place. As they did before, none of them makes any move to start the interrogation. They just stare at the captive with unblinking eyes, intentionally trying to keep Sarducci ill at ease.

After a time, Steve breaks the tense stillness. "You look a little rested," he says kindly. "I see that they let you take a shower. Did you have anything to eat?"

"Yes."

"All right; that's good. I'm sure you like this better than what was going on before, so let's get started. Here's what's going to happen. If you want to continue being treated well, you're going to have to cooperate with us. If you refuse to answer our questions, we'll have no choice but to let this tattooed gentleman and his friends continue to do things their way. Do you understand what you have to do?"

"*Sì, io capisco*," Sarducci replies grudgingly. "But I cannot say anything to you. My family in Sicily is being watched. And me? I am a dead man, whether you kill me or someone else does. But my wife, my daughters...my parents... If I talk, they will also be killed."

Steve cocks his head to one side. "It's amazing to see how concerned criminals are about their families when they get caught. Did you think about them before you decided to become involved in the first place?"

Raphael leans over to whisper something to Accola, who looks back at him with raised brows. The colonel whispers what he just heard to Steve.

"Well," says Steve, looking at Sarducci. "It seems that your wife, your daughters, and your parents are here in Rome, in protective custody. They arrived about thirty minutes ago."

"What? How?"

"We'll let you see them if you tell us what we need to know. If you don't, they'll be returned to Sicily, and the Ravens will take over here. Then, if you somehow survive our friends' questioning, you will also be sent back there."

Giuseppe's eyes widen, then he shudders with great, heaving sobs that shake him to the core.

Though the mobster looks pitiful, no one comes to his aid. They let him cry for as long as he wants, knowing that this strong reaction may mark a turning point.

Minutes pass before Sarducci calms down. "*Grazie.* Thank you," he says, sniffling and blinking tears from his eyes. "I am grateful that my family is safe. I will tell you what I know, but only after I see them in person."

Steve thinks for a moment. "Okay, I can agree to that," he says, rising from his chair. "We'll take a break now so you can visit with them. We'll return in a few hours, and at that time, we expect that you won't hold anything back. It's your choice whether your family lives in peace or dies in Sicily."

Outside the room, it finally dawns on Steve why the cold and dank underground passageway seems familiar every time he steps off the elevator. He realizes that it reminds him of the catacombs where the early Christians hid to avoid persecution and death, and he has no trouble imagining Colonel Accola and Raphael as Roman oppressors.

Steve shakes his head to return to the present. "We have a couple of hours before we need to come back here, so I'm going to poke around outside and check in with Angie, John, and Kate."

"Va bene," says Accola. "I will call Caputi from my office to check on that list of apartments. I just hope Sarducci gives us something useful."

"If he knows anything, he may pass it on, now that his family is here."

A chill wind is blowing across Vatican City when Steve exits the Palace of the Governate of the Vatican State, so he zips his jacket up as he crosses the cobblestone courtyard.

In Saint Peter's Square, he looks for familiar faces in the crowd, but doesn't see any until he gets to Piazza Pope Pio XII, where he spots Frank at a souvenir booth.

"You actually thinking of buying this stuff?" he asks, edging up to his friend.

"I need a souvenir for my refrigerator," Frank shrugs. "How'd it go with Sarducci?"

Steve picks through some rosaries. "They damn near killed him. But the Ravens got his family out of Sicily, so I hope he'll start talking once he sees they're all right. I'm giving him a couple of hours to decide to play nice."

Frank barely responds to Steve's commentary. He merely gives him a noncommittal grunt, as he's continuing to look through the inexpensive trinkets on display, which surprises Steve. He's never pegged his friend as a refrigerator magnet-kind-of-guy.

While Frank continues to dither, Steve states quietly,

"You know, I took a good look around the square. It's gonna be damned near impossible to secure it properly."

This time, Frank makes no reply at all. He's still trying to choose something.

Steve exhales loudly through pursed lips. He's impatient to get going, but he knows that Frank won't leave until he makes his purchase. He has no interest in anything for himself, so he puts down the item he was looking at and hopes his friend makes a decision soon. But over and over, Frank picks up an object, looks at it, then puts it down again.

Steve groans loudly; he's tired of watching this futility. "Come on, decide on something already," he complains. "I'm hungry. Let's get something to eat."

"Okay, okay," Frank replies, knowing that he's wasting time. "Guess I'll take this one."

While Azim rings up a small magnet in the shape of Saint Peter's Basilica, Frank looks at him closely. Something seems familiar, but he can't place his finger on it. And with Steve still urging him to hurry, he has no time to figure it out, so he just leaves the booth.

A few paces away, the men catch sight of Kate and John. "You want to join us?" Frank asks. "We're going for breakfast."

"Hell, yeah," says John. "We could use some strong coffee. It's gonna be a long day."

While they look for a café, Frank notices that the weather is getting colder and that he's underdressed, as usual. The only apparel he's wearing against the brisk Roman air is a light sweater, so he shivers and pulls the garment tighter. "Can we eat somewhere inside?" he grumbles. "This weather is for shit!"

"Then how you gonna manage living here full time?" asks Kate, casting a dubious glance Frank's way.

The warm-blooded Floridian's mood improves when he's seated at an indoor table. "You know what?" he says to Steve. "I'm gonna call George to see if he'll join us."

"You better be prepared for a tongue-lashing," Steve warns.

"Oh, he should be up by now."

Frank clicks on George's number, then waits while it rings and rings. When George finally responds, Frank chirps, "Rise and shine, sleeping beauty! Meet us at a place called Feffo Roma. My treat."

Frank listens to George's response, then ends the call with a chuckle. "I think I woke him up. He wished me a good morning, but then he threw in a rather nasty verb and pronoun."

"Told ya," says Steve.

CHAPTER TWENTY-SEVEN

When breakfast is over, Kate elbows John and nods at the door. "Time to get back to work, ace," she says. "If we're not in the square soon, the boss is gonna have our hides." Fixing her eyes on Steve, she asks, "You're paying for us, right?"

"Yeah, I got it."

Kate nods again and tips an imaginary hat, then she and John return to work, leaving Steve and Frank with George.

Earlier that morning, Frank's call woke their friend up from a deep sleep. He remained awake long enough to talk to Frank, but as soon as the call ended, he went right back into dreamland. Now he's overtired and on his third cup of cappuccino. And because he arrived late, he missed Steve's update.

"So tell me what happened," George urges, stifling a yawn. "Did Sarducci talk?"

"He hasn't said anything yet," says Steve. "But his family is here now, courtesy of the Ravens. I'm gonna check on him in a couple of hours. He said he'd talk after he's sure his family's okay."

George yawns deeply and takes another sip of coffee.

"Angie," says Steve, "Kate and John are monitoring the square, so I'd like you to check with Caputi about the rentals."

George yawns again, so Steve asks, "You gonna wake up sometime today, Geo?"

"Yeah, I'll be all right."

"You sure? You're looking mighty poorly, son."

George flips Steve the bird, then finishes the last of his coffee.

"Stick with me this morning, Geo," says Steve. "You can hook up with Raphael at the interrogation room; he's still there with Sarducci."

Steve needs to kill time before returning to the interrogation room, so he and George wander around the square for a while, eventually stopping at the enormous obelisk in the center. Like many others, they study it curiously and wonder why it's there.

"Seems out of place, don't you think?" comments George.

"There must have been a reason they put it here, but I'll be damned if I can figure it out," remarks Steve.

Leaving it a mystery, they turn around and join the large crowd entering the basilica.

Inside the massive church, the two friends marvel at the size and majesty of the place. They walk from statue to statue, reading information signs and getting a sense of what's there.

When it's time to go, Steve says, "Follow me and let me do the talking. I have to make peace with the Swiss Guards again."

Outside the church, Steve walks up to the guardhouse at the cobblestone courtyard's entrance, fully expecting to have to explain his reason for being there again. But the Swiss Guardsman merely nods and waves him through.

"Huh! That was weird," Steve remarks as they enter

the courtyard. "I guess they can't forget handsome faces like mine!"

"Rubbish!" retorts George, sniffing the air in mock disgust. "They just don't want to have to talk to your ugly mug again!"

Though the men arrive at the underground room at the time Steve specified, Raphael doesn't bring Sarducci back until early afternoon.

"Where the fuck were you?" Steve snaps at Raphael. "We've been here since eleven!"

"It took longer than we thought to bring the family together. There were some...complications."

"Really? I don't believe it. You mean the Ravens have problems? What a concept."

"It is unusual. But here we are, so you can begin your questioning now."

"Grazie, kind sir," replies Steve tartly. Then he turns to George. "Sarducci may get distracted if you come in with me, so I'd rather you stay out here. You can watch everything on the monitor, okay?"

"Aye, aye, captain," replies George crisply.

While Giuseppe watches, Steve enters the now-familiar room, taking the same seat he used earlier in the day. "Here we are again," he quips to the anxious mobster. "You've had more than enough time to visit with your family. I trust they're well?"

"They are fine, under the circumstances."

"Good. You promised to answer my questions after seeing them, so here's the first one: Who leased the apartment for the assassins?"

Up above, the driver of a small Fiat shows a forged pass

to a uniformed officer in Saint Peter's Square. The officer accepts the document as genuine, and the car goes through the checkpoint under one of the colonnades.

At first, the car moves slowly. But suddenly, it speeds up and barrels through a gap in the barricades, directly toward a group of tourists strolling through the square.

When the sightseers see the car coming at them, they scream and scatter in all directions, and the commotion elicits an immediate response from the Swiss Guardsmen. In a flash, they rush toward the crowd with their automatic weapons at the ready.

But the driver turns the car around and directs it right at the papal guards. In response, they aim for the driver, but the automobile is now empty.

With no one to guide the car, the unmanned "missile" continues toward the guards, who are desperate to stop it. They shoot at it repeatedly, hoping to disable it before it can damage precious objects in Saint Peter's Square.

But it just keeps coming. And then, it erupts like Mount Vesuvius.

The explosion is so forceful that it causes the ground around Vatican City to shake, and the rumbling is felt in the interrogation cell deep below.

"What the hell was that?" asks George, bursting into the room he's not supposed to enter, while at ground level, Colonel Accola yells "Merda!" and grabs his desk phone.

When Steve's phone rings, the colonel shouts, "I think a bomb just went off in Saint Peter's Square! There is a cloud of smoke, and police, Ravens, and guardsmen are running toward it!"

"Holy crap!" exclaims Steve. "We felt it way down here!"

Raphael shouts orders at the other Ravens. "Lock this

man up and move his family to a safe place!" he commands. "We cannot let anyone get to them! I am going up to see what happened!"

When Steve, George, and Raphael reach street level, Colonel Accola is waiting for them at the elevator. "Andiamo!" he yells. "They targeted the Swiss Guards! Two of them are dead!"

"Fuck! They could be testing security! Anyone else hurt?"

"I am not sure! There were very many people in the square!"

Among the panicked crowd are a pair of mob soldiers, but they aren't tourists. They were sent to Vatican City today to watch their boss' assignment play out and to relay the details to him.

While Vito's soldier gives him a play-by-play account of the chaotic scene, he listens intently and studies the photos the other soldier sends. The blast marks the first time in modern history that Vatican City succumbed to an attack, and he's ecstatic. He knows that his men achieved a historic milestone this day. He doesn't care that two guards were killed, many tourists were injured, and a guardhouse, several early Roman iron railings, and many ancient stones lining the historic piazza were destroyed. All he knows is that the pope and everyone else now understands the supreme power of Cosa Nostra.

As they take stock of the damage, George, Steve, Raphael, and Colonel Accola stop to aid the wounded as best they can. But some injuries are too much for them.

"This one needs help!" yells Steve to a nearby policeman. A woman lying beneath some chairs has a leg wound that's bleeding heavily. "Don't worry; I'll wait with you," he tells her, though he's not sure she understands.

Steve leaves when the woman in good hands. Then he

begins to walk away, just as his phone vibrates in his pocket. "Babe! Where are you?" he asks nervously.

"I was in the dining room when the entire hotel shook!"

"Stay put!" he orders. "It's a war zone out here!" Then he hangs up quickly.

Not far away, Frank and George are helping a man into an ambulance, so Steve joins them. And to his surprise, he sees Frank making the sign of the horns, an age-old Italian gesture to ward off further evil.

"I saw the driver bail; then all hell broke loose!" Frank confides. "Now I can't hear shit! Do you think it was the assassins?"

"It was either them or the fucking mob saying hello!" says Steve.

"When the driver bailed," Frank adds, "the FBI guys took off after him. He was heading for the Tiber. Geez! When that fucking bomb went off, I thought I was back in the Delta!"

"Go see the EMTs, Angie. Your ears must be ringing something fierce!"

Unexpectedly, John DeMaria appears at Steve's side. "The fucking driver swallowed a bullet," he reports wearily. "Kate is gonna stay with the Carabinieri while they process the scene. I think he was Mafia. I bet they're pissed at us for grabbing Sarducci."

"Could be," replies Steve, placing a toothpick from the restaurant between his lips. "I was about to question Sarducci when the whole place shook, so I better find Raphael and get back there. I want to finish up with him before something else happens."

Near the square, the assassin-hopefuls study the hectic scene from their booth. "This is wonderful!" they whisper to each other over and over. "Our Mafia friends have placed much fear in the infidels' eyes!"

"The Mafia is a worthy collaborator!" they all agree.

"Allahu Akbar!" they chant together softly.

It's now dusk, and the temperature is beginning to drop, but neither Steve nor Raphael is aware of the change. At this moment, they're plummeting well below Vatican City, hoping to get crucial information out of their captive.

In the quiet of the underground hallway, their footsteps and the whoosh of the closing elevator door announce their arrival to the Ravens standing outside the interrogation room.

"*Sarducci ist zur Zusammenarbeit bereit,*" they tell Raphael, which Raphael translates as "Our Mafia man is ready to talk."

Steve nods and spits his toothpick onto the floor. "I hope so," he responds. "Let's get in there before he changes his mind."

At Raphael's direction, a colleague pushes a button on the wall, which responds with a loud buzz. Inside the room, Sarducci watches impassively as the men take their seats.

"I have decided to tell you what I know," he begins. "Henri Franchi was our man. He kept us well informed of what you were doing, so we were always able to stay one step ahead of you. That is why you could not do what you wanted in Sicily, Calabria, and Rome. We always knew that you were watching us."

"We already discovered that much," states Raphael, unimpressed by the mobster's admission of collaboration with one of their team. "What else do you know?"

"Vito ordered me to take care of the Muslims. He said a man named Enzo Carducci leased an apartment for them in Rome, so I arranged passage for them from Sicily. Now before you ask, I do not know where the apartment is. Enzo took them there himself. I had no part in that."

"Are you seriously telling us that you don't know where your boss' killers are hiding?" Steve asks.

"I do not know where they are. Vito is careful to keep things separate so one person does not have too much information."

"Yeah, yeah," replies Steve. "What else?"

"When Enzo told me they were settled, I went back to Cefalù to report to Vito, and that is all I know. Torture me, kill me, do whatever you want; I am a dead man anyway. I do not know any more than this."

Raphael studies the man, then leans over to Steve. "I think I believe him," he whispers. "Let us talk outside."

In the hallway, Steve looks skeptically at Raphael. "Why do you think he's telling the truth? He's Vito's right-hand man, and he was sweating something fierce in there."

"I know. But if he is as concerned about his family as he says he is, he would have told us much more."

Steve sighs. "He's probably an expert liar. I'm not as confident as you are, but time is slipping away fast, so I'm willing to go with you for now. We should keep him in custody in case we need him later. You okay with that?"

"Yes. We can reinterrogate him if we need to."

"He didn't give us much," says Steve. "I was really hoping for an address. I think we should set up some raids as soon as Caputi gets that list."

Raphael chuckles at Steve's comment, but his expression

is anything but happy.

"What's wrong?"

"I know Signore Caputi said he would get that information for you, but it will take days, even weeks, to get anything meaningful out of our Italian bureaucracy. Did he not tell you that?"

Steve rubs the side of his head. "No, he did not. Well… Can't the Ravens help? I had high hopes that Sarducci would tell us where they're holed up, so now, all we can rely on is a reliable list. And we damned well can't wait for bureaucrats to sort it out."

"No, we cannot. I will do what I can."

"I have faith in you, buddy. If there's anyone who can 'nudge' things along, it's you. Oh, and we also have to get Sarducci and his family out of Italy. You'll arrange that, too, right?" Steve pats Raphael's arm firmly, confident that the Raven will comply.

"Yes," confirms Raphael.

"Excellent. Well, there's nothing more for me to do here tonight, so I'm going home to my wife. We'll meet at eight a.m. in Caputi's office — if I don't hear from you sooner."

"Va bene…Stefano."

Saint Peter's Square is still lit up with flashing blue and red lights in the cold November evening. The square is now clear of victims, but forensic teams are hard at work scouring the area. Cleanup crews are also washing down the stones, and construction teams are repairing some of the damage. To avoid the work crews, police officers direct Steve to a secure back entrance to the basilica. They tell him to walk through the church and exit through the main doors.

Tonight, an eerie stillness fills the enormous space inside the most prominent structure in Italy. Though it's getting late, there should still be some tourists inside the building. Instead, only a few people are wandering around, mostly police and clergy, and the quiet is unnerving.

Steve hurries past prominent statues and the tombs of past popes with no time to stop. A police officer requests ID to enter the square, so he shows his temporary government credentials before exiting through the main entrance.

At the top of the church's steps, he spots George, Frank, John, and Kathryn standing together near the tall central obelisk, so he makes his way toward them.

"How are your ears?" Steve asks Frank when he reaches the group. "Still hear the ringing?"

"Nah," Frank replies. "It's almost gone now. I got an uneasy feeling about this, Chic. I know those ragheads were here; it's like we were being watched. But one of the cops said the Mafia took responsibility for the explosion. Did Sarducci say anything?"

"Ya mean 'Three Fingers?' You were right; the Ravens did a number on him. But all he told us is that a guy named Enzo Carducci rented or bought the apartment where they're staying. And conveniently, he doesn't have the address. So, we need Caputi to get that list."

George overhears the conversation and asks, "We gonna track down that Enzo guy?"

"Yeah, we need to do that. And another thing. According to Raphael, Caputi is probably ass deep in government bureaucracy, so I suggested that the Ravens give him a hand. Look, I'm tired. We start again at AISI at eight a.m. tomorrow, so I'll see you all then."

"Okay, get some sleep," says George.

As the group disperses, news crews from around the world are finally being allowed into Saint Peter's Square, and the newscasters are in a tizzy. The team members find themselves dodging between reporters and support teams scurrying around to stake out the best spots for their location shots. All of them want to be the first to broadcast reports about the first time in recent memory that a deadly incident occurred in Vatican City, and the Swiss Guard lost members to an outside force.

Salvatore Caputi is shocked when he learns of the event in Vatican City. He spent most of the day inside, trying to get the list the group needs at the MEF building, located near the "wedding cake," the famous monument to Victor Emmanuel II. He overheard people talking about the incident while he was shuttling between sub-agencies of the Italian Ministry of Economy and Finance.

Now, at the end of the day, Salvatore is tired and frustrated, with no more answers than when he began. So he's not looking where he's going when he exits the building.

"Umf! I am terribly sorry," he apologizes when he runs into a huge man blocking his path.

"You are a hard man to track down, signore," declares Raphael. "Do you have the list?"

"No, I do not have the list! They say they are 'working on it!' Bureaucrats — our worst enemies!" spits Caputi furiously.

"Who told you this?" asks Raphael.

"Most of our fine civil servants said this same thing, so I went to the top. However, neither the head of the State

Property Agency nor the minister himself was willing to talk to me. Both of them told me to return on Monday, even after I explained that I'm with AISI! I even gave them a few details of the terror plot! I cannot believe it! I demanded answers from each of them, but they both shrugged and dismissed me. They said I got to them too late in the day! I am so angry! They are preparing to leave as if there is nothing urgent going on!"

"Where are their offices?"

"The clerks told me to go to so many different places today that I am not sure if I can find them. But the State Property Agency chief was on her way out behind me."

Though the arrogant Raven knows all too well about the frustrations of dealing with the Italian government, he also knows how to get things done.

"Do not worry," Raphael advises the older man. "Follow me back into the building. We will have that list before the night is over."

Giovanna Cardone, the head of the State Property Agency, looks down at her watch while she pushes at the door of the Ministry of Economy and Finance. She has certain things on her mind, like what to wear to dinner that evening, so when Raphael shoves her back inside, she almost loses her footing.

"What the..." she says, intending to let out a string of expletives; however, the words stick in her throat. The sight of the imposing Raven staring at her through mirrored sunglasses stifles all complaints.

But Giovanna's temper flares anew when she sees Salvatore Caputi standing next to him.

"You again," she says reproachfully. "I told you to come back tomorrow." Giovanna purses her lips and looks at Salvatore with smug confidence. She knows that her boss, Filiberto

Belladonna, is on his way to the exit and that he will have a few choice things to say.

The attractive chief of the State Property Agency is confident that her boss will get rid of the pesky civilian. She's aware of the considerable clout she has with the Minister of Economy and Finance, but inexplicably, doesn't consider that her affair with him is the deciding factor in her rapid climb up the ladder.

Giovanna smooths the skirt of her business suit and taps her foot impatiently. She expects Filiberto to handle the matter, so while she waits for him, she runs a hand over some stray hairs that escaped her elegant coiffure.

"Are you all right?" asks a concerned Filiberto when he catches up to his mistress. "I saw what happened to you!"

"I am fine," replies Giovanna haughtily, directing Filiberto to Salvatore with a roll of her eyes.

Filiberto sees Salvatore but turns instead to the man who caused the problem. "Who are you?" he asks imperiously, puffing out his chest with importance.

The sixty-year-old man wants very much to be Giovanna's knight in shining armor. But when he catches sight of Raphael's tattoo, he abruptly changes his tune. Instead of defending his lover, he says, "Ah, hello again, Signore Caputi. I see that you are back with a companion."

Filiberto knows that he's fallen a notch in Giovanna's esteem, but he's more aware of the situation than she is.

"This is my good friend," replies Salvatore with a satisfied smirk. "He wants to see that list I asked for as much as I do, but unfortunately, Monday is not an option for him."

The property agency chief is confused by this exchange. She expects Filiberto to rebuke the impertinent citizen, so she asks crossly, "Aren't you going to say something? We already told him—"

"Be quiet, Giovanna," Filiberto declares in a firm voice. Then he addresses Salvatore. "It will take us a while to get the information. Hours, I think."

Raphael removes his mirrored glasses to stare hard at the Economy and Finance minister; however, the tone he uses is unusually congenial. "We are happy to help," he says pleasantly. "Shall we begin now?"

Giovanna gasps and grabs the minister's arm. "We have an evening dinner reservation tonight, remember? We can't just—"

Filiberto shakes his arm free and locks eyes with Giovanna. "Dinner can wait," he insists. "*Il signore e il suo amico...* I am sorry, I do not know your name."

"Raphael. I am called Raphael."

Filiberto clears his throat. "Sì, ah, Raphael. Giovanna, the needs of these men are more important than our dinner plans."

Salvatore is impressed by the rapid turn of events over the bureaucrats. "You should not go hungry because of us," he says. "Please have one of the night guards fetch us food and something to drink. If we are to be here for hours, we will need to eat, yes? Now, shall we go to the office of Signorina Cardone? I believe she has access to what we need."

"Um..." Giovanna is still unsure, so she looks one more time at Filiberto, who gives her a stern glance. "Yes, we can access the records from my computer."

The State Property Agency leader still doesn't understand what's happening, but she knows that Filiberto expects her to comply.

On the way to Giovanna's office, Filiberto tries to explain his actions. He leans close and whispers urgently, "Raphael is with the Order of the Raven."

At the clandestine group's name, Giovanna's eyes widen, and she lets out a gasp, then immediately clamps a hand over her mouth to stifle it.

When the would-be assassins return to the apartment, they tell a shocked Josef what happened. "Turn on the television!" they urge. "It must be on the news by now!"

Josef scrolls from station to station, finding broadcasters on every channel reporting live from Saint Peter's Square.

"We saw it; we were there when it went off!" claims Moammar, Azim, and Amid, not for the first time. They want Josef to understand how close they were to the devastation at the infidels' shrine.

"It was glorious!" declares Azim, raising his eyes to heaven.

"Oh, yes! But it was so small!" argues Moammar. "When it is our turn, we will give the Italians a real demonstration of Allah's power!"

"Yes! And it will happen in just a few days, *inshallah!*" agrees Amid. "Now turn on the porn channel! I am tired of this!"

Josef shakes his head at his comrades' interest in adult movies. "I am going to sleep now. If I am hungry, I am not content to watch someone else eat."

CHAPTER TWENTY-EIGHT

Rome awakens the day after the car bomb like a hungry child — irritable and impatient for solutions. Many of its citizens watched reports of the devastation late into the night, and this morning, they're looking to their government for answers.

For breakfast, Steve and Diane take advantage of the small hotel restaurant's complimentary breakfast. While the restaurant's employees huddle together in small groups, presumably discussing yesterdays' events, Steve eats a selection of cured meats, and his wife chooses fruit and yogurt at the buffet table.

Steve thinks, *Things are closing in now, but I have to remember the good times*. Closing his eyes, he reminisces about his first encounter with Diane on the side of busy I-595 in South Florida.

When Diane returns to the table, she smiles and flips back her blond hair. "What were you thinking about? There was a funny look on your face."

"Oh, I was just remembering the day I swept you off your feet. You know, it was only four years ago. Can you believe how much has changed since then? We're together and living in Italy now! Babe, I want to invite my kids here for Christmas; I miss the grandchildren."

Diane spoons yogurt into her mouth and looks at Steve critically. "If you want to see your kids again, I'm gonna say this one more time: Don't do anything stupid!" For emphasis, she points the spoon at Steve and shakes it. "No matter what you think, the years are creeping up on you... And on me. And make sure Frank and George don't do anything stupid, either. Those two are part of your family, too."

Diane chews a few pieces of fruit, then looks at her watch. "Uh, oh! Are you finished eating yet? You're late for your meeting!"

"Madam, you've obviously mistaken me for someone else," Steve claims. "Today, I'm going to take my time getting there. If they don't like it, they can kiss my grits."

Steve places his napkin on the table and rises to begin another eventful day. "Don't spend too much money today, babe. We're going out to dinner tonight — just you and me."

Missing from the conference room this morning are Steve, Salvatore, and Raphael. None of them have shown up yet, even though it's almost eight-thirty.

"Where's your Raven, Colonel?" Frank calls over his shoulder as he pours himself another cappuccino.

"I do not know. Where is your friend?"

"Buon giorno, everyone," announces Steve, strolling casually into the room. "As for Raphael, I wouldn't be surprised if he's sleeping a little longer today. He and Caputi butted heads with the Italian bureaucracy until the wee hours of the morning."

"If they were there that long, I hope they got what we need," replies the colonel. "And what about you, Steve? Did you get anything from Sarducci when you went back there after the explosion?"

"No, he didn't have much to say. All he gave us is the

name of the guy who set up the terrorists' apartment. It's someone named Enzo Carducci. Anyone heard of him? He says that's all he knows."

"*Questo è ridicolo!* scoffs Accola. "That asshole is close to Vito, but he does not know anything else? Impossible!"

"Well, Raphael believes him."

The colonel is dumbfounded that the skilled Raven would accept such an absurdity, but he prefers to think that he has a reason for it. "Va bene," he utters. "We should start looking for this Enzo."

"Yeah, but we can't depend on that. Things are moving too quickly now."

"Then we should wait to see what they got from the Ministry Department. While we wait, I have news for you, Steve. I made arrangements with the pope's staff to grant you access to the roof of the basilica on Sunday. There is a small room up there that they will furnish with a cot and warm bedding. You can set up your sniper position during the day and sleep there overnight."

"Excellent!" responds Steve, walking over to the coffee table. "Geo, you're still with the Ravens, and everyone else should resume their surveillance positions today."

While they wait for Salvatore and Raphael, the room retreats into silence, each man turning to his own thoughts.

Before long, the door opens, and the missing members join the group. Both look tired and disheveled; their hair looks like it was combed hastily, and their clothes are wrinkled, a highly uncommon sight in fashion-conscious Italy.

Uncommunicative as usual, Raphael grabs a chair and sits down. However, Salvatore is ecstatic. "We got them!" shouts the AISI agent gleefully. "We know where the apartment is!"

"Where? Tell us!" shout the crew with varying degrees of excitement.

"When Franchi tipped Cosa Nostra off to our raid, they moved to an apartment about ten minutes from Saint Peter's Square. The address is Vacanze Alba, Number 201. Raphael ordered his men to watch it. And guess who owns the apartment?" asks Caputi, before answering it himself. "Giovanni Sarducci!"

Steve stares daggers at his silent rival. "So that fucker was holding out on us after all! And you believed him!" he shouts accusingly. "Who knows what else he didn't tell us!"

Caputi asks, "What do you want to do now?"

"We need to storm that place, and soon! Get yourself cleaned up, Raphael! You and Geo are joining that team!"

"Wait; let us think about this," interjects Vincenzo. "We should check the apartment out before we go in there. They most likely have explosives."

"Yes, you're right," says Steve, more calmly now. "You have any ideas?"

"We could send in an undercover team."

"Okay, how do you propose to do that?"

"We can disrupt their power or water, then one of our men can pose as a maintenance worker."

"That is good," agrees Salvatore. "We can fake a water leak. In fact, an emergency in their apartment will make them call *us*. We can work with the building manager to get in there."

"That could work," replies Steve, to nods from everyone around the table.

"We can probably get inside in a couple of hours," says Salvatore, continuing his thought. "Do you want to lead the team, Steve? Are you skillful with plumbing tools?"

Steve laughs, "Oh, no! You do *not* want me anywhere near the plumbing! But I can sure fake it for a while."

"Bene. Let me talk to my team. I will try to set it up for this afternoon."

"Good. We'll raid the place after we get a clear picture of the inside. Set up your assault for tonight." Steve stops suddenly and slaps his forehead. "Oh, crap, I forgot! I'm supposed to take Diane out to dinner tonight!"

CHAPTER TWENTY-NINE

Unexpectedly, the pope's staff readily agreed with Colonel Accola's request to grant Steve access to the basilica roof. So, thinking he had nothing to lose, he also asked for unrestricted access to the Passetto di Borgo for George and Raphael, and once again, they dispensed with their usual hesitation. The church officials understand that the ancient, elevated passageway running between Vatican City and Castel Sant'Angelo is a good place for the pope's defenders to watch for threats.

The Passetto is a long, covered corridor that was built over seven hundred years ago as an escape route for popes. It was most recently used in that capacity in 1527, when Clement VII fled the city during the Sack of Rome. The significance of that event is not lost on George as the two men enter the ancient structure.

"Looks like you're prepared to be here a long time," George says, walking behind Raphael. "What are you carrying? The popes didn't take anything when they were here."

Raphael just keeps walking, as if he didn't hear George.

"You don't like my little jokes, do you?" George asks. "I'm just trying to lighten the mood, big guy."

Raphael sighs. "I have various supplies with me, George: catalytic heaters, battery-powered torches, blankets, and food. The walkway is cold and damp even during the day, so we will need illumination and warmth while we are here."

"Okay, gotcha. But won't anyone see us?"

"Not at this time of year. The Passetto is only open for a limited time during the summer."

The lookouts scout the walkway for good vantage points, then begin their tedious jobs. Each one takes up a station in front of a narrow opening in the wall to watch for signs of their prey in the street below.

Meanwhile, in an apartment building across from the Passetto, Salvatore is trying to convince the manager of the assassin's building that he and Steve are policemen, even though they're dressed as plumbers.

"Our department received a tip about Unit 201," says Salvatore, flashing a phony ID while Steve does the same. "An anonymous informant says a ring of car thieves is renting it. Before we take our investigation to the next step, we want to get in there to make sure he is right. And we want to do that without raising suspicion."

"*Allora*, what do you want from me?" asks the manager suspiciously.

"We want you to give us access to the apartment above it."

"*Perché*? If the robbers are in 201, why do you want to go into 301?"

"We are going to create a leak in the ceiling so they will let us into their apartment," says Salvatore to justify their actions. "That is why we are wearing plumbers' uniforms."

"Ah," replies the Sicilian. He is intrigued but not yet convinced.

Salvatore goes on with his fictional story, leaving out the real reason they want to get into Unit 201: to check the place for firearms before raiding it later that night. Instead, he tells the manager, "When the occupants call you to report the leak, all you have to do is bring us to them. We will do the rest."

The manager crosses his arms over his chest. "What about the damage you will cause?" he probes. "A water leak is very serious. What will you do about that?"

Salvatore thinks quickly. "Do you have a business card or a spare piece of paper?"

The man pats his pockets and produces a receipt for something he bought that morning. "This is all I have."

Salvatore writes an address on the back. "Send us a bill for the repairs. We will reimburse you."

"Pfft. I do not believe you," scoffs the manager. "No one in the government would be so willing to fix a problem. Who are you, really?"

Once again, Salvatore must come up with a believable excuse to make this work. "This is a critical investigation," he states gravely. "The city has had enough of these car thieves, so we are authorized to do whatever we need to secure your help. Will you work with us to catch these criminals? I guarantee that you will get your money."

"Hmm, this will cause many problems. But my car was stolen last year, and my tenants have also lost vehicles." The manager looks into Salvatore's eyes for a long moment. Then he places the vital address deep into his shirt pocket. "Bene. I will help. And this is your lucky day, officer; I can let you in right now. The tenant in 301 is away for the month, on a business trip to Switzerland. He asked me to keep an eye on his saltwater aquarium."

"Grazie," says Salvatore, motioning for Steve to pick up a folding ladder emblazoned with the name of a non-existent plumbing company, while he picks up a toolbox with the same name.

Inside the third-floor unit, the tenant's saltwater aquarium occupies a prominent position in the living room. The tank is large, at least seventy-five gallons, and it contains a collection of brightly colored fish swimming gracefully around artificial plants and corals.

The display is impressive, but the 'policemen' ignore it. They head directly for the kitchen, where they set about opening and closing cabinet doors.

When they find two large pots and an oversized pitcher, Steve starts filling them with water. The manager watches, apprehensive about what will happen next.

As the containers fill, Salvatore clears a space under the sink and uses a knife to remove a glob of putty from around the water pipe. Then, he pours the containers' contents into the hole.

On the floor below, Josef suddenly hears an unusual sound while he relaxes in his bedroom. He listens intently and follows the noise to the kitchen, where he is dismayed to see water dripping from a large spot on the ceiling.

"Damn!" he curses in his native Farsi. "Come quick, Azim! And bring towels! There is a leak in the kitchen!"

Azim drops the weapon he was cleaning and wipes his hands on a rag. In the kitchen, he's startled to see dripping water and a pool forming on the floor. "I will call the manager," he snaps after uttering a few choice phrases in Punjabi. "You know where the towels are. Start mopping up this mess. I need to secure our weapons before we can let that Sicilian bastard in."

Azim and Josef are the only ones in the apartment at the moment. The other two had to return to the booth because they forgot to tally up the day's take for the booth's owner.

Upstairs, Salvatore pours more water into the hole, and soon, the building manager's cell phone rings.

"That was them," the manager informs the men he

thinks are policemen. "I will tell them that you were already here to check on another unit."

At apartment 201, the door opens a crack, and a man eyes the toolbox and ladder. "That was quick," he says suspiciously.

"You are lucky," the manager replies with a thumb pointed at Steve and Salvatore. "They were about to leave. There was a problem with another tenant's faucet."

"Huh," replies Josef. He's wary, but he needs help. "Well, come in. I think a pipe burst."

Steve takes in everything he can as they walk through the unit. He doesn't see weapons, but there's a heavy odor of gun oil and cleaner fluid in the air.

Inside the kitchen, water is now gushing out of the hole, and the building manager is worried. "Look at this mess!" he shouts at Salvatore, shaken by the consequences of the phony plumbers' actions.

"Do not worry," says Salvatore, making sure that Josef hears him. "It is probably coming from the upstairs apartment. We will take a look, but we can probably fix it today. Do you need help mopping this up?"

"No!" responds Josef forcefully. "My roommate is here. We will clean it up." Josef is anxious for these people to leave; Azim is still hiding evidence of their plot.

Outside in the hallway, Steve and Salvatore thank the manager again.

"Sì, sì," he replies. "But now I need to call a real plumber and a contractor to fix the mess you made! I hope they will fix it before my tenant returns! You will definitely get my bill!"

While the manager marches back to his apartment, Steve says to Salvatore, "Did you smell the gun oil and solvent?"

"Sì, and did you see the overstuffed backpack? I think I saw a wire."

"Yeah. Who knows what's in that thing? The raid tonight has to be quick and precise; we have to assume they have explosives. The doors of two rooms were closed so they could be hiding anything in there. I'll let the team know what we suspect. You going to set up your SWAT unit?"

"Yes, we will be ready. Will you join the raid?"

"Nah, I'm just gonna observe. Tonight, I'm gonna let the younger guys handle the dirty stuff."

At six o'clock that evening, the woman Josef met at the Italian *supermercato* is getting ready for her upcoming date, while across town, Josef has just started to prepare for it with a quick shower.

Earlier that afternoon, Josef worked up quite a sweat mopping the kitchen because Azim didn't want anything to do with it. Lately, his coconspirator's only interests seem to be cleaning the rifles and watching adult movies, so Josef was left to wipe down the floor and walls himself. As an excuse to leave the apartment, Josef told Azim that he's going out later to pick up some tea because they have none left for the next day.

Across the street, Raphael and George are still holed up in the Passetto. It's now bone-chilling cold inside the old stone structure, so George takes his eyes off the street to turn up one of the catalytic heaters.

"Who knows how this will turn out?" he says, knowing that Raphael can hear him even though he probably won't respond. "We know there are only two men in the apartment right now, so we have to wait for the others to appear."

As the evening matures, a rare sight greets Romans and tourists alike: snow. Puffy flakes, descending onto the ancient stones, dance haphazardly in swirling gusts from a winter storm that catches the city unawares.

Regina is dismayed by the sight. "Damnit, not to-night!" she mutters dismally. With a deep sigh, she rummages through her closet for a heavy coat, then heads downstairs.

When Josef sees the snow, he's already in the lobby of his apartment building. "Huh? Snow in Rome? I did not know it snows here. It is going to be cold out there," he mumbles grumpily.

Rushing back upstairs, he rummages through a pile of clothes to find more shirts to layer himself with, since he doesn't have a coat. He was already wearing his gray hoodie, the only warm outerwear he owns.

Moammar and Amid are happy that they finished their accounting before the snow started. "I am so weary of this place," Moammar complains through chattering teeth as they scurry toward home. "It is much too cold to be out here any longer!" Amid agrees.

When the pair arrive at their building, they're surprised to see Josef hurrying to the lobby door. Looking up, Josef sees them as well. "I am going to buy more tea," he explains, passing them as quickly as possible.

Outside, Josef raises his hood and puts his hands into his pockets. Shivering in the frigid air, he runs across the street in front of the building, his only thought to get to his destination as soon as possible. He's so uncomfortable in the cold that when two cars collide in the intersection behind him, he merely shoves his hands deeper into his pockets and keeps going.

Above him, George and Raphael watch in consternation as the accident unfolds, knowing that they're powerless to do anything about it. The event held so much of their interest that neither of them saw Josef crossing the street.

Regina is sitting alone at the gelateria, waiting patiently for her date. She arrived early, so she's not worried that Josef isn't there yet. The weather is colder than she likes, so she hurried all the way from her apartment, even though the snow stopped, and the wind went to sleep.

When the bell at the door jingles, she happily waves Josef over.

"I am sorry to be late," Josef apologizes as he removes his hood and fixes his hair. "I did not know how cold it was going to be, so I had to go back upstairs to put on warmer clothes. You look nice."

Regina smiles shyly. "Thank you. I am glad you are here. Which flavor of gelato do you like?"

"Ah, I cannot ever make up my mind. Everything looks so good!"

CHAPTER THIRTY

When the snow stopped, the U.S. FBI special agents and Italian SWAT team members were greatly relieved. Tonight's raid will be much easier if they don't have to deal with the white stuff, too.

Frank and Steve are also there, around the corner from the assassin's building, even though neither of them has a direct role in tonight's activities. They couldn't stay away. There's too much at stake.

The seasoned professionals are careful to stay well out of sight while they don bulletproof vests and recheck their weapons and communications gear. The mission is critical; they periodically look to Vincenzo Bennini, the raid's leader, for the go signal. They know what's expected of them, and they're restless.

Up in the Passetto, George and Raphael keep watchful eyes on the area. The wall's narrow slits give them a birds-eye view of the front of the building, so Vincenzo ordered them to monitor tonight's activities. But they're uncomfortable. The temperature keeps dropping, and the old walkway, constructed of bricks and tuff, is getting colder and colder.

The entire time they've been there, Raphael has been his usual uncommunicative self, and George can't stand the quiet. He fills the silence with whatever's on his mind, even if it always turns into a one-sided conversation. He complains about being bored, whines about being hungry, and pesters Raphael with questions the stoic Raven won't reply to.

So he's stunned when Raphael suddenly declares out of the blue, "I do not trust those, how you say, 'rag heads.'"

George turns his head sharply in Raphael's direction. "Neither do I," he replies, happy to get a few words out of the man. "And now that I have your attention, I have to say that I don't know why you volunteered to come up here tonight! It's fucking freezing in here!"

While George was speaking, his breath came out in cold puffs, which annoyed him greatly. Grabbing a blanket, he wraps it tightly around his head and shoulders and curses again.

Looking on, Raphael knows that George is unhappy, but all he does is chuckle quietly at his plight.

"Fuck you!" George grumbles. "This is the worst stakeout I've ever been on!"

At the end of their date, Josef offers to accompany Regina home, and she accepts. The two continue to talk on the way, and Regina becomes more and more comfortable with Josef. When they reach Regina's door, she shyly asks if Josef would like to come in for something to drink.

Once more, Josef is unsure of what he should do. His tiny brain tells him to stay, but his indoctrinated mind urges him to leave the infidel. He enjoyed his time with Regina and wants to prolong it, but his extensive training wins in the end.

Josef responds, "I would like to come in, very much so. But I need to go home. My work starts early tomorrow morning."

Regina is surprised. "On a Sunday?" she pouts.

"Yes. But please, another time?" Josef knows there will

never be another date, but he can't make himself deny the possibility.

Though Regina is disappointed, she clings to the hope of seeing Josef again. "Yes, another time," she responds brightly, leaning in for a kiss.

When the door closes, Josef stares at it for a long moment, replaying the kiss over and over. In his mind, he alternates between wanting to tear the door down to continue that good feeling and knowing that he should spend the night alone in his lonely bed. Eventually, he sighs and leaves the building.

It's almost ten when Josef begins his long walk home.

At the assembly point, Vincenzo finally gives the go signal, and the team splits up into two groups of five, each making its way quietly up to the second floor. One uses the elevator, while the other ascends the stairs.

In front of Unit 201, the lead officer kneels on the floor to slide a thin camera probe under the door. On a small screen, he sees two men casually watching TV and another leaving the room.

Slowly and quietly, he retracts the probe and moves some distance away to report his findings. "Only three suspects are visible," he announces to Vincenzo. "Shall we proceed?"

Bennini receives the transmission in an armored command vehicle at the staging area, where Steve and Frank are looking on. "Do you have any thoughts?" he turns to Steve. "They don't see the fourth one, but he may be there. I am inclined to tell them to enter."

"Damned if we do and damned if we don't," answers Steve with a shrug. "I say go for it."

Bennini gives the command.

While an officer swings a battering ram at the door, the three men watch on a small monitor and hold their breaths.

Inside the apartment, Amid and Moammar are taken by surprise when the door opens with a thundering crash. With no time to react, they freeze in place on the sofa, making it easy for the cops to shove them to the floor and handcuff them at gunpoint.

Azim is another matter, however; he's in the bathroom when the commotion starts. When he hears the officers' commands and his comrades' shouts, he rushes into a bedroom, slams the door behind him, and gets ready.

"I will get him!" calls an officer when he sees Azim dash through the hallway. The policeman goes to the bedroom door and shoves at it. But when it opens, he stops instantly.

Standing in the middle of the room is Azim, holding a detonator attached to a backpack.

The next moment, a huge explosion rocks the building with a shock wave so strong that it shakes the armored command vehicle parked around the corner.

"What the hell was that?" yell the three men inside it. Shouting, they rush toward the front of the building, while George and Raphael leave their posts inside the Passetto at a dead run.

Josef is still some distance away when he hears the blast. Alarmed, he sprints the rest of the way, only stopping to catch his breath when he's under the Passetto.

Unsure of what he will see, Josef peeks out from under an archway but can't make anything out through a mass of thick, swirling smoke and debris. Coughing repeatedly, he waves a hand in front of his face to clear the air, and before long, catches sight of a gaping hole in the front of his building.

When Vincenzo sees the damage, he races back to the van to contact the raiding team, but no one responds to his frantic calls.

"We gotta get up there!" shouts Frank, looking up at the damage.

"I'm going up with Vincenzo!" yells Steve.

While additional law enforcement begins to swarm the area, Steve and Vincenzo cautiously head up the stairs. On the second floor, they see that the explosion ripped through two apartments and that three dead and two injured officers are lying in pools of blood.

While Bennini calls for EMTs, officers pick through the debris. Soon, they announce three severely burned bodies in 201 and a dead man and woman in 202.

Near the hole in 201, an officer shouts, "One of the dead in here is ours! I do not know who the other one is! And there is one more in another room!"

Steve makes his way to the gaping hole, saddened by the deaths of two innocent people and some of the elite team. Through the hole, he spots the crumpled body of Moammar Sanjoni lying on the ground two stories below under a street-lamp.

Steve assesses the situation so far. "The two unidentified bodies up here must be the assassins," he mutters to himself. "So, if there are two up here and one outside, where's the fourth?"

Suddenly, a distinctive smell permeates the area. "Ruptured gas line!" call officers from the kitchen. "Everyone out!"

As Salvatore runs down the stairs with the others, he shouts orders into his phone. "Shut off the gas before this entire building goes up!"

Outside, Vincenzo waves at George and Raphael when they finally make it to the scene. "It is bad!" he tells them. "Do not go inside! There is a gas leak!"

Across the street, Josef is still staring at the destruction from the shadow of the Passetto, safe from the mayhem and the ever-growing crowd of spectators drawn to the scene. Cloaked in the darkness, he watches as television personalities begin to broadcast live reports.

Standing on the sidewalk, Steve screams in frustration. "We fucking blew it again! FUCK!"

"It's not all bad!" shouts Frank over the wail of sirens. "Three of them are dead, right?"

"Yeah, but how come there's only three?" retorts Steve with narrowed eyes. "Unless one of them vaporized into thin air, we still got one alive!"

Steve suddenly looks around, trying to spot someone in the mob of people. "Hey, where's Raphael? I haven't seen him yet."

"Huh?" responds George, searching the crowd curiously. "He was here a few minutes ago. We ran out of the Passetto together and got here at the same time. I have no idea where he is now."

While Josef continues to hide, he tries to decide what he should do now that his hideout and possibly all of his companions are gone. *I may be the last one left*, he thinks, *so I must continue the mission alone. It is good that we put supplies in the van, but I cannot stay there until Monday. Where can I go now?*

Soon, an idea forms in his mind, and he begins to smile.

Clinging to the shadows, Josef makes his way to the garage where the group's van is parked. Thankful that he always keeps the keys on him, he climbs into the vehicle and directs it north — to Regina's apartment.

Minutes later, he's knocking on her door.

When Regina heard the explosion, she turned on the TV to see what happened, and she's been watching the news coverage ever since. So when there's a noise at her door, she jumps.

Cautious by nature, Regina looks through the peephole first and can't believe her eyes: Josef is standing at her door again! Though she's happy to see him, she isn't sure why he returned, so she only opens the door enough to peek out.

"Regina, I need your help," Josef pleads through the narrow opening. "I am sorry to be here so late, but I do not know what to do. Did you hear the explosion? It came from my building! It was damaged, and they are not letting anyone inside, so I have nowhere to go. I had a few things in my car, but that is all I have now. Would you mind… Can I stay here for the night? I promise that I will leave in the morning."

Regina opens the door wider. "Of course!" she replies, trying to disguise her delight at seeing Josef again. "I am so sorry about your apartment. You can stay here as long as you like."

"Hold still, or I will not be able to help you!" demands an EMT in highly accented English. The emergency technician noticed that Steve was bleeding while he was tending to Agent DeMaria's wounds from the apartment blast. The special agent is stable now, but he has several injuries that need more attention.

When Steve complies, the technician gets back to work.

But Steve's phone rings, so the technician has to stop again.

"Yeah, I'm fine," says Steve. "I know; it happened again. Some people died, and others were injured, including one of the FBI guys from our team. He's pretty banged up. They're taking good care of everyone, but I think the FBI agent is probably out of the fight now."

Frustrated, the EMT motions for Steve to end the call.

"Listen, I gotta go," Steve tells Diane. Then he clicks off and once again submits to the EMT's ministrations.

When he's cleaned up and bandaged, he turns to his crew. "Okay, guys, fill me in."

"We thought it'd be a piece of cake," explains Agent Samuels. "When we breached the door, Amid and Moammar were shocked to see us. Neither of them put up a fuss; they just stood up and surrendered. But when one of the guys went looking for the third one, all hell broke loose. The next thing I know, I'm lying on the floor, staring up at the ceiling."

"Yeah," adds DeMaria. "Azim yelled, 'God is great,' then, boom!"

Some distance away, Vincenzo pats the shoulder of an employee from Roma Gas, then looks for Steve. When he spots him talking with the other Americans, he threads his way through a crowd of evacuated tenants and Roma Gas trucks.

"What's the status of your team?" Steve asks when Vincenzo joins them.

"Three of our men and two tenants from the adjoining apartment are dead because of those fools! And there are injuries among the tenants and damage to more than a couple of units. We will have to close the building for a while, so many of these people have nowhere to go."

"It's a mess," admits Steve.

Standing beside him, George pipes up with the question everyone wants to ask. "What about Igmani? Was he there?"

"He was not among the dead or injured," says Vincenzo.

A gloomy silence grips the group until George speaks again. "So, we know they had an explosive device. Did you find any other weapons up there?"

"They had an arsenal of rifles and handguns and a second IED. That one must have exploded when the first one went off. That is why the blast was so large."

"Ah, hell," remarks Steve glumly. "As much as I hate to say it, this isn't over yet. One assassin is still out there, so Monday's gonna be hell. We need to continue with our plans. I'm gonna set up my sniper position on the basilica's rooftop tomorrow, and I'll sleep up there that night. Right now, I'm going home."

Steve looks over at John DeMaria, who's still being treated for his wounds. "Special Agent, you've done enough. Thanks for your assistance, buddy. Get yourself home to Pennsylvania as soon as you're able. And hey, make sure you bring your wife some fancy gifts from Italy, along with your handsome self!"

Steve shakes the agent's hand, then starts walking to his hotel, happy to leave behind the blue and red lights bouncing off buildings and wet pavement like a bizarre firework show.

At Saint Peter's Square, he's surprised to see that sturdy iron fencing is being erected across the piazza's formerly open expanse. It looks like it's intended to funnel visitors through manned entrances where everyone can be searched.

"Look at what we've come to," Steve murmurs with a shake of his head at the precautions that are now necessary at this major religious shrine. "A couple of looneys can change everything. I hope this won't be permanent."

When Steve reaches his hotel, Diane is downstairs waiting for him by a roaring fireplace. The couple clings tightly to each other, wishing they can find a way to shut out the crazy world around them.

CHAPTER THIRTY-ONE

When Steve wakes up the next day, he pads around the hotel room as quietly as possible in the dark, hoping not to wake Diane. Steve's an early bird by nature; he doesn't mind being up before sunrise. But Diane is a night owl. She needs the sun to get going.

Despite Steve's efforts, Diane is wide awake. Most mornings, she knows when Steve is up and can easily go back to sleep. This morning, however, she's too tense to relax. While the water runs in the shower, she stares up at the ceiling, her mind going a mile a minute. She can't stop thinking that in only one more day, either all hell will break loose, or Steve and his team will catch a devious assassin, and a tragedy beyond measure will never occur. Either way, Diane knows that Steve could be in grave danger, and that's keeping her awake.

To Diane's relief, her racing thoughts eventually quiet down. She told herself that worrying won't solve anything, so now, she's able to roll over to catch a few more hours of shut-eye.

While Diane snores softly, Steve shaves and splashes on aftershave in the bathroom. Then he dresses and exits the steamy room fully dressed and ready to go. Treading lightly, he moves to the closet to retrieve a large military duffle bag, then leaves the hotel room.

On the way downstairs, Steve reviews everything that still needs to be done before Monday. The stakes are high, and his stomach is in knots. Forgoing breakfast, he asks the concierge to request an Uber and sits down to wait for it.

While Steve is already starting his day, Josef is squirming on Regina's living room couch for the umpteenth time. It's not the most comfortable place to sleep, but he doesn't mind. He knows that he's close to Regina — she's only in the next room — and that makes all the difference.

As night gives way to morning, Josef stirs again, and his mind fills with thoughts of the nearby woman. Initially, his impure reflections bother him greatly. He knows he shouldn't be thinking about Regina like that — especially today, the day before he completes his mission. But the ideas in his head are too delightful to dismiss.

In the long run, the possibility of enjoying his last day on earth to the fullest consumes Josef to the exclusion of everything else. He settles on one of several enticing options, then relaxes and goes back to sleep until daybreak.

When Steve arrives at AISI, he sets his duffle bag on the floor to fix himself a cup of coffee.

Strangely, the place fills up quickly this morning, even though it's Sunday. However, the mood is depressing. There is none of the usual good-natured banter that has preceded past meetings.

When everyone is seated, Steve looks at the gloomy faces before him. "I know you're upset, and so am I," he begins in a somber tone. "It's no secret that the raid didn't go off as planned. We fucked up, big-time. People were killed, others were injured, and the public was caught up in the entire mess. My condolences go out to the families of all who died — the people in the neighboring apartment and the AISI and law enforcement officers. I also pray for the speedy recoveries of all the injured, including Special Agent DeMaria, who is now headed home."

"He was injured that badly?" asks Vincenzo.

"Yes, unfortunately. Your medical team did an excellent job taking care of him, but he's in no shape to continue with us. However, we're still here, and we have work to do. We have every reason to believe that Igmani is still out there, so we have to keep going until we find him."

Salvatore Caputi raises his head to speak. "We are all troubled by the casualties. But we must remember that three of those who died are the ones who wanted to kill our pope, and that is a great relief."

While murmurs of agreement spread around the room, the team's spirits lift.

"We will not give up trying to find that last bastard," Salvatore stresses. "We stationed officers outside the apartment building in case he tries to go back there. And la polizia received a good tip late last night."

"What did they find out?" asks Frank.

"The owner of a parking garage not far from the building flagged down one of the officers. After the explosion, he remembered that a van had been sitting in the same spot for a while and hadn't been moved. He said he never thought about it before, but now he is suspicious."

Steve is intrigued. "Did the officer inspect the vehicle?"

"It was gone when they got there. But the owner gave us the license plate number."

George asks, "Did you issue a BOLO?"

"What is BOLO?"

"It means 'Be on the Lookout.'"

"Sì, we sent the plate number to all law enforcement agencies."

"Was it back in the garage this morning?" George asks.

"No, it has not returned."

Steve glances at his longtime friend and catches a familiar look. "Well, that tells us something," he remarks. "If that asshole has the van, he could be anywhere. It's even possible that he left the scene altogether and is now with other accomplices we don't know anything about."

Now, the faces around the table are worried again.

"Angie, I'm gonna put you with Sal," Steve decides. "Work with him and the police to trace that van. We have no time to waste, so let's get back to it!"

Sunday Mass will be starting soon, so Regina needs to leave her apartment. But she hasn't seen Josef yet. She heard the water running behind the closed door of the bathroom a while ago and assumed he was taking a shower. But he hasn't come out yet, and she's getting impatient.

Hearing a noise, Regina looks up to see Josef standing in the middle of the room wearing nothing but a towel.

"Oh!" Regina splutters, flushing beet red at the nearly naked man. "Um… I am sorry, but I must leave now. Mass will be starting soon, and I do not want to be late. But you can stay," she adds hastily.

Josef knows that Regina is embarrassed, but he doesn't care that he has made her uneasy. "I took a shower while you were dressing," he explains nonchalantly. "I will be leaving soon as well. I want to see if I can get into my apartment this morning. After that, I need to go to work."

"Yes, I remember," responds Regina.

"I will be at a souvenir booth at Saint Peter's Square. My cousin owns it, but he had to go to Sicily. He asked me to operate it while he is gone."

"Oh. Okay," replies Regina, trying not to look where she knows she shouldn't.

"Please stop by the booth later."

"Um, I... Um, where is it?"

"Do you know where the bookstore is? The one in the plaza near the square?"

"Yes, I think I know the one you mean."

"The booth is outside of that store."

Regina nods. "Okay, I can go after Mass. You know, you can stay here as long as you like. I have an extra key..."

Turning around, Regina fishes through a drawer and holds out a spare.

"Thank you," Josef replies. "You are a kind woman."

When Josef takes the key, he squeezes Regina's hand and brushes his fingers lightly against her cheek.

Regina blushes again, but before she leaves, she kisses Josef lightly on the lips.

When Regina is gone, Josef calmly removes a fresh change of clothing from the escape bag he brought with him. It's one of the duffel bags he and his accomplices stored in the van for emergencies.

After dressing, he snoops around the apartment to make sure it will be safe to stay there. Satisfied that there's nothing to worry about, he digs through his escape bag to make sure his 9mm Beretta is still there.

Ready now to head outside, Josef locks the door and descends the stairs. On the sidewalk, he keeps his head down on his way to the parked van.

Assuming that it would be better not to go back to the garage, he parks his vehicle a few blocks away from his building and takes his time walking there. As he goes, he scans pedestrians, cars, and everything he passes. He wants to have enough time to change direction if he spots anything suspicious.

Behind him, a pair of Carabinieri patrolling the area spot the van after Josef is already around the corner. They position their car behind the suspicious vehicle and call the plate in.

Soon, a K-9 unit and other law enforcement vehicles filled with armed officers arrive with Frank and Salvatore.

Following established routine, everyone hangs back while the dog handlers approach the van. The dogs circle the van sniffing repeatedly, while the K-9 officers hold tight to the leashes of their partners.

"Looks good!" calls one of the officers at the German Shepherds' excitement.

"Yeah, keep going!" replies another.

When the dogs reach the back of the van, their behavior changes dramatically. They pull at their leashes, bark furiously and sit, a sure signal that explosives are nearby.

Residents of the area who heard the barking wonder what's going on. They peek out of their windows, curious to see officers and patrol cars on their street.

As a crowd begins to gather, Frank becomes afraid for their safety. "We need to get those people out of here," he urges Salvatore. "The bomb squad's coming; anything could happen."

"Sì, they will make an announcement."

Soon, a line of policemen pushes the onlookers away, while other officers order everyone living nearby to stay indoors and keep away from the windows.

Frank pulls out his phone to call Steve. "Hey, we found the van!" he tells him. "Dogs got a positive hit. We're waiting for the bomb squad now."

When Steve gets the call, he stops what he's doing at his perch on the basilica's roof to listen to Frank's report. "Call me after it's breached," is all he says before he slides the phone back into his pocket.

Steve is pleased that they found the van, but he's worried. "We don't need more bombs," he mumbles quietly. He shakes his head to stop himself from thinking about what could happen and concentrates instead on fastening a Leupold Mk IV M3 10x42 mm scope onto a suppressed Remington M24 SWS rifle.

If the former FSA director has a choice, the M24 is the gun he always chooses for jobs like this. It's highly accurate at 900 yards, and that distance can be stretched to over a thousand, if needed.

After the scope is on, Steve attaches the rifle to a Harris bipod. He leaves a box of .308 Winchester rounds in his duffel bag until he'll need it.

With the gun in place, the sniper puts his eye up to the scope to fine-tune the focusing. "Ha, I see you," Steve whispers when he spots Agent Kathryn Samuels standing near one of the large fountains in Saint Peter's Square. He uses Samuels as a target to make the necessary adjustments.

While he's doing that, Josef passes just outside of his line of vision, and Steve misses seeing him. Samuels doesn't see the assassin, either, as she's busy taking a photo of a couple of tourists who asked her for help.

With the gun sight ready for business, Steve turns on his communications gear. "Love your earrings," he says softly into his mic.

When Kathryn hears Steve's voice through her earpiece, she turns around to scan the basilica roof. "There you are," she says when she spots a head peeking over the wall. "It's hot down here. Can't believe it snowed yesterday."

"Yeah, go figure. We found the terrorists' van," Steve informs her. "There may be explosives inside, so I'll let you know if it pops."

Steve moves the gun's sight away from Samuels and uses it to scan the square. "Hey, where's the damage?" he mutters to himself.

He's surprised that he can't see any obvious signs that a car bomb recently exploded there. The only changes he notices are a missing guard shack and a new patch of concrete. Other than that, he sees nothing else amiss — until he trains his scope onto a couple of Swiss Guardsmen.

"Well, would you look at that!" he whistles quietly. Turning on his mic again, he says, "Hey, Samuels! Take a look at the Swiss Guards. I never thought I'd see modern weapons combined with centuries-old Renaissance dress uniforms!"

"Yeah, I saw that earlier. Looks funny, but I'm glad to see they're carrying. Ceremonial lances wouldn't be much help in a gunfight!"

Frank and Salvatore move behind a line of police tape where a group of people is watching a bomb squad officer guiding a tank-like robot to the rear of the van.

The crowd holds their breaths as the robot creeps toward its target, then stretches out an arm-like probe up to the window. Through a tiny camera, the explosive ordnance disposal officer sees an automatic rifle, some clothing, and two backpacks scattered across the vehicle's floor, but no people. Exploring further, he moves the robot to the driver's side window, but there is no one inside there either, so the officer directs the robot to retreat.

Simultaneously, two men waddle toward the van in heavy armor and protective gear. At the back doors, the Explosive Ordnance Disposal officers first test the door handle for booby traps. Finding nothing suspicious, they try to open the door, but it's locked, so one of them drills through the outside panel to unlock it manually.

Minutes later, the EOD team is x-raying the two backpacks inside a large, cast iron and steel enclosure in the bomb disposal truck, and a forensic team is swarming the vehicle.

While this is going on, Steve is on the roof overlooking Saint Peter's Square, searching for anything unusual in the ever-increasing crowd of people flocking to the famous tourist site. When his phone buzzes, he answers it with a tense, "Talk to me."

"We got into the van; no problems there," says Frank. "But there were a rifle and two backpacks filled with explosives inside it. The bomb guys are destroying the backpacks now, and forensics is working on the van."

"Okay, good," says Steve.

"Yeah, but there's something else. They also found clothing, wigs, and makeup. So Josef must be out there in disguise."

"Crap! That's just fuckin' great!" wails Steve. "How're we gonna spot him now, if we don't even know what the fucker looks like anymore?"

"Welcome to another day in this fucked-up world," retorts Frank cynically.

Wearied by the continual setbacks the team keeps coming up against, Steve lets out a heavy breath through tightly clenched teeth. "All right, listen," he says. "Sounds like the van's being taken care of, so come over to the basilica. I'll meet you at the bottom of the main steps."

When Mass ends, Regina hurries toward Saint Peter's Square. The unusually warm weather is delightful, and so are her thoughts about Josef. But her mood changes when she comes upon the damaged apartment building.

"Oh! How horrible!" she gasps, stopping to survey the destruction. "I hope that huge hole is not near Josef's apartment!" Regina shudders against the incomprehensible hatred that could cause such damage and makes the sign of the cross, then hurries to leave the building behind.

Near the square, Regina comes upon barricades in places they've never been before and somehow knows that they're related to the damaged building. Sucking in a breath, she winces at the sight of officers patrolling with dogs, and Carabinieri patrolmen cradling automatic weapons. With her head down, she makes a beeline for the bookstore where the booth is located.

"Hello!" Josef smiles broadly when he sees Regina. "I am happy you came!" he says, grabbing Regina's elbow to steer her away from a browsing customer. "Listen," he says quietly, "I was only able to get a few things out of my apartment. Can I stay with you, at least until Tuesday?"

"Yes, of course," Regina responds. "I passed your building on my way here, and it looks terrible! A man at my church said organized crime is to blame. He said the news is reporting that they are responding to the pope's excommunication decree."

"Oh?" replies Josef with feigned indifference. "Who knows about these things. Can you do me a favor? I am the only one here, and I need to step away for a minute. I do not want to shut the booth down, though."

Regina looks startled. "Uh... Are you asking me to take care of your customers? I do not know..."

"Oh, it is easy," Josef insists. "The bookstore permits me to use their bathroom, so I will not be long. All the items are marked with prices, so you do not have to do anything but take money. You just put the costs into the register and hit this button. Everything is automatic. Look, I will show you."

Regina watches closely as Josef repeats the instructions several times. "All right, I can do that," she says. "But do not be long."

At the same time as Josef is talking with Regina, Frank is weaving through strolling pedestrians in the square. Spying George reading a brochure, he sneaks up behind him and exclaims, "Well, I'll be damned! Is that you, George Jackson, being all touristy?"

George recognizes the voice and spins around with one finger raised in the air. "Who wants to know?" he asks crossly.

"Whoa, baby!" laughs Frank with his hands up in mock surrender. "I'm on my way to meet Steve. You wanna come?"

On the rooftop, Steve packs up his weapon and stows it inside a small closet that Vatican officials outfitted for his use.

The room is tight, but all he needs is a rollaway bed for one night. *I hope no one saw me out there,* he mumbles.

At ground level, Steve greets Frank and George, who are waiting for him at the foot of the steps in front of the large basilica doors. As they talk together, a middle-aged man approaches with a wide smile. "Hey, you guys are American, right?" he asks in a distinctive southern drawl. "Always happy to hear English when I'm overseas."

"Yeah, we're American," responds George. "Where are you from?"

"Born and raised in Louisiana!" the stranger responds proudly. Then he looks at Steve and says, "I saw you up on the roof a little while ago with a pretty large gun. I'm ex-Marine, so I know a sniper weapon when I see one. What's going on? There are tons of police all over the place, and the Swiss Guard is armed to the teeth."

The trio sizes up the squared-jawed man, trying not to show surprise that he saw Steve on the roof and wants to talk about it.

Having no recourse but to respond, Steve gives the man just enough information, so he'll go away. "The pope's gonna hold a public audience tomorrow with members of the G7, and we're helping with security," he explains.

"You had a suppressed .308 up there," smiles the jarhead. "That's some help. You guys expecting trouble?"

"Look," says Steve, "I don't know when you arrived in Rome, but the Mafia recently detonated a bomb here. So, from one ex-Marine to another, I advise you to avoid tomorrow's dog and pony show."

"Gotcha," responds the man, giving Steve a fist bump. "Semper Fi," he adds, waving to them as he walks away.

"That was uncomfortable," comments Frank. "Hope no

one else wants to question you."

Steve shrugs. "Nothing I can do about it. But let's find a better place to talk."

Under one of the colonnades, Steve asks his friends, "Now that Josef's apartment is wrecked, do either of you have any thoughts about where he would go?"

"Maybe he's spending time at the Grand Mosque," suggests George. "They could have a place there where pilgrims can sleep."

Steve raises his brows in thought. "That sounds interesting. Get the Ravens to scope that place out again, would ya, George? But don't go in until Caputi gets permission for us to be there."

"Will do. I'll go find Raphael."

"All right. Aw, shit. Look at the time!" Steve exclaims. "I haven't had anything to eat yet. Let's round up the guys for a late breakfast at my hotel. Can you find Samuels, Angie? Ask her to join us."

"Yeah, sure."

"Thanks. I'll meet you at the hotel."

Suddenly, Steve realizes that he didn't invite George to breakfast, too. "I owe you, Geo!" he calls out as George walks away.

"Yeah, more than you realize!" George calls back.

CHAPTER THIRTY-TWO

As promised, Josef returns to the booth quickly, bringing food for himself and Regina. The booth is busy this morning, so they try to consume the sparkling water and fresh fruit he brought between customers. But it's not easy. T-shirts, rosaries, magnets of famous Roman sites, and other trinkets are popular with the visiting crowd.

Josef edges up to Regina. "I am sorry," he says. "We can sometimes get very busy. I am happy that you are here to help."

"You are welcome," Regina replies. "It became easier once I remembered my retail training. I once worked in a store in my hometown."

Steve notices a crowd gathering around a particular souvenir stand on the way to his hotel and recognizes it as the one Frank bought something from the other day. Curious, he considers stopping to see why it's so popular, but then he remembers that his friends are waiting for him. "Aw, we don't need any of that stuff anyway," he mutters, and continues on his way.

This morning, Diane is trying to ignore the pointed stares of people passing through the hotel lobby. She knows they recognize her, so she's happy that she spent a little extra time getting ready for the day. Though she didn't put the glam on, she's still stunning in a more casual way. Today, she's wearing a yellow sundress she bought in Rome, and she caught her blonde hair up in a loose ponytail.

At any other time, Diane would be happy to talk to her fans. But right now, she hopes no one wants to chat; she's not in the mood. She's hungry, and Steve is late.

Tapping her foot impatiently, she wonders yet again, *Where is he?* And with a heavy sigh, she rechecks the time on her wristwatch, even though she knows it couldn't have changed much from the last time she looked.

At that moment, a familiar screech snaps her head up. Searching the lobby for the source, she widens her eyes when she sees her former personal assistant pointing at her excitedly from the elevator bank.

"Tammy!" Diane cries, running toward her longtime friend and business associate.

"Diane? What on earth are you doing here?" Tammy screeches, reaching out to hug Diane.

"Really?" asks Diane, placing her hands on her hips. "Have I been gone that long? Did you forget that I moved to Italy?"

"I didn't forget, you silly woman!" Tammy shouts. "I can't believe that I ran into you at my hotel!"

"Your hotel? Are you staying here, too? What, are you working for a celebrity who's in the country?"

"No, I'm not working!" Tammy replies, grabbing Diane's hands and jumping up and down like a child with a secret. "I finally took the plunge! I did it, Di! I took advantage of all the vacation time I banked and came to Italy! You know how much I always wanted to come here! I'm treating myself to a grand vacation!"

"That's fantastic!" cries Diane happily. "I know that going to Italy has been on your bucket list for years!"

"Yes, but how weird is it for us to see each other in a random hotel?" Tammy holds her hand up to stop Diane from answering. "Wait," she says. "Before you say anything, I have to tell you that you're looking fabulous, my friend! *La dolce vita* must really be true!"

As the women chat, Steve approaches them with a broad grin. "Well, well, well," he declares. "I can't believe I'm seeing you in Italy, Tammy! You've been talking about coming here for as long as I've known you!"

Seeing Steve, Tammy screeches again and holds out her arms. "Now, you!" she squeals, squeezing tightly. "Oh, I've missed you guys terribly!"

"I bet you missed me more," teases Steve. "We were just about to get breakfast. Why don't you join us? It'll give you two a chance to catch up."

"Oh, I wish I could!" Tammy replies with her smile fading quickly. "I'm on a tour, and our bus is taking our group to Pompeii this morning."

"Oh, you're going to love Pompeii," remarks Diane, "but it won't take all day to see it. What are you doing after that?"

"We're going to Sorrento and the Amalfi Coast."

Diane inhales sharply. "We live on the Amalfi Coast, Tammy! You should have let me know you'd be here! I could have given you a personal tour!"

Steve has an idea. "How much longer will you be in Italy?"

"Today's excursion is our last one. We'll be back in Rome late tonight, and then we stay here for another five days before flying home."

"Hey, that's perfect!" exclaims Steve. "That means you have time to visit with Diane! Dee, you can bring her home for a visit. You know we only live an hour away."

"Well… I don't know," says Diane. "What if you need something and I'm not here?"

"Dee, I'll be busy for another couple of days, so I won't be seeing much of you, anyway. And if I need anything, I have plenty of people to call upon."

"But Steve—"

"I'll be fine, Dee; I won't be alone. Catch up with Tammy. Take her home with you tomorrow. If you book an EasyJet to Naples tonight, I'll arrange for a chopper to take you the rest of the way." Turning to Tammy, Steve asks her why she didn't let them know she was coming to Italy.

"I didn't want to bother you guys. You two live here, but I'm just a tourist."

"That's ridiculous!" insists Diane. "It's wonderful to see you! We miss our friends from home!"

Steve knows the ladies want to talk, so he hugs Tammy goodbye and tells Diane that he's going to get them a table.

"Okay, be there in a minute," says Diane.

On the way into the restaurant, Steve sees Frank Angelo and Agent Kathryn Samuels entering the hotel. "Hi, guys. I was just going to get a table. Diane will join us in a minute."

When Diane joins the group, she takes the empty seat next to Steve. "I'd really like to catch up with Tammy," she says, "but I don't want to leave y—"

Steve stops her with a finger over her lips. "No worries, Dee. Have fun."

Frank overhears their conversation and asks, "Are you going somewhere, Diane?"

"Her former assistant is here in Rome," Steve explains. "She's with a tour group that's headed to the Amalfi Coast today. After that, she has five days in Rome to do whatever she wants."

"Wow, she should see your villa while she's here," comments Frank.

"That's exactly what I said!" laughs Steve, looking pointedly at Diane. "And I'm trying to convince Dee to take her to our house for a few days."

"That's a great idea," agrees Frank. "Don't worry, Diane. I'll watch Chic for you."

"Oh, great," laughs Diane. "Now I'm really worried! The coyote watching the fox? Yeah, that'll work!"

At that moment, the waiter arrives to take their orders just as George runs up to their table. "Chic!" he pants. "Can we talk? In private?"

"Yeah, what's up?"

Excusing himself, Steve follows George into the lobby. "Why aren't you with Raphael?" he asks, pointing to a couple of chairs near a stone fireplace.

"Accola said he put the Ravens on high alert."

"Uh, oh. Why'd he do that?"

"His Holiness' schedule for Monday has changed. He's no longer going to greet the French and German leaders on the steps of Saint Peter's. The pope's office decided that the people should see the pontiff alone first, so he's going to do his usual tour through the crowd in the popemobile. After the people greet him, he's going to pick up the two leaders in the popemobile and bring them to the basilica."

"What?" exclaims Steve. "Colonel Accola agreed to this?"

"No, he objected, but they ignored him."

Steve moans and holds his head in his hands. "What are they thinking? Now Josef won't need to get too close! Depending on where he stands in the crowd, they could drive right past him! And then, he'd get three birds with the price of one! Fuck!"

"I know," George says glumly. "It'll be a miracle if we can prevent a tragedy. Colonel Accola was livid. So, what do we do now?"

Steve runs his fingers through his hair while he thinks.

"Status quo," he replies. "We do what we came to do. But we're going to need more assets in the square. Go back to the Ravens. I'll get the others and meet everyone in the conference room." Steve rises from his chair and looks toward the restaurant. "Diane's gonna have a fit!" he moans again.

Back at the table, Steve doesn't sit down, so Diane knows something's up. "What is it?" she asks with a frown.

"Honey, we gotta go," he says, pointing at Frank and Kathryn. "Don't worry; it's nothing serious." Looking around, he beckons the waiter to the table. "Let me know what you arranged with Tammy. I'll get that AISI chopper for you."

Steve informs the waiter that they have to leave unexpectedly. "Can we take our meals to go?" he asks.

"*Sì, subito*," replies the young man, hurrying off to bring them disposable containers for their "family bags," as they're called in Italy.

When Steve is ready to leave, he leans over to his wife for a hug.

"You're such a lousy liar," Diane whispers into his ear. "I always know when something's wrong. Do I have to remind you again to be careful?"

Inside the AISI conference room, Steve holds his family bag high so everyone can see it. "Hey, everyone! We brought our breakfasts with us today! Hope you don't mind loud chewing!"

Steve is trying to sound cheerful before starting to discuss more serious matters. However, Colonel Accola isn't interested in light banter.

"I vehemently tried to change the pope's mind," the commander states bitterly, "but he insists on good optics. He said he appreciates my concerns, but in the end, he agreed with his office's decision. Signore Ciccone, this team has been hit with obstructions from day one, so I will not hold it against you if you want to leave us."

"Huh? This is highly unusual coming from you, Theodore. What is fueling this change of heart?"

"His Holiness will now meet the foreign leaders at the far end of the square. Then, all of them will drive through the crowd together."

"What about security?"

"Pope Urban is confident that a larger than normal police presence will deter anyone with 'bad intentions.'"

"Who's advising him that way?" grumbles Steve.

"His people may have told him that there is only one terrorist now."

"Oh, great. Don't they know that one person acting alone is much harder to stop than a group? And if Igmani follows the pattern of other terrorists, this 'one guy' knows that it's all up to him now, and that will make him willing to do anything necessary to complete the job."

Steve turns to his friends. "Angie and Geo, I told you from the start that you're not obligated to be on this team. I asked you to join the group as a favor to me. But it's getting dicey now, and I don't want to put you at any more risk than you feel up to. I'll be up on the rooftop, far away from the killing zone, but the rest of you will be right down there in the mix. People may be killed or injured on Monday. You can back out if you want."

Frank and George look at each other with raised brows; they're surprised by Steve's statement. They've never heard him talk like this before.

George says, "I understand what you're saying, Chic, and I appreciate the warning. But I know the risks and I'm willing to stay. Anyway," he adds, glancing sideways at Frank, "you can't live forever, right?"

But Frank isn't as optimistic. "Chic, this is too screwed up for my taste," he responds, shaking his head at George. "Thanks for the heads up, but I'm not going to stay. I don't want any more of this bull crap. Sorry, old man. I don't want to take a chance of dying or getting injured; I just want to enjoy my retirement in peace. So I'm gonna take you up on your offer. I'm out. I'm going back to Sorrento."

When Frank stands, George pulls on his arm. "Whoa, where do you think you're going, *amico*? You can't leave without saying goodbye!"

George rises to his full height and grips Frank's shoulders, hugging him tightly. "I'll be back at your house as soon as this is over," he tells his buddy.

Then Steve moves in for his own farewell. "No hard feelings, pal. Wish I was going with you. This thing went south real fast."

After Frank says goodbye to each member of the group, he walks out of the room, closing the door gently.

"There goes the only smart one," sighs Steve as he and George retake their seats. "But we have a job to do, so let's get back to it. We're going to need extra K9 units on patrol in the entire area. And can we get more officers from other..."

Steve suddenly stops talking. He spies George out of the corner of his eye, slowly sliding Frank's breakfast over to join his own.

George wonders why Steve is no longer speaking, so he looks up to find everyone staring at him. "My mother always said, 'Never let good food go to waste,'" he declares with a sheepish grin.

As George takes everything out of the bags, the usually tight-lipped Raven dons his mirrored sunglasses. "I respect the American for being honest," he says, surprising everyone. "Mr. Angelo is brave for speaking his mind. But with God's help, we will prevail against this foe. Now, I must also leave to prepare my team. And that includes you, Mr. Jackson."

George frowns at the two containers of food in front of him. "Fuck," he grumbles. "Guess I'm gonna be too busy to eat this morning. Anyone want some free breakfast?"

CHAPTER THIRTY-THREE

The next day, Diane and Tammy take the EasyJet flight Diane booked the night before. Their trip will take them to Naples Airport, where a helicopter arranged by AISI will shuttle them the rest of the way to the Ciccone's house in Ravello.

Tammy is too excited to sit still on the short flight to Naples. Between gossiping with Diane about the latest goings-on in Hollywood, she looks down every chance she can get at the Mediterranean Sea and the rugged Italian coastline. Oohing and aahing, she points at what she says is beautiful, even though she can't make out any details from so high up in the sky.

Diane is happy that she's able to show her friend a good time. But she's also worried. During the rare moments that Tammy isn't chattering about something or other, she mutters short prayers for her husband and the others who are putting their lives on the line to defend the pope.

Somewhere below the Easy Jet, Frank is also enjoying himself. After he left the AISI building, he rented a classic Alfa Romeo Duetto Spider for the trip back to Sorrento, and now, he's driving along the Amalfi Coast with the wind whistling through his hair.

The rental agency clerk advised Frank that the speed limit on Amalfi Drive ranged from 28-45 kph, which equates to a more familiar 18-28 mph for the American. The slow speed limit surprised Frank, until he remembered that he wouldn't be on the autostrada, but on a twisting and narrow road with dizzying drops and spectacular scenery.

Though Frank is usually a cautious driver, he can't help flooring it as much as he dares. Whenever there's a break in traffic and no blind spots ahead, he lets the car go. His intention on this trip home is not to drive fast, but to fly low.

In Rome, Steve is back at his sniper position on the basilica's roof. The day is warm and pleasant, so he removes his jacket before setting up his rifle again. *Hey*, he thinks, *if the temperature holds into the evening, I'd love to sleep under the stars above Saint Peter's! Maybe I can move my bed outside tonight.*

Steve attaches his rifle to the bipod, then checks the scope's focus by looking down at the square. *There better be a ton of undercover officers among the pilgrims tomorrow*, he muses.

Steve remains up on the roof for the rest of the day, only leaving for short periods of time. He packed his bag with enough snacks, sandwiches, and water to get by until the following evening, if necessary.

Later, when dusk closes in, the activity in the square shifts to more and more police and fewer and fewer visitors. Because of the dwindling crowd, Josef decides to close up shop early and go back to Regina's apartment. He suspects that the police will bring in the K9 units again, so he doesn't want them to find his gun in the kiosk.

On the way to Regina's apartment, Josef's mind turns to the last time he saw his companions alive. He remembers how they talked through their plan and made sure their weapons worked perfectly. Naturally, they didn't know that paradise would call them sooner than they thought. He wonders fleetingly if they would have done anything differently if they had known.

When Josef nears the Passetto, his mission turns into stark reality as the tangible evidence of his comrades' martyrdom hits him full force.

"Allahu Akbar," he murmurs appreciatively at the sight of the gaping hole.

Up on the roof, Steve continues to look down over the thinning crowd and the growing presence of law enforcement. He notes that in one area, some of the officers are directing the placement of temporary barricades around the rows of chairs set up for the papal audience. In another place, he sees two policemen beginning their patrols from opposite ends of the square. Watching them curiously, he sees them weave through the chairs and meet at the obelisk, where they chat and have a smoke.

Steve isn't happy. "Doesn't look like they're taking this too seriously," he mutters dismally.

Behind him, Colonel Accola appears, holding a large bag. "I thought you would like a hot meal," he says.

"Thanks," replies Steve, looking over his shoulder at the Colonel. "That smells great!"

"What have you seen so far?"

"It's the calm before the storm. You know, I thought I

was done with this shit, but here I am in Rome, staring down the barrel of a high-powered rifle again."

Accola pops the caps on two cold Peronis. "We have always tried to make this church one of the safest places in the world," he tells Steve, handing one bottle over. "Yet tomorrow, it may become a place no one would recognize."

Steve downs half of the popular Italian beer, then peeks into the bag of food. "Well, you know that history repeats itself. Ever since this started, I had the feeling that we were fighting the crusades again."

When Josef enters Regina's apartment at the end of the day, she's cooking a meal of fresh fish and vegetables. "I hope you like this," she says. "I am trying to become a better cook."

Josef drops his backpack on the floor next to the couch. "On the way here, I passed my apartment building and stopped to talk to the manager," he says coolly. "The police are letting people back in, so this will be the last night I will be staying here."

In the pre-dawn hours, the moon dips below the horizon while the sun starts its daily climb. Though the sky is beginning to lighten, it's still early, and most residents of the Italian peninsula are sleeping.

However, Diane is already up. Worry for the love of her life kept her tossing and turning much of the night, so she decided not to fight it anymore.

In the kitchen, Diane yawns and pours out the last bit of

coffee from the Moka pot. The simple stove-top coffee maker is a symbol of Italian culture and a staple in many homes, but it can be a little tricky to use. Every Italian they met urged them to buy one, so Diane learned how to use it pretty quickly.

Yawning again, Diane turns up the heat for another pot. Today, she's going to need more than a couple of cups of rich coffee to keep her going. Suddenly, her cell phone ring-tone pierces the villa's stillness, and she answers with a quick "Pronto!" hoping the shrill sound won't disturb Tammy.

"Hi, it's Ang. I hope I didn't wake you; I couldn't sleep."

"What's wrong? Is Steve okay?"

"Yeah, I guess so, but I'm not in Rome anymore; I'm back in Sorrento. I've had my fill of danger and excitement. All I want now is a nice, quiet retirement. So I'm here if you want to talk, or if you want some company today. I know you're probably worried."

"Angie... You quit the team? But today is Monday!" Diane is astonished that one of the musketeers has turned away from a career built on acts of courage on the very day of the pope's public appearance.

"Yeah, it's time, and there are plenty of others who can do what I do," Frank contends. "I know you think I'm letting Steve down, but you may have noticed that I'm moving a lot slower lately. My body ain't what it used to be, and it could be dangerous for a lot of people if I don't acknowledge that. I don't want to jeopardize anyone with my slowing reflexes, especially my good buds. You know I love those guys."

Diane sighs wistfully. "I guess that makes sense. I just wish it didn't happen today."

"It'll be all right. I wouldn't have done it now if I weren't sure there were enough skilled professionals on the team."

"I know," says Diane. "I wish Steve would slow down,

too, but you know him. I appreciate your call, Angie, but Tammy is staying with me for a couple of days, so I'm going to be busy showing her around. She always wants to be on the go, so there probably won't be much time for me to think too much."

"All right, that's good. But remember my offer."

"Thanks, I will. Take care, my friend."

This morning, Josef is also up early, though he had no trouble sleeping through the night. As soon as his eyes popped open, he tossed the covers aside and tiptoed through the shadowy apartment, hoping not to awaken Regina. He used the weak light of the rising sun to find his way to the bathroom and turned on the water for a shower. Today is the day he's been planning for a long time, and he can't wait to get started.

As quiet as Josef was, Regina still heard him moving around. She's not used to having someone else in her home, so the slightest sound woke her.

Though Regina is awake, she remains in bed, listening to the sound of the running water. *I cannot believe there is a man in my apartment!* she reflects with wonder. *I only met him a few days ago, but he seems nice. It is a pity that he must leave today. I want to let him know that I like him and would like to keep seeing him, but how can I do that without seeming desperate? Oh, I know! I will leave him a note!*

Regina wants to carry out her plan before Josef comes out of the bathroom. So, clad only in her short nightie, she jumps out of bed and pads into the living room to write a short message.

Now, where should I put this so he will be sure to find it? she wonders, looking around the room. When her eyes light upon the backpack, she grins. *That is perfect! He keeps that with him all the time!*

Hoping that Josef will be surprised, Regina bends down next to the bag and pulls on the zipper. But as the opening widens, her eyes grow larger and larger.

For several heart-stopping moments, Regina stares un-believingly at something that looks very much like an explo-sive device attached to a jacket filled with nails. "What the...?" she mutters, suddenly afraid of the man she knows nothing about.

At that moment, a pair of strong hands wrap tightly around Regina's head and mouth, forcing her to fall backward onto the floor. Naked and wet from the shower, Josef tries to keep a firm grasp on the panicked woman, but Regina kicks and squirms in every direction.

Minutes ago, Josef thought he heard a noise when he shut the water off in the bathroom. Hungry for breakfast, he hoped it was Regina moving around in the kitchen, so he cracked the door open and peered out. Instead, what he saw shocked him: Regina was snooping in his assassin's bag!

Josef was furious! This person he thought he could trust had found his terrorist equipment! In a wild rage, he flew out of the bathroom, intending to do whatever was necessary to stop the woman from sounding an alarm.

Now, Josef is holding Regina down while trying to keep away from her feet. She's been kicking at anything she can to get out of his grasp, and he knows she could do him some harm, so he looks for an effective way to keep her quiet.

That will do, he presumes, settling on a brass sculpture on a bookshelf. It seems like just the thing to knock Regina out with, and it's only a few feet away.

Grunting heavily, Josef drags the thrashing woman over

to the shelf where the heavy object sits. When it's within reach, he releases one of Regina's hands, grabs the statue, and smashes it against her temple.

When Regina goes limp, he drags her into the bedroom and works to catch his breath. Though he's tired from his exertions, he knows that Regina could regain consciousness at any moment, so he hurries to the kitchen to find something he can use.

After rummaging through several drawers, he rushes back to the bedroom and stands over Regina's inert figure for a long moment. *It is a shame that you found out,* he mutters angrily. *You should not have done that.*

As Josef stares at the unconscious woman, an urgent need builds, one that he knows will not subside until it's satisfied. To still the urge, he persuades himself that he will not be content until the infidel has been taught a lesson, and lifts Regina onto the bed.

With duct tape from the kitchen, Josef binds Regina's hands and feet to the bedposts, then stuffs a dishcloth into her mouth and secures it with more tape.

Hungry for release, the assassin rips off Regina's underwear and rapes his victim mercilessly. The violence of the act brings Regina back to consciousness, but her muffled screams only increase Josef's pleasure.

When Josef is finally satiated, he stares down at his handiwork, confident that he has performed his duty against the prying infidel. He's proud of his accomplishment; happy that he could do this last thing before going to his reward.

With unseeing eyes, Josef gazes at his victim. Then, after a moment of strange calm, he turns away and leaves the room.

The pope's surviving murderer is now on high alert. While Regina cries and moans in the other room, he wriggles into his suicide vest and tapes the detonator to his right arm, exactly the way he practiced it hundreds of times. Then, he pulls on a roomy hockey jersey and a gray hoodie and tucks a 9mm Beretta into his waistband.

While Josef slips his backpack over his shoulders, he glances briefly toward the bedroom, but Regina's whimpering still has no effect on him. With single-minded determination, he pulls the hood low over his forehead and leaves the apartment, making sure to lock the door securely behind him.

CHAPTER THIRTY-FOUR

Inside Vatican City, Steve munches on a protein bar and sips from a bottle of water *non-gassatta* — non-carbonated. He likes seltzer products, but the gas sometimes makes him belch, so he tries to stay away from it.

Down below, the square is relatively empty — it's still early. Only a few police officers are on duty at the moment.

However, by the time Steve slips into a fresh shirt and stows his sleeping bag, a smattering of pilgrims has begun to line up outside the checkpoints leading into the square. Seeing them, Steve chuckles; *Guess they want the good seats.*

The pope's defender grabs his rifle and settles into position. With his eye up to the scope, he swings the gun around in a wide sweep to check the square for suspicious activity, and stops when the souvenir booth comes into view. "Now, there's an enterprising guy," he mutters. "The early bird always catches the worm, I guess."

Steve trains his eye on Josef while he opens the booth for the day. But there is nothing unusual in the man's activities, so he moves on.

It seems that Josef made a good choice when he got dressed that morning. The hood he's still wearing low over his forehead kept Steve from getting a good look at him.

Before George leaves his room, he clicks on Special Agent Kathryn Samuels' number. "A bunch of us are gonna meet one last time," he tells her. "So you should be there, too. It'll be the last chance for anyone to raise concerns."

"All right. Same café as before?"

"Yeah. A bunch of Ravens will be joining as well. By the way, they'll be packing heavy."

At the café, Kathryn quickly spots concealed 9mm Uzis on the hips of all the Ravens. *George was right,* she thinks, recalling his heads-up. Though the weapons are small and compact, the FBI agent knows what to look for.

Remarkably, Raphael takes charge of this meeting since Steve isn't there. He says, "I know all of you are professionals, and I have confidence in every one of you. However, it bears repeating that every one of us needs to be on exceptionally high alert today. When you arrive at the square, spread out and keep in constant communication with each other."

"Are there any extra precautions this morning?" asks a Raven.

"Sì. The police will be using large dump trucks as barriers to prevent unauthorized vehicles from entering the area."

"Va bene."

"And as you know, we also have snipers set up on the rooftops. Other questions?"

Kathryn speaks up. "Is there any information on our suspect?"

"Nothing so far. Anyone else?"

Another Raven asks, "Did the police put extra officers on

duty?"

"Sì. Extra police and Carabinieri came in from neighboring cities."

Raphael waits a minute for other questions, but there are none. "All right," he continues. "Remember, when we find our man, we neutralize him and isolate him immediately. The square will be crowded, so we need to do everything possible to prevent accidental involvement of bystanders."

George raises a finger. "Raphael is right. But our best hope is to prevent Josef from breaching the barricades at all. There is no way we can fail at this today!"

At the booth, Josef closely monitors this morning's activities. He's alone now, with no backup, so he needs to be alert.

Today, more than the usual number of tourists, Roman citizens, law enforcement officers, and camera crews are scurrying around because the pope's general audience was moved to this day, and heads of state are expected to appear with him. To Josef, these people look like an army of ants swarming over discarded sweets, instead of excited visitors hoping to witness the pope's popular weekly tradition.

It doesn't take long for the streets around Saint Peter's Square to fill with even more people wanting to go through the temporary security checkpoints. Now there are thousands, and the souvenir stand is busy with people buying trinkets to remember their visit.

When all available chairs inside the square's secure zone fill up, police direct the remaining pilgrims to find a place to stand on the Via della Conciliazione. Most are willing to follow instructions; however, some balk at not getting one of the coveted seats. Police officers remain patient, but they don't give an inch.

When Pope Urban IV finally arrives, the crowds are thrilled. As he cruises by in his famous popemobile, people click cell phone cameras and jostle for space with others who tearfully cry, *"Viva il Papa!"* In some sections, spontaneous songs of joy break out, while people in other areas try to stand out by waving small flags and banners in the pope's direction.

While this is going on inside the square, George and Agent Samuels make their way into the mass of people standing around the souvenir booth. Here, the crowd is so thick that it's hard to keep an eye on everyone, but they do their best.

When the pope approaches this area, Josef removes his hoodie and leaves the booth. To get to where he needs to be, he pushes roughly through the crowd, but it's hard going. Everyone is focused on the pope, and no one wants to give up their place.

Nearby, Kathryn notices movement out of the corner of her eye. She cranes her head in that direction and spots a young man elbowing people aside and forcefully inserting himself into every small space he can find. Thinking that it's odd to see someone behaving so rudely in this crowd, she eyes him closely.

Suddenly, Kathryn whispers into her mic, "I got him. It's the guy running the booth behind us. There's a small metal box with a red button in his hand, and he's wearing an oversized jersey that can cover anything. There may be a bomb under his shirt."

With widened eyes, George looks at Kathryn, who nods in Josef's direction.

"I see him," replies George. He's not wearing a disguise."

Kathryn alerts nearby Ravens while she and George circle around the assassin as best they can. In front of them,

Josef continues to push his way forward, closer and closer to a place where the pope will likely pass by.

When several Ravens arrive in the already packed space, people around them become annoyed. But the Ravens don't notice.

Suddenly, George broadcasts an urgent message: "He pressed the button. No aggressive moves. Keep calm in the crowd."

This morning, most shops within Vatican City have suspended operations until the papal audience is over. However, it's business as usual in the surrounding city of Rome.

At the Deutsche Bank near the Grand Mosque, manager Helmut Muller notices an empty desk. "Where is Regina Cappelli?" he questions his head teller. "Did she call in sick today?"

The German woman shakes her head. "No, Mr. Muller, we have not heard from her."

"Did anyone call her?"

"Yes, but she did not answer."

"Hmm. She is usually dependable. You would agree, would you not?"

"Yes, sir. It is not like Regina to ignore a call from the office. She will usually notify us before the start of her shift if she will be out for any reason."

Muller reaches into his pocket and hands the woman a key to his Audi. "We should check on her. Ask Security to go to her apartment."

When Steve heard George's alert, he swung his scope around to track the assassin from above, and the other snipers did the same.

Below them, George is shouldering his way as close to Josef as he dares. He needs to be extra cautious because Pope Urban is standing nearby, outside the protection of his armored vehicle. Against advice, the pontiff wants to greet Germany's and France's leaders at their limousines, where they've been waiting for him at the edge of the square.

Josef mindlessly continues to push people aside as he creeps closer and closer to the pope. Now that his martyrdom is so close at hand, his religious training is taking over, and he's no longer fully aware of his actions. But he's still nervous and stops often to wipe a sleeve across his forehead.

While keeping an eye on his target, George assesses the risks of acting in such close proximity to dignitaries and innocent bystanders. If he waits too long, the assassin will surely detonate the bomb and there will be many deaths and injuries, including several high-profile ones. And if he acts too soon, the bomb could still go off, with the same devastating effects.

In the end, George decides that it's best to move quickly. *If I can keep the killer's hand closed, he won't be able to arm the bomb.*

With no more time to waste, George lunges toward Josef, and in one swift move, clamps his hand tightly around the hand holding the detonator and bends Josef's arm around his back.

George's action throws Josef off-guard for a moment, but the killer won't allow himself to be stopped. The mission is the only thing that matters to him, so he fights George like a crazed tiger, trying every way possible to break George's grip.

As the men thrash about, the people around them scatter frantically, preventing anyone on the team from getting close enough to help.

Soon, chaos reigns everywhere. People shout, "Bomb!" and run through the square, causing panic among the seated crowd. Without thinking, everyone exits the square en masse. In the bedlam, terrified people surge around the limousines, trapping the frightened dignitaries inside their vehicles.

Thankfully, Josef's intended target is no longer in harm's way. The instant the pope's guards learned of the struggle within the crowd, they ushered the pontiff back into the popemobile and raced him into the safety of Vatican buildings.

The Deutsche Bank security officer is careful not to react when the head teller hands him the key to the bank manager's car. "Be protective of it, Franco. Return quickly, and do not damage it," the woman stresses in her stiff German manner.

Though the woman is unpleasant, the security chief is much too excited to get behind the wheel of the Audi A8 to let her brusque manner spoil his day. Driving the Audi will be much better than taking his old scooter, and it will be a pleasant distraction in his boring workday, even though he doesn't understand why he's going out in it at all.

When the security officer is inside the car, he leans back against the leather seat with a contented sigh. "I could get used to this," he murmurs, luxuriating in the comfort of the high-end vehicle.

The bank employee turns the radio on and runs his hand over the smooth leather of the steering wheel. But reality soon hits. He knows his meager salary and the high price of gasoline place a car like this out of his reach, so he sighs with disappointment and turns to the business at hand.

Reaching into his pocket, he pulls out the address the teller gave him. "Oh, damn. This is close; it is a shame that it is not further away. I was hoping to spend more time in this beautiful machine."

At Regina's apartment building, the guard finds her unit and rings the bell, wondering again why the manager sent him there. *She's probably sick and overslept. That's why she didn't call the bank.*

When no one answers, he knocks and presses the bell again. But there is still no response, so he pounds on the door and calls out Regina's name.

Unexpectedly, muted sounds come from inside the apartment, making the hairs on the man's arms stand up. Cocking his head toward the door, he listens closely and is sure he can hear someone crying.

"Regina?" he calls again, loudly. "It is Franco…from the bank! Are you all right?" When the crying increases, he shouts, "Can you open the door? We are worried about you!" But the door stays closed, and the sounds continue. "I am coming in!" he yells.

Concern for his co-worker compels the overweight security guard to do something he never thought he'd do.

Using his shoulder as a battering ram, he shoves at the door with all his might, but he only gets a wave of pain for his effort. Switching tactics, he kicks forcefully at the doorjamb, and this time it opens.

The crying sounds lead the bank guard to Regina's bedroom, where he hesitates at the partially closed doorway. Modesty makes him wonder if he should barge in or not, but the continued whimpering propels him forward.

"Wha...?" he chokes out, his eyes bulging out of his head as the door swings open.

In front of him, Regina lies spread-eagled on the bed, gagged, and tied to the bedpost. "What on earth...? Who did this? What happened to you?" asks the guard while he removes the tape and gag from Regina's mouth.

"Il Papa!" shouts Regina. "You must tell the police! He is going to kill the pope!"

Though George is thirty years older and twenty pounds heavier than the would-be terrorist, he easily tackles Josef to the ground and pins him there when his adrenaline takes over.

Under George's weight, Josef can only move his arms and legs, so he wriggles as much as possible to shake George off. However, the man won't budge. Fleetingly, Josef wonders whether the infidel restraining him is as strong as he seems, or, can it be — horror of horrors — that Allah has abandoned him because he failed at his mission?

George keeps his hand over Josef's, even amidst the ruckus below him, while he strains to keep his balance on the moving target. Grunting heavily, he keys his mic and shouts, "Hey! You gonna take this guy down already? I don't know how much longer I can hold on!"

Steve keeps his gaze steady. "Too risky; I might hit you instead."

"Look; I'd rather be shot — in a non-critical area, mind you! — than be blown to bits by this fucker's vest! Crap! He won't stay still! I think I'm losing my grip!"

"Okay," says Steve. "Hold onto that detonator... Don't let it go for any reason."

Steve concentrates on the image in his scope, exhales slowly, then holds his breath as he squeezes the trigger between heartbeats.

Instantly, a suppressed .308 round penetrates George's back just beneath his collarbone and exits into Josef's temple. George screams in pain and slumps over the assassin but keeps a tight hold on Josef's hand.

When Raphael sees George fall, he rushes over and clamps his hand over George's. "I got it," he says. "You can relax now."

On the rooftop, Steve throws his rifle aside and bounds down the stairs two at a time, cursing and praying at the same time. When he reaches ground level, he runs through the empty church and exits through the massive doors at the front — straight into bedlam. All around the square, frantic people are climbing over tipped chairs and barricades in a headlong rush to get away from unseen danger.

At George's side, Agent Samuels applies pressure to her colleague's wound while Raphael works on the detonator. Slowly and steadily, Raphael exchanges his hand for George's, all the while keeping the red button pressed.

"Ooooh, oww...damn, this hurts!" moans George through excruciating pain. "Shit. Chic owes me more than a steak dinner this time! Maybe I should ask for a Ferrari!"

George grits his teeth when another wave of pain takes over. "I swear, I really gotta get out of this business," he groans.

When Steve arrives, he's relieved to see his friend alive and breathing. Kneeling close, he asks anxiously, "How ya doin', pal?"

George smiles weakly at Steve's red and teary eyes. "Got allergies?" he asks.

"Yeah. What color Ferrari ya want?"

Soon, explosives professionals take over and force Steve and Agent Samuels a safe distance away.

"This guy is dead!" declares an officer hovering over Josef. "But the vest is active!"

Another shouts, "Get the wounded man out of here so we can deactivate that bomb!"

When George is out of the way, men in heavy padding surround Josef and Raphael. Some study the vest, while others discuss the best way to coax the detonator from Raphael's grip.

While the professionals work, international news crews try everything they can to get close to the story. They try cajoling and bullying the Ravens and the armed Swiss Guardsmen keeping them back, but nothing they do breaks their ranks.

Suddenly, a reporter spots a group of robed men approaching and notifies the others, who surge forward in a crazed frenzy. "It is the pope!" they cry, pointing their cameras and mics in his direction.

Unconcerned by the commotion he's causing, Pope Urban strides confidently through the crowd directly toward George, protected on all sides by colorfully striped Vatican soldiers and black-robed clergymen.

Bending over the stretcher George is lying on, the holy father blesses George and whispers into his ear. Then, he embraces Steve. "I am very grateful for all of your vigilance," he declares sincerely. "This day would have unfolded very differently if not for the watchful eyes of you and your associates."

Steve declares, "We are happy that you're safe, Your Holiness." Then he kisses the pontiff's ring.

Over the pope's shoulder, Steve sees Raphael watching them from a place far from other people. He knows that no one will ever acknowledge the man publicly for his bravery, so to show his gratitude, he does the first thing that enters his mind. Moving aside, he comes to attention and snaps Raphael a smart Marine salute.

The poker-faced man understands Steve's gesture. However, in his typically reserved fashion, he merely slips on his mirrored sunglasses and melts away into the crowd.

When Steve climbs into the ambulance to accompany George to the hospital, he says, "I guess I better call Diane."

"Yeah, she's gonna kill you, you know."

Unsurprisingly, Diane answers on the first ring. "Oh, my God! Steve! Are you okay?" she shouts, almost hysterical with relief. "We've been watching it all on TV! It's on every channel! Tammy is freaking out, too!"

"I can imagine; it's crazy here!" replies Steve. "But we got him, babe! The pope is safe! I have to tell you something, though, and I don't want you to be upset."

"Honey! Are you—"

"No, no, I'm fine. But Geo was injured. I'm going to the hospital with him now."

"Is it bad?"

"He'll be okay," answers Steve. "Pissed off, but okay. Would you tell Angie? Oh, and babe, I'm coming home...to stay. This is my last job. I'm definitely done with this shit! Call the kids and ask them to fly over for a visit, our treat. All I want now is to be a grandpa!"

EPILOGUE

While a light drizzle falls over the Mediterranean, Diane putters around the kitchen, humming as she works. Grabbing a spoon, she stops to taste the meal she's preparing for the three musketeers and smacks her lips approvingly.

In the next room, George is staring at the clouds through the French doors. One arm is still in a sling, which annoys him to no end, but the weekly physical therapy his doctor insists on is doing wonders.

Behind him, Frank brings a tray of salami and various cheeses in from the kitchen. "So, Chic," he asks, "when are your sons coming over?"

Steve places his bottle of Peroni down to exchange it for a chunk of creamy Mozzarella di Bufala cheese on a savory cracker. "The grandkids are in school now. They're coming during Christmas break."

Diane joins the group with a glass of Prosecco. "I still can't believe you intentionally shot Geo," she remarks. "I thought you guys were good buddies!"

"Yeah, some friend he is!" laughs George. "And where the hell's my Ferrari?" he adds with mock seriousness.

A sudden knock at the door interrupts the light banter.

"Are you expecting anyone?" asks Diane curiously.

Steve shrugs and opens the door a crack. Quietly, he asks for identification, then slips outside and closes the door behind him.

When Steve is gone, Frank asks, "He doesn't know that the rest of the team is coming today, right?"

"No," Diane replies. "But not all of them can make it. Salvatore and Colonel Accola are due soon, but Special Agent Samuels is already back in the states. I hope it wasn't them at the door."

"What about the Ravens and Vincenzo Bennini?"

"The Colonel said the Ravens don't do parties, and Vincenzo is in Milan."

When Steve reenters the villa, there's a sly smile plastered all over his face as he walks over to George. Tossing him a key fob, he states matter-of-factly, "It's not a Ferrari, but I don't think you'll notice. Merry early Christmas, ace."

With eyes the size of saucers, George stares at a black key fob etched with a silver and red chevron. "You didn't!" he shouts.

Steve shrugs. "Check it out, bro."

Excited beyond belief, George rushes outside, followed closely by the others.

"Go around to the side!" Steve hollers after him.

Puzzled, George rounds a corner of the villa, then comes to a complete stop. Parked on the grass is a bright red, mid-engine Corvette, with an enormous red bow fastened to the roof.

While the amazed group crowds around the car, a black Mercedes pulls into the driveway, unnoticed by everyone.

"I'll be damned!" sputters George, standing in front of the Corvette. "It's an American Ferrari!"

"Uh, uh," corrects Frank. "That would be a Ford GT, my friend," he says, to laughter from his friends.

As Colonel Accola and Salvatore Caputi join them, George unlocks the car door and squeezes behind the wheel. "Thank God it's my left arm in the sling," he says, eyeing Steve. "I'd kick you to kingdom come if I couldn't drive this right now."

George fires the engine up while Colonel Accola takes Steve aside. "We found another Mafia mole," the colonel says solemnly. "This time, inside the Vatican."

"You're kidding. Who is it?"

"A cardinal...Cardinal Carlotta. He is one of the three clergymen associated with the Ravens."

"Holy shit! Even the freakin' Ravens were compromised? Man, what I'd give to see Raphael's face the minute he finds out!"

The men cut their conversation short because they can no longer hear each other. George is revving the V8 over and over, with a big smile plastered on his face.

Steve excuses himself and walks over to the car, prompting George to roll down the window. "Too bad your Corvette ain't here!" George says. "We could race each other around Italy!"

"Won't be long now," Steve retorts. "She's on the way!"

Amid the noise, no one notices that Diane has run into the house. When she returns a minute later, she walks up to Steve and eyes him angrily. "The State Department is on the phone for you," she announces icily.

Steve is aware of the troubled look on his wife's face, but curiously, he smiles back at her with a joyous twinkle in his eye.

"Fuck 'em!" he whoops, defiantly raising his fist in the air. "I don't give a damn! I'm retired!"